Return to Summerfield

Return to Summerfield

Dianne H. Lundy

Primix Publishing
11620 Wilshire Blvd
Suite 900, West Wilshire Center, Los Angeles, CA, 90025
www.primixpublishing.com
Phone: 1-800-538-5788

© 2023 Dianne H. Lundy. All rights reserved.

No part of this book may be reproduced, stored in a retrieval system, or transmitted by any means without the written permission of the author.

This book is a work of fiction. Names, characters, places and incidents are the product of the author's imagination or are used fictitiously and any resemblance to any actual persons, living or dead, events, or locales is entirely coincidental.

*Cover "Quietude" by Hooshang Khorasani, www.hooshangstudio@suddenlink.net. (used by permission)

Published by Primix Publishing   06/14/2023

ISBN: 978-1-957676-48-7(sc)
ISBN: 978-1-957676-49-4(e)

Library of Congress Control Number: 2023909960

Any people depicted in stock imagery provided by iStock are models, and such images are being used for illustrative purposes only.

Certain stock imagery © iStock.

Because of the dynamic nature of the Internet, any web addresses or links contained in this book may have changed since publication and may no longer be valid. The views expressed in this work are solely those of the author and do not necessarily reflect the views of the publisher, and the publisher hereby disclaims any responsibility for them.

Other Books by Dianne H. Lundy
The Girl from Nip 'n' Tuck (autobiography)
Summerfield Series:
*Summerfield
*Return to Summerfield

**The Billy Allgood Story
**Property of Louisiana Christian University
Available through https://bookstore.lcuniversity.edu

My Novel Critique Group

Pictured left to right: Dianne H. Lundy, Norma Franklin, Debbie Hancock, and Rebecca Jemerson.

Dedication

THIS BOOK IS DEDICATED TO the ladies in my novel critique group, Norma, Debbie, and Rebecca, who helped me immensely with their patience and feedback as I progressed through the writing of these stories.

Contents

Part I: Introduction 1
   Return to Summerfield. 3

Part II: "The Return" Luci's Story, Part 2 5
   The Return 7

Part III: "Smooth Sailing" Regenia's Story. 127
   Smooth Sailing. 129

Springtime in Summerfield
   Preview to my next book
   Part I: "Catnip" Cody and Jennifer's Story 211

Lagniappe: Favorite Family Recipes. 217

Part I

Introduction

Return to Summerfield

THE LADIES OF SUMMERFIELD ARE back with new and exciting stories with some familiar faces and some new ones. Follow them on their journeys as their lives change from unexpected events that lead them to making some crucial decisions that affect, not only them, but also other members of their families and some of their friends as well. Enjoy the emerging characters who hold the promise of even further adventures as life in Summerfield progresses through the years.

Part II

"The Return"
Luci's Story, Part 2

The Return

JEREMY CLARK UNLOCKED THE FRONT door of his house and stepped inside. It was totally dark, and he was greeted by a heavy silence. *What is going on?* he wondered. Luci hadn't mentioned going anywhere. He was expecting her and the children to be home. He was returning from a trip to Washington, D. C., where he had received an award as Outstanding Young Businessman of the Year. It had been quite an honor, and he had wanted his wife by his side when he accepted the award. She had been unable to attend due to a pressing case in the law firm where she was employed, so he had taken his secretary, Belinda Hargrove, instead.

His original plan had been to return home the same night as the awards banquet, but their plane had been delayed due to inclement weather, so they had to take a later flight. Now here he was, holding his suitcase in one hand and his trophy in the other, but there was nobody to show the trophy to. He turned on the hall light and set the suitcase on the floor, placing the trophy on the table near the entrance, thinking the family could see it later.

He walked down the hall and into the kitchen in the mood for a beer or at least something cold to drink. As he flipped on the light, something in the middle of the table caught his eye. He walked to the refrigerator, opened the door, and removed a beer, twisting off the cap as he headed towards the table. That's when he saw it—a picture of himself and Belinda plastered on the front page of a tabloid. He set the beer down quickly and picked up the paper, unable to believe what he was seeing.

He remembered it all now. He had been so enthused about the award he had hugged Belinda and kissed her on the cheek just before he went up to accept the trophy. He had seen a flash going off. Then all he could see was spots until he caught sight of one of the paparazzi heading out the back door. If he could have caught the little weasel, he would have wrung his neck, but the guy was too fast. Besides, he was stuck in front of the audience, making an acceptance speech.

He had put the incident out of his mind until now, and now it was too late. Luci had evidently seen the picture, and that explained why she and the children were gone. There was no note, just the picture in the middle of the table. That was enough of a message. She didn't have to spell it out for him.

He began mentally kicking himself for letting it happen. When Luci had informed him she wouldn't be able to accompany him on the trip, the first person he had turned to had been his mom, Maude, but she, too, had begged off because she was fighting a cold. The two tickets had already been ordered and paid for, so he opted to take Belinda, reasoning that a day away from the office would do her good. They hadn't planned to stay overnight, so there didn't seem to be any harm in having her come along. The problem had started when their flight had been delayed, and he had to scrounge around for hotel rooms. Of course, they had occupied separate rooms, but Luci had no way of knowing that. Nevertheless, she should have trusted him, he reasoned. He had never cheated on her and he wasn't about to start now. Luci was the love of his life, the only woman he wanted.

Blast the paparazzi! There was no telling how many marriages they had ruined with their rush to get pictures and be the first to have them published, regardless of the circumstances. Getting the picture printed in the paper the next day was a record, even for them. Furthermore, how did Luci get a copy of it so fast? She never read the tabloids. In fact, she hated them. Did somebody send her the picture? Who was taking such an interest in his affairs? *What really happened?* he wondered.

It wasn't the first time he had been photographed with a beautiful woman other than his wife, and it wouldn't be the last. At first, it had been just the regular newspapers because the Clark name was recognized internationally due to his father's business dealings. But when he had taken over the reins of the company, being a young, handsome businessman who seemed to attract women wherever he went, the tabloids had circled around him. His brief fling with a socialite who was well known in the upper crust of the New York society had not helped matters. There had been rumors and more rumors, but he had always convinced Luci that's all they were, and she had always forgiven him. This time it was different. This time it was a woman he worked closely with every day.

He and Belinda were just friends, nothing more. She was engaged to her college sweetheart, and the wedding was just a few months away. He had promised to give her away, as her parents were deceased, and she had no close relatives. Hardly a day had passed when he hadn't heard something about the wedding plans. It was all Belinda could talk about. He had listened patiently, nodding in all the right places, but with his mind sometimes a million miles away.

Well, it was too late to do anything about the situation tonight. He didn't know where Luci and the children had gone, but he would bet his fortune she had headed straight for Summerfield and her parents' home. He wasn't going to upset the whole family tonight, but he and Luci were going to have it out tomorrow. Whether by phone or in person, he hadn't decided, but one way or another he was going to contact his wife and he was going to get her back!

⬥❖⬥

LUCI CARLITO CLARK SET HER bags down in the foyer of her parents' home and glanced around her surroundings, marveling at how little had changed since she had moved away twelve years ago following her marriage to Jeremy Clark. Their wedding day had been one of the happiest days of her life, yet here she was, walking out on Jeremy and returning to her Italian roots. *How could things have gone so wrong?* she wondered as she blinked back the tears.

She glanced down at her left hand, her ring finger now empty. She had removed both her engagement and wedding rings, storing them in their original boxes that were tucked into their house safe back in New York. She simply could not and would not wear them now. Not after what had happened.

Her two children, Brian and Jennifer, had run ahead to the kitchen, following their noses as the delicious smell of teacakes drifted into the rest of the house. Her mother, Rosa, was an excellent cook whose food was usually gobbled up quickly by anyone who happened to be in the vicinity whenever it was on the table. Never in Luci's thirty-three years had she known her mother to produce a dish that wasn't mouth-watering.

Her train of thought was interrupted as the two children ran back into the room, each clutching a cookie and smiling broadly. Their Grandma Rosa was one of their favorite people. They didn't know why they were suddenly coming to visit her when it wasn't even Christmas, but it didn't really matter because they always had so much fun at her house.

"Mama, Mama, look what Grandma gave us," they yelled in unison.

"Oh, teacakes! They're my favorite, too," she exclaimed, trying not to let her depression rub off on the children.

Mama Rosa followed the children into the room, her eyes questioning Luci, but she wisely held her questions for later when the children would be otherwise occupied. She had known they were coming because Luci had phoned ahead. The call had been brief, but she could tell by Luci's voice something was wrong. Very wrong. It would take some time to get the whole story, but she knew eventually the truth would come out. Luci had always been honest with her parents, and she wasn't about to start lying to them now. Of that Mama was certain.

"Luci, it's so good to see you again," Mama exclaimed as she hugged her daughter gently. "Let me help you take your luggage upstairs."

"No, Mama. They're too heavy for you. I can manage," Luci assured her.

"Will you be staying for long?" Mama inquired.

"I don't know right now. I'm thinking of moving back here and setting up my own law practice," Luci responded as she began to manipulate the heavy bags upstairs.

"Your own law practice? What about the firm in New York?" Mama Rosa called out after her as Luci topped the stairs and disappeared into her former bedroom.

"I can't talk about it right now. I'll take my bedroom, and the children can sleep in Anthony's old room, if that's okay with you," Luci yelled as she disappeared from sight, her voice fading in the process.

Mama Rosa stared at the empty space at the top of the stairs. Her instincts had been right. Something had gone awry between Luci and Jeremy, but what? It was going to take some time to get the information out of her daughter. Luci could be stubborn at times, and this appeared to be one of them. Mama was fully prepared to bide her time until the whole story was revealed. No matter what had happened, she wasn't about to stand by and let Luci make the biggest mistake of her life. There was no doubt in her mind that Luci and Jeremy belonged together.

She shook her head and waved her hands, muttering in Italian as she began walking back to the kitchen after peeking into the living room to assure herself that the two grandchildren had settled in front of the TV. Luci had come home to her parents in a silent plea for help. Mama Rosa didn't know what she could do to help her daughter, but right now it was time for some comfort food. That's what she would prepare tonight—Luci's favorite dish, spaghetti and meatballs. Everybody always felt better after a good meal, and a good meal was what they all needed.

⬩◆◆◆⬩

DINNER THAT NIGHT WAS A far cry from the usual camaraderie that was so typical of the Carlito table. Papa D'Armon had come home in a jovial mood, delighted to see his daughter and grandchildren for an unexpected visit. His happiness had been short-lived, though, quashed by a frown Mama had tossed his way. He had soon realized there was more to the story than met the eye. Luci's coming home without Jeremy meant something was amiss. Mama had kept the details of Luci's phone call to herself, preferring to wait until her daughter arrived to find out the real source of the problem.

So, the adults sat at the table in their usual places, eating quietly, each lost in their own thoughts. The children, unaware of any impending crisis, chattered continuously, breaking the silence that hung over the room like a heavy blanket. They quickly gobbled up their portion of the spaghetti and meatballs and asked for seconds, a request that brought a smile to Mama's face. She always enjoyed watching people consume the food she had prepared. "Problems cannot be solved on an empty stomach," she often told the family.

Luci pushed her food around on her plate, eating only a few bites. Not even Mama's offer of apple pie for dessert could tempt her this time. The wounds went too deep. All she could think about was Jeremy and his betrayal. Only extraordinary self-control kept her from bursting into tears.

Her parents knew her every mood. The expression on her face spoke volumes. Luci was both troubled and in trouble. Whatever it was, Jeremy was involved. Jeremy, the man they had accepted into their family and loved like a son. He was the cause of their daughter's unhappiness, but exactly what had brought on the crisis was unclear.

Luci had never complained about her marriage. It had seemed to be an ideal union that had produced two wonderful grandchildren. Both Jeremy and Luci had established themselves in successful careers. As far as the Carlitos could tell, everything had been running smoothly. What had gone so wrong that Luci had come running home to her parents? They were restless, anxious to learn the whole story whenever they got Luci alone, hopefully as soon as the children were in bed.

The meal ended abruptly as the children polished off their slices of the apple pie, excused themselves, and jumped up from the table, running back into the living room to watch TV. Luci offered to help with the dishes, but Mama declined, insisting that Luci needed to rest after her long trip.

Papa went into the living room and settled in his easy chair to read the paper, while the children lounged in front of the TV. He smiled as he watched them arguing over who would be in charge of the remote control. It was good to have young voices in the household again. He didn't see enough of his grandchildren, he decided.

Luci appeared in the doorway and announced it was bath time for the children. A dispute then ensued as to who would be the first to miss part of their favorite TV program. Jennifer, being the youngest, was the loser, and she reluctantly followed Luci upstairs and down the hall towards the bathroom.

Brian's triumph was fleeting, however, because Jennifer reappeared in less than thirty minutes, decked out in her pajamas and bathrobe. She stuck her tongue out at her brother as she skipped into the room. He moaned as Luci entered the room behind her daughter.

"Okay, young man, you're next. Upstairs now. Your bath awaits."

"Aw, mom, do I have to?" he protested.

"Yes. No arguments. Hurry up and then Papa D'Armon will tell you a bedtime story."

The last statement was all it took to get Brian up and moving. Bath time was no longer a problem, Luci noted. Papa D'Armon was a master storyteller, and the stories of his childhood in the old country were eagerly anticipated by the whole family—the same stories she and her brother, Anthony, had listened to when they were growing up.

Less than an hour later, with the dishes washed and both children in their pajamas and bathrobes, the whole family gathered in the living room to listen to one of Papa's stories. Luci had turned down the lights, and Papa had lit a fire in the fireplace. The children settled down in front of Papa's chair, while Mama sat on the couch with her knitting. Luci nestled in another large chair, legs tucked underneath her. It was just like old times, she reflected.

She leaned back in the chair and closed her eyes as Papa began his story. She felt her body relax as she was transported back to Papa's childhood days. It was the first time she had forgotten about her current marriage problems since her initial glimpse of that picture of Jeremy and Belinda on the front page of a tabloid. Papa's voice droned on as the story unwound, having an almost hypnotic effect on everyone listening.

Soon the children were nodding, and Luci could barely keep her eyes open. She snapped back to reality as the hall clock chimed the hour—9:00 p.m. Mama was smiling at the children as she worked on her latest knitting project, her favorite pastime besides cooking. Mama and Papa exchanged glances, happy that their grandchildren and Luci were back under their roof, no matter what circumstances had brought them there. It was an act that did not escape Luci's attention, although she knew they were dying to know why she and the children were suddenly back home without Jeremy.

She roused out of her stupor, realizing she was still a mother and there was work to do.

"Okay, children, time for bed. Give Mama Rosa and Papa D'Armon a goodnight kiss and I'll tuck you in."

The children offered little resistance this time, rubbing their eyes as they rolled to their feet, obediently shuffling over to produce the goodnight kisses for the grandparents. Luci rose from the chair and began to follow them upstairs, glancing at her parents as she climbed towards the top step.

"I think I'll just take my bath and go to bed," she told them. "We'll talk tomorrow. I promise."

A long soak in a hot bath proved relaxing, and Luci thought she was headed for a peaceful night's slumber until her head hit the pillow. Then it all came back to her—the tabloid photo, the rumors of Jeremy's cheating over the years, her doubting him, their arguments about other women. Suddenly, she was wide awake.

She couldn't get the tabloid photo out of her mind. She had been headed out to get the morning paper when she saw it lying beneath the mail slot in the front door, all neatly folded with the photo on top. Somebody had put it there, but who? Why was it so important that she see that particular photo? She had seen plenty of pictures of Jeremy with other women, but it was always business. Was something really going on between him and Belinda, a girl much younger than he was? Why did it bother her so much?

All she could do was toss and turn. She couldn't remember spending such a sleepless night since the time Jeremy had proposed to her and she had promised to give him an answer the following morning. Well, that and the first night of their honeymoon. That was a night to remember, also, she thought regretfully as she fluffed her pillow for the umpteenth time, hoping to induce the much-needed sleep.

The sandman never came, and Luci was still wide awake at 7:00 a.m. when her cell phone, which she had placed on the nightstand beside her bed, began ringing incessantly. She didn't have to look to know who the caller was. She knew there was no way Jeremy was letting her go without a fight, but she was prepared to do battle. If she couldn't live with him, she was going to start over and build a life for herself and her children back in her hometown of Summerfield She had been formulating the idea in her head ever since boarding the plane from New York. She was licensed to practice law in her home state, so setting up a law office wouldn't be too hard to do. Besides that, she still had connections in the community. Many of her friends and acquaintances from high school and college still lived in Summerfield or in neighboring towns. Once word got around, she would be sure to get some clients. In fact, practicing law in a small town might prove to be more interesting than working for the big law firm in New York.

The phone continued to ring to the point where she could not ignore it. Although she had set it to go to voicemail, Jeremy was evidently ignoring that feature and continually hitting the redial button. The only way to stop the calls was either to answer the phone or shut it off. She might as well answer it and get the showdown over with.

"Hello," she spoke reluctantly as she took the call.

"Luci, where are you?" She didn't need Caller I. D. She would recognize Jeremy's voice anywhere, anytime.

"I'm in Summerfield at Mama and Papa's house."

"Luci, I found the picture you left behind. You didn't give me a chance to explain."

"Explain? That's what you've been doing for the past twelve years, explaining why you were with all those other women."

"And you always believed me. I told you I never cheated on you."

"Jeremy, honestly, I don't know what to think anymore. It seems every time I turn around it's either a picture of you and another woman in the news or else I'm hearing some kind of rumor about you having an affair."

"Just because there are rumors doesn't mean it's true. You know how the media loves to sensationalize everything, especially the tabloids."

"Still, I need some time to think. Jeremy, I'm going to stay in Summerfield for the time being."

"Luci, you can't do that. I love you. I want you and Brian and Jennifer with me in New York."

"I didn't say it was permanent…"

"I don't care if it's permanent or temporary," Jeremy interrupted her in mid-sentence. "There's no way I'm letting you go."

"I've made up my mind, Jeremy. I need to have my space. Please send me the children's birth certificates. I'm going to enroll them in school here."

"No, I won't do it. I'm not sending you anything. Don't do this, Luci. Please, I'm begging you. Give me another chance."

"If you won't send me the papers, I'll get them another way. Don't forget you're married to a lawyer."

With that last remark Luci disconnected the cell call and turned off the phone. She just hoped that her family didn't overhear the somewhat loud conversation.

<hr />

"Luci…Luci…" Jeremy continued to yell into his phone until he realized he was talking to dead silence.

Frustrated, he threw the phone against the wall. Seeing it shatter into little pieces gave him some satisfaction, although he realized he would be out more money for a new phone. At this point it didn't matter. Money had always been of little consequence to him and was even less so now.

She was determined to leave him. He could see that now. He would have to win her back, court her all over again. The first time had been hard enough, and that was when they were working together on his restaurant when he had talked her into assisting him in the remodeling project. What excuse could he come up with for reinserting himself into her life? What if she refused to see him anymore? It was too much to think about now. He had pressing business, and it was time to get ready for work. Maybe work would take his mind off his family troubles. Yes, work, that was where he belonged now.

An hour later he walked into his office only to find it cold and dark. There was no Belinda. No coffee. No doughnuts. Belinda was always sitting behind her desk, waiting to greet him with her usual bubbly smile. Plus, she always had a pot of freshly brewed coffee to give him a burst of energy from that jolt of caffeine.

What now? he wondered as he pilfered thought the cabinets looking for coffee filters and a bag of his special brew. He had skipped breakfast, and his stomach was letting him know about it. He had no appetite, but his stomach had other ideas. Even if he couldn't have a doughnut, at least he could make himself a pot of coffee. He wasn't totally helpless, despite Belinda's jokes to the contrary.

"Aha, I knew I'd find you," he announced triumphantly as he finally opened the right door. *Great, now I'm talking to myself. I've really got it bad,* he mused as he snatched the filters and coffee from the cabinet and headed towards the coffeepot.

Just what is the ratio for water to coffee for a perfect brew? he wondered as he stood with coffeepot in hand. *Come on, Jeremy. It can't be that hard. Read the package directions. Why are men so dependent on women for every little detail?*

Moments later he felt a slight degree of satisfaction as he listened to the steady drip of the coffee coming through the pot, and the aroma of the fresh brew began to penetrate the room. He had located the sugar, creamer, and cups while waiting for the process to finish. How did women make all these things seem so easy? Furthermore, where was Belinda? She was never late and never missed a day of work. She had proven to be a competent secretary and they had a good working relationship. It just wasn't like her to be tardy. He needed her today more than ever. He was already under enough pressure from his troubles at home. Now he had problems with his secretary. What else was going to go wrong to ruin his day?

That question was answered before he could even pour himself a cup of coffee. The door burst open and Belinda practically fell through it, sobbing hysterically. She headed for her desk and threw herself into the chair, not even bothering to close the door behind her.

"Belinda, what's wrong?" he asked anxiously, hurrying to pat her shoulder, his coffee totally forgotten.

"It's Matt," she sobbed, grabbing a handful of tissues from the desk as she spoke.

"Matt? What about him?" Jeremy inquired as he walked from behind the desk and closed the door.

"He says the wedding's off. He saw a picture of you kissing me in one of those tabloids. Somebody left a copy of the paper in his mailbox."

"I can't believe he'd do that. You've been dating since college. He doesn't trust you?"

"Not where you're concerned. He doesn't like me working for you. He says you're way too good-looking and way too rich. Besides, there are always pictures of you with other women in the news."

"I didn't realize Matt Collins was keeping such close tabs on my personal life." Jeremy couldn't resist the sarcastic dig.

"I told him you're like a father or a big brother to me, but he won't believe me. He still thinks there's something going on between us."

"Matt needs to grow up!" Jeremy exclaimed. "Not every boss has an affair with his secretary."

"That's what I tried to tell him, but he's not accepting it."

"Well, then, I guess I have something to tell you, too. Luci has left me. She went back home to Summerfield, back to her parents' house. She saw the picture, too."

"Oh, Jeremy, I'm so sorry. I had no idea."

"I'm still getting used to the idea myself. I'm not letting her go, though. I'm going to get her back. I just haven't figured out how yet."

He walked over to the coffeepot, poured two steaming cups of the brew and added creamer and sugar.

"Here, take this," he said, handing one of the cups to Belinda. "You need something to clear your head, and, God knows, I certainly do."

"Thanks, Jeremy. You're the best," Belinda responded, dabbing at her eyes before she accepted the cup. "I'm sorry I wasn't here earlier to make the coffee for you. How did you know I like sugar and creamer?"

"You've been working here for three years. I do notice a few things that go on around the office," he teased.

"And I thought you couldn't survive without me," she countered.

"Don't worry, Belinda. We're going to fix this. I don't know how, but I'm going to get my family back. I promise you that."

—◆◇◈◇◆—

IT WAS TIME TO TELL her parents what was going on. Luci realized that as soon as she hung up the phone. She would talk to them over breakfast before the children were up. They would take it hard, she knew, because they both adored Jeremy. But she was their only daughter and they would stand by her, no matter what. Family was the most important thing to them and always would be.

The smell of cinnamon rolls wafted up the stairs and began to tickle her nose. She had to smile, remembering how Mama Rosa insisted on everyone's eating a good breakfast. She never let anybody leave the house on an empty stomach.

Mama knows cinnamon rolls are one of my favorites. She's doing everything she can to whet my appetite. I think it just might be working, Luci thought as she felt her first pang of hunger since walking out of her home in New York and boarding the plane for Summerfield. Luci knew nobody could stay around Mama Rosa long without working up an appetite for her delicious cuisine.

Well, it was time to face her parents and get it over with. She threw on some casual clothes and walked into the bathroom, splashed water on her face and ran a brush through her hair. Makeup was not needed for this occasion, although Mama would be sure to notice the dark circles under her eyes from lack of sleep. Well, it was all just part of the picture. No sense in trying to hide anything from her parents. It was better to get it all out in the open. Maybe she would feel better if she told somebody instead of keeping everything all bottled up inside. There was really nobody else she could talk to. Her so-called best friends were all in New York, and she certainly couldn't confide in the children. Her parents were the only recourse.

She pasted what she hoped was a passable smile on her face as she walked down the stairs and headed towards the kitchen. She knew Papa would be sitting at the table, drinking his first cup of coffee. Mama would be bustling around, getting all the food ready for him and the visitors. She pushed open the door to view the familiar scene.

"Luci, good morning," Mama said as Luci poked her head through the door.

"Mama, Papa, good morning to you both."

"I made cinnamon rolls, one of your favorites," Mama informed her.

"I know. I could already smell them. That's what brought me down here so early." Luci smiled again as she spoke.

"Luci, come and have some coffee with me," Papa insisted, waving her to the table as he spoke.

"Yes, the rolls are about to come out of the oven," Mama added as she poured Luci's coffee.

"Mmmm...I can't wait," Luci exclaimed. "I think I'm getting my appetite back."

Luci sipped on the coffee as Mama removed the rolls from the oven and placed them on a plate that she sat in the middle of the table. Luci and Papa both reached for one at the same time, an act that brought a grin to both of their faces. It was almost like old times when she and Anthony had fought over who would get the first cinnamon roll at breakfast.

They made their selections and began to munch on the confections, a melt-in-your-mouth experience.

"Now I remember why Jeremy was so insistent on buying all your recipes for his restaurant," Luci observed, referring to the fact that Jeremy had used Mama Rosa's recipes as the basis for the menu for the vacant restaurant he had bought in Summerfield.

"Speaking of Jeremy...where is he? Why didn't he come home with you and the children?" Papa inquired, opening the door for Luci's explanation of the situation.

"I have something to tell you," Luci began. "Jeremy and I are separated for the time being. I'm going to move back here and start my own law practice."

"But why? Why would you want to do that? I thought you and Jeremy loved each other. And what about the children?" Mama asked.

"It's a complicated situation, Mama. I can't go into all the details now. You'll just have to trust me. I know what I'm doing. I've been thinking about it for some time. I'm going to enroll the children in school here. I'm licensed to practice law in this state, and I still know lots of people around here, so I'm sure I can get some clients. Jeremy and I just need some time apart. I don't know if it's permanent or not, but I just need my space right now."

Her parents sat in silence, absorbing the information. Then Papa posed a question.

"Luci, what did Jeremy do that caused you to leave him? He's our boy now, and we all love him so much."

"Papa, there have been many rumors of infidelity over the years. I just never told you and Mama about them. Jeremy has always assured me that the rumors are false, and I believed him, but I was hurt just the same. This week there was a tabloid picture of him kissing his secretary during a trip to Washington, D. C. It was the final blow for me, the last embarrassment."

"Kissing his secretary? I can't believe Jeremy would do such a thing. Are you sure the picture wasn't altered? They can do things like that now, you know," Mama commented.

"Well, I couldn't believe it either, but there it was, staring me in the face. Somebody pushed it through my mail slot—somebody who wanted me to see it," Luci mused.

"Who would do that? Is there somebody who would want you and Jeremy to break up?" Papa asked.

"Hmmm…I never thought of that angle, but you may be right. There are many women who would give anything to have Jeremy, to have what I have."

"Then if that is true, maybe you need to give the whole situation some more thought," Mama suggested.

"I will. I promise, but for now I'm staying in Summerfield. My mind is made up. I'm a lawyer, so I know how to do investigations. I will get to the bottom of this."

"Well, it's time for me to get to work. We're glad to have you and the children stay with us as long as you like. You know you are always welcome here," Papa told her.

"Yes, Papa, I know. I'll stay here for the time being, but eventually I want to get my own place, either a small house or an apartment. Today I'm going to start the paperwork I need to get the children enrolled in school."

"I know they'll be excited about that," Mama joked.

"Yes, they will protest, but they really do enjoy school. Maybe they'll make some new friends, so things won't be so boring for them. Maybe some of my old schoolmates have children about the same age as Brian and Jennifer. Wouldn't that be nice? They could play together sometimes."

"I'm thinking of several people now," Mama said.

"Well, goodbye. I'm headed out to the taxi station," Papa announced, grabbing his lunchbox off the counter as he spoke.

"Goodbye, Papa. I'll see you tonight," Luci responded.

"Goodbye, D'Armon," Mama added as Papa kissed her cheek before walking out the door.

<hr />

JEREMY MOVED THROUGH HIS MORNING meetings mechanically, almost in a stupor. Belinda had recovered enough from her crying jag to regain her composure and take control of the office. The girl was a wonder. That was one reason he had hired her. That, plus he had known her parents for years before they were tragically killed in an auto accident. His other secretary had left to raise her family after she had gotten married and become pregnant. Belinda had happened along at just the right time. He hadn't regretted his decision to hire her, not at all. In fact, he had rather enjoyed his role as a father figure in her life when her parents were no longer around.

The girl didn't have a mean bone in her body. *So why is somebody messing around with both our lives?* he wondered. It was too much of a coincidence that the photo of him kissing Belinda was in the possession of both Luci and Matt. He didn't know exactly how Luci got hold of the photo. He would bet somebody had sent it to her. Somebody was out to ruin his marriage. He was sure of it. Belinda was just an added casualty, extra insurance for the perpetrator. He wasn't going to get Luci back until he found out who had sent the tabloid to both her and Matt.

He was going to hire a detective, he decided. He didn't have time to investigate the case personally. Not if he kept up with his business demands. He had the money, so he might as well use it. The sooner he got to the bottom of the problem and got Luci back, the better. He was missing his family already, and they hadn't even been gone a whole day. And then there was the problem of Belinda and her fiancé. The wedding had been scheduled for only a few months away, so he had to get the matter straightened out before then. He would never forgive himself if Belinda's wedding was permanently cancelled because of his actions.

LUCI DECIDED THAT ROUSTING THE children out of bed after the long plane trip would be too much trouble. Going to the school alone and scouting out the situation would be the best thing to do. The children could stay home with Mama Rosa, and she would take them to school the following day. She could get a list of the supplies they would need and take them shopping. At least getting some new things would get them somewhat excited about going back to school, she hoped.

After informing Mama of her plans, she headed back upstairs to change into more suitable clothes. Thirty minutes later, dressed in one of the suits she usually wore to court, she peered into the mirror, satisfied that she had successfully concealed the dark circles under her eyes.

She smiled as she remembered the old adage, "A little powder, a little paint, makes a woman what she ain't." Then she sighed. If only the school registration process could be taken care of as easily. She didn't know how she would manage without the proper papers, but she would just have to give it a try and see what developed. After all, she *was* a lawyer, and a darn good one at that!

She slipped into her heels and grabbed a matching handbag, thankful that she had at least remembered to pack some decent clothes. She could send for the rest of her clothes later, or buy some new ones if Jeremy refused to let her have access to her belongings. But he wasn't a spiteful man. She had to give him that much credit. Plus, he had always been generous where his family was concerned. There were so many qualities about him to love. Was leaving him the right thing to do? Well, no more time to think about that now. She had to get moving if she wanted to get the children registered for school.

She headed downstairs, calling out to Mama as she reached the bottom step.

"I need to borrow the car, Mama. Where are the keys?"

"They're hanging here in the kitchen on the key rack," Mama informed her.

"Okay. You don't mind, do you? I won't be gone long."

"No, no, I don't mind at all. Take your time. I'll just enjoy cooking for my grandchildren when they get up."

"Don't let them sleep too late now. We don't want to get them off their schedule, especially if they have to get up tomorrow morning for school," Luci chided softly, kissing Mama on the cheek as she grabbed the keys and headed out the back door.

She hit the unlock button on the key ring and then opened the door and slid inside the roomy sedan. It was a far cry from the old days when all they had was a rusty pickup truck and two broken down taxicabs. Thanks to Jeremy's investment in Mama's recipe collection, Papa had been able to buy two new cabs, and the fleet had now grown to a total of five cabs, complete with drivers. Buying the new sedan for Mama to drive about town had been one of Papa's proudest moments.

Luci started the car and listened to the smooth hum of the engine, a sound which few people appreciated, much less paid attention to, she mused. She was grateful that she could drive up to the school in style. It wasn't that she was conceited, she told herself. She just didn't want anybody to think her children were from a poor family, something she had experienced in her younger days.

Soon after that, she found herself pulling into the school's parking lot. She brought the car to a stop and paused to take in the view. The transformation that had taken place over the last few years was amazing. The former school building where she had attended classes as a child had been replaced with a modern structure. If she didn't know she was in her hometown, she wouldn't have recognized the place. It was a little sad. Nothing ever stayed the same, but at least she had her memories, she reasoned. Just like she had her memories with Jeremy.

Annoyed that the thought had even crossed her mind, she forced herself to think of other things. Looking around the modern playground as she exited the car, she headed up the sidewalk, following the sign directing her to the front office. She pulled the door open and walked to the office, where she came face-to-face with one of the school secretaries.

"Hello. May I help you?" the secretary inquired.

"Yes, I want to see about registering my children for school," Luci responded, trying to figure out why the girl looked so familiar.

"Let me get you some registration packets. How many children do you have?"

"Two," Luci replied, holding up two fingers.

"Fine. Two packets. You just fill these out, and then I'll show you in for an interview with our principal, Mrs. Noreen Andrews," the secretary informed her, handing over the packets as she spoke.

Luci soon found herself seated at a table in the corner of the office, leafing through the papers as she filled them out. But her mind kept wandering back to the name that had struck a chord somewhere in the recesses of her past. *Noreen Andrews? I have met just one person in my entire life named Noreen. Could it be the one-and-only Noreen Watson, the girl I was always competing with for the top academic awards in my classes?* she wondered. *She never did like me very much, especially when I beat her out for class valedictorian.*

Her train of thought was interrupted as the secretary approached, flashing a friendly smile.

"All through with the packets?" she inquired as Luci shuffled the papers together.

"Yes, I think that about does it."

"If you will just follow me, Mrs. Andrews will see you now."

Luci rose to follow the secretary, smoothing her skirt and straightening her jacket in the process, a subconscious gesture from her courtroom days. She put on her best poker face, another trait she had learned to project during some challenging trials in which she had been the lead attorney.

The secretary's brisk pace quickly brought them to a door labeled *Noreen Andrews, Principal.* A brisk knock was followed by a crisp voice instructing them to come in. Luci had little choice but to enter the room as the secretary introduced her.

"Mrs. Andrews, this is Mrs. Luci Clark, one of our new parents." She glanced at the name on the card as she spoke. "Mrs. Clark, our principal, Mrs. Andrews."

"Thank you, Miss Carter," the lady behind the desk replied, rising to extend her hand as she spoke.

As Luci shook the hand that was offered, she looked into a pair of the iciest blue eyes she had ever seen. She felt a slight chill run down her spine as she released the principal's hand.

It's Noreen, all right. Same old, same old. She hasn't forgotten or forgiven me.

"Mrs. Clark…Luci, please be seated."

Luci eased herself into the chair, maintaining an erect posture, preparing herself for battle, if necessary—mental battle. She knew Noreen would never lower herself to attack her physically.

"Well, well, well. Luci, what brings you back to this sleepy little town? I thought you shook the dust of this place from your feet a long time ago."

"I've never forgotten my roots, Noreen. I just moved on to another life. But now I've decided to come back home and open my own law practice. So, I would like to get my two children enrolled in school as soon as possible. Is there a problem with that?"

Noreen flipped through the papers before she answered. "It appears you have filled in all the correct information. However, we will need copies of your children's birth certificates, immunization records, and records from the last school they attended."

"Of course. I'll get that information for you. We just arrived in town, and I haven't had a chance to send for the papers yet. Will there be a problem with the children starting to school tomorrow?"

"No, not at all. Just get the records to us as quickly as possible.

I'll have the secretary summon one of our teacher aides to show you around the school before you leave," Noreen responded, rising as she spoke to indicate the interview was over.

"Thank you," Luci replied as she exited the office, maintaining her erect posture just to make a statement.

She shook off the chill as she walked back into the main office. The icicles that were encasing her chest began to melt when she observed the secretary, who was now greeting her with a warm smile.

"You don't remember me, do you?" the secretary asked.

"I'm trying to think. You look so familiar," Luci told her.

"I'm Darlene Carter. You used to be my babysitter when I was a little girl. It took me a while to realize who you are. You're still so beautiful. I used to wish I could grow up to look as beautiful as you."

"Don't flatter me now," Luci teased. "I have been racking my brain, trying to figure out who you are. Little Darlene, all grown up now, and you did turn out to be beautiful."

"I've already sent for one of our teacher aides to show you around. Oh, here she is now," Darlene exclaimed as a robust figure burst through the door.

"Sorry, sorry, I was way over in the kindergarten class when you paged me." The woman puffed as she tried to catch her breath.

She paused as she glanced at Luci, who was staring intently at her. Then both women rushed towards each other with outstretched arms.

"Oh, my God, what are you doing here?" they shrieked simultaneously, hugging tightly.

"Luci Carlito Clark, as I live and breathe. I never thought I would see you setting foot in a school in this town again." Maxine smiled with the same gap-toothed grin that had become her trademark.

"Maxine Gates, I can't believe I found you again," Luci exclaimed as she stepped back to view her best friend from her childhood days. Maxine had hardly changed at all. Not only did she still have that same contagious grin, but her broad face still sported a generous sprinkling of freckles across her nose and cheekbones, and her head was topped with that wiry, unmanageable, mousy-brown hair. Age had not improved her figure either, Luci noted.

But looks had never mattered to Maxine. That's what had made her so popular among her classmates. She could always be counted on to supply the punch line for a joke, and Luci could never remember seeing her depressed or unhappy.

"So, how many kids do you and Tyler have now? Luci inquired, referring to Tyler Gates, Maxine's husband, who had been the fullback on the football team.

"Four, all boys. Tyler wanted to start his own football team, but four was all I could handle," Maxine joked. "What about you?"

"I have two, a girl and a boy. I'm here to enroll them in school today."

"Here...in Summerfield? I thought you had a big cushy job in New York," Maxine lowered her voice as she spoke.

"It's a long story," Luci whispered.

"Mrs. Gates, I called you in to show Mrs. Clark around the school. Principal Andrews requested it," Darlene interrupted the conversation.

"Of course, I'm so sorry, but I was just so excited to see my friend again. Come, Luci, and let me show you our wonderful new school. Nothing like the boxcars we had when we went here." Maxine opened the door to the hall as she spoke, and she and Luci stepped out of the office. Luci was relieved to be out of earshot of the general public. She didn't want her problems known to everyone in Summerfield.

"Okay, girl, tell me what's up," Maxine ordered as they walked down the hall and towards the gym.

"Believe me, Maxine, it's a very long story and I can't get into it here, but Jeremy and I are separated, and I'm coming back to Summerfield for the time being. I plan to open my own law practice."

"It must be serious if you're back here alone because you and Jeremy were so much in love."

"Yes, it is serious. Very serious. I just don't know what I'm going to do yet. I had to get away to think. This is the best thing I can do right now. I can't just sit around. I'll go crazy with nothing to do. That's why I decided to open a law practice right here in Summerfield."

"Well, you know best. We'll have to get together soon, and you can tell me all about your problems, but right now let me show off the school."

Luci was impressed as they walked about the school. It was quite modern, and she was satisfied that her children would receive a quality education at the facility. But she couldn't quite get rid of the hostile vibes she had felt when she looked into Noreen's eyes. *Why was such a cold-hearted person appointed principal over innocent children?* she wondered. It was hard to keep her mind on what Maxine was saying as they passed through the different departments. Almost before she knew it, they were back at the front lobby.

"And that, my friend, is our little school," Maxine informed her.

"It's a very nice facility. I'm sure my children will love it here, once they get settled in," Luci responded. "But I do have one question for you. What's up with Noreen…Principal Andrews? She seems so cold and distant. She was always a little snobby, but now she's different, almost like she doesn't care about anybody or anything. At least, that's what I sensed during my brief interview with her."

"You think you have a long story. Hers is even longer. She married some big-wig politician. They have lots of money. She tried and tried to have a baby. Even went through invitro-fertilization, but nothing happened. She's just bitter about it because her husband refused to adopt."

"How do you know so much about Noreen?"

"You forget. It's a small town. Everybody knows everybody's business."

"Yes, it's been so long since I lived here. I had no idea about Noreen. You don't suppose she would ever do anything to harm a child, do you?" Luci asked worriedly.

"I don't think so," Maxine responded slowly, pondering the question as she spoke.

"Well, she didn't seem very happy to see me again."

"Probably brought back the old memories. Not only did you beat her out as valedictorian, but you also won prom queen, and she had her heart set on that."

"I had forgotten all about that. Yes, she was pretty mad at me for a long time after that."

"Principals have to go through a long process before they're appointed. I'm sure Noreen met all the requirements, or they would never have given her the job," Maxine assured Luci.

"I hope so. I would hate to think that she might take out her vengeance on my children because of me."

"I'll keep a close eye on them for you. I promise."

"I'll be bringing them to the office first thing in the morning."

"Okay, I'll make it a point to be there, and I will personally escort them to their classes," Maxine told her.

"Great. Let me head back home and see what my family is up to. I still have to find a location for my law office, and I also need a place to stay beside my parents' house."

"I'll think about it tonight and see if I can come up with any good ideas for you."

"Okay, goodbye then, and I'll see you tomorrow morning," Luci said as she pushed open the front door and headed back to her car.

<hr />

BELINDA GLANCED UP FROM HER computer screen as the office door swung open. She almost did a double take but managed to keep her countenance under control as she observed the curvaceous, provocatively-dressed woman who glided through the door as if she were strolling down a runway at a fashion show.

"May I help you?" Belinda inquired, inwardly cringing because she knew from past experiences that her boss would not be happy to see his former fiancée. She had heard the story of how he broke up with Sheba James after he met Luci. The parting had not been amicable.

"Yes, I'm here to see Jeremy…Mr. Clark on important business." The reply came in a husky tone that was the envy of many a woman, Belinda included.

"I see. Let me check his appointment calendar," Belinda responded, stalling for time. She knew her boss was on the phone with a detective, starting the work on the case involving the mysterious appearance of the tabloid pictures.

"Mr. Clark is currently in conference. Perhaps I could schedule you for another time," she suggested.

"No! I must see him right away." The retort came rather sharply.

Ah ha, the cat's claws are showing. Jeremy is about to get scratched, Belinda thought as Sheba swept past her desk and headed towards Jeremy's door.

"Never mind. I'll see myself in," she informed Belinda.

She opened the door, pausing for dramatic effect as the door swung open to reveal Jeremy, who looked up in surprise with the phone glued to his ear. He stopped talking in mid-sentence.

"I'll have to get back to you," he said as he quickly disconnected the call, rising from his chair as he spoke.

"Sheba, this is an unexpected visit. What can I do for you today?" he inquired.

"I have business to discuss with you," she informed him, closing the door as Belinda craned her neck to take in the scene.

"And just what would that business be?"

"I'm interested in forming mergers with some of my companies. I know you have experience in that area, so I'm here to ask you for advice."

"Why me? Surely, you have competent lawyers who can handle the case for you. My expertise is in business, not law."

"Oh, the mergers haven't occurred yet. I need somebody to negotiate the deals for me, and I think you're the man for the job."

"Well, Sheba, I handle the business for my own company. I haven't been involved in assisting other people with their business takeovers…" He hesitated as he stalled for time.

"I know, but you're the one person I feel I can trust. If you will help me, I'll make it well worth your while, even though I know you don't need the money."

Jeremy laughed. "Everybody can always use more money. You know that, but my time is limited right now. I have other problems to worry about besides my business."

"Other problems…oh, my, are things not going well with you and the little wife?" She spoke softly, but Jeremy could swear he saw the briefest hint of a snarl on her face. He was not fooled. Not this time. He had made a mistake once before, thinking he loved her, but that was before he met Luci. There was no comparison between the two women. Luci was a warm and loving person, whereas Sheba was well suited to her namesake from the Bible. She would stop at nothing to get what she wanted, even if it meant betraying the people she supposedly loved. The question was, why was she showing up now, right after the mysterious tabloid incident? Could she somehow be responsible for the whole mess? It was definitely something to think about.

"Earth to Jeremy...where did you go?"

"Sorry, Sheba. What were you saying?"

"I was explaining exactly to you what companies I want to merge my businesses with. I think the best thing to do is to have my lawyers send the papers over to you and then you can see what you think about it. Will you help me, as friend to friend?"

He looked at the woman who was sitting in front of his desk. She was still as beautiful as ever with her long, carefully styled red hair, green eyes, accented heavily with eye shadow and mascara, and an almost porcelain complexion. The fragrance of her perfume permeated his nostrils. He didn't know what the scent was, but it was bound to be expensive, like everything else in Sheba's life. He almost sighed as he remembered how Luci always smelled like strawberries. He had been taken in by Sheba's beauty once, but now he could see that it was only superficial. *How could I have been so blind?* he wondered.

"All right, Sheba. I'll see what I can do. But this is a one-time thing. I hope you understand that. I have a company of my own to run."

"I understand perfectly. But I am ever so grateful for your assistance."

She rose gracefully from the chair, and Jeremy followed suit, reaching the door just in time to open it for her.

"Goodbye, Sheba," he said firmly, hoping she would take the hint that he had no further romantic interest in her.

"Goodbye, darling. I'll be in touch," she replied, touching his cheek softly as she turned and walked out the door, the scent of her perfume leaving a lingering trail.

He resisted the urge to cough and then gave in, almost hating himself for letting it happen.

A silence filled the room as the outer office door closed behind her. Jeremy turned to find Belinda staring at him, her mouth agape.

"What?" he asked.

"Oh, nothing. Nothing at all, Mr. Clark," Belinda replied in her most proper secretarial voice as she calmly reached over and turned on the small fan she kept on her desktop.

"It's just that I was thinking...don't you find it rather strange that she showed up here so soon after we both got those tabloid pictures? I know she used to be your fiancée."

"Yes, I'm thinking about that also. It is strange. Very strange. Excuse me, but I have another phone call to make."

He walked back into his office, shaking his head as he went. Women! He had enough trouble with just one woman, and now there were three of them to deal with. He still had to win Luci back. Then there was the matter of getting Belinda back together with Matt. Now, as if he didn't have enough problems, his former fiancée had to show up on the scene. Well, one thing was for sure. Life was never dull around his office.

<hr/>

THE FOLLOWING MORNING LUCI WAS up early, rousing the children out of bed and getting them ready for school. Although they weren't overly enthused about going to a new school, shopping for supplies and a few new school clothes had helped to soften the blow, as she had predicted. Her children were very good students and were always popular with their classmates, so she was sure they would adjust to their new surroundings shortly.

Less than an hour later, she found herself driving them to school in her mother's sedan. They chattered excitedly as they peered through the windows from the back seat. Even though they had visited their grandparents many times, they had never actually seen much of the town where their mom grew up. Their endless questions were starting to give her a headache as she pulled into the school's parking lot.

"Okay, kids, here we are. Hop out and we'll go to the front office and find out where your classrooms are," she told them.

They wasted no time in following instructions, and the trio headed up the sidewalk at a brisk pace. Luci sincerely hoped Maxine would keep her promise to meet them and take them to their respective classrooms.

She was not disappointed when they walked into the front lobby and saw Maxine standing by the office door, sporting her familiar grin.

"Brian and Jennifer, this is one of my good friends from the days when I went to school here. Her name is Mrs. Gates, and she's going to take you to your classrooms today."

"Hello, Brian. Hello, Jennifer. I'm so glad to meet you at last. Your mom has told me so much about you. Are you ready to meet your teachers?" Maxine asked.

"Yes," the children responded in chorus.

"Well, I just happen to have your schedules right here. Your mom got everything all set up for you yesterday. All she has to do is go and sign you in, and we will be ready to go."

"Thank you so much, Maxine. You have no idea how much I appreciate this. I'm going to go and look for office space this morning," Luci informed her in a low voice, thankful that her kids were distracted by the large bulletin board that adorned the wall by the office.

"Don't worry. We'll be just fine," Maxine assured her. "Just sign them in, and you can be on your way."

❖

LUCI HAD SCANNED THROUGH HER laptop the previous night and discovered that several of her former classmates were now in the real estate business. She had a hard time deciding which one to pick, but she finally went with Linda Kay Spurgeon, a girl who had been on the cheerleader squad with her. The office was located downtown, and she headed the car in that direction as soon as she had signed her two children into school.

She looked about as she drove through the familiar streets, amazed at the changes that had taken place in the past few years. Many of the original buildings had been either replaced or renovated, giving the town a fresh, new look. Although Summerfield was a small town, its standing as a community was boosted by the location of a private college situated on the outskirts of town. It was right across the river from a larger town named Brooksville. She was sure between the two communities she could find enough clients to support herself and her two children.

She didn't know what time the real estate office opened, but it should be open by the time she got there. Linda Kay had always been such a peppy person. Somehow, Luci thought that selling real estate would suit her. Luci just hoped Linda Kay could find the right office space for her. The ad had been rather impressive, so she hoped the company lived up to its promotion.

Peering through the side windows as she drove slowly down Main Street, Luci looked for the company sign and street address. There seemed to be a lot more numbers now than when she was growing up. Nobody paid attention to the numbers then.

Well, I guess that's a good omen. The more people here, the more potential clients for me, she thought.

Just then she spotted the sign advertising S & J Real Estate Company. It was posted on a neat, brick veneer building of modern design with a glass door at the entrance. She pulled into the parking lot and exited the car, hitting the lock button as she walked towards the doorway.

She took a deep breath before she pulled the door open. She was about to embark on a new chapter in her life—a chapter without Jeremy. Leaving New York had been the first step. Now she needed a place to set up her own law practice. Maybe Linda Kay could also help her find an affordable house, something to start off in for her and the children. She couldn't stay with her parents forever and getting out on her own would probably be the best thing she could do. Two important decisions awaited her in selecting those two dwellings. So far, things had been working out for her. She just hoped that trend continued.

She was pleasantly surprised when she walked into the office. It was cheerful and tastefully decorated with all the latest trends in design. But then she should have expected no less from Linda Kay, who was always one of the best-dressed girls in school.

"Welcome to S & J Real Estate. May I help you?" inquired the receptionist, who was sitting at a desk near the front door.

"Yes, I'm looking for a place that would provide adequate space for a beginning law office, preferably something in the downtown area," Luci responded.

"Do you have an appointment?"

"No, I just arrived in town a couple of days ago. My name used to be Luci Carlito. I was one of Linda Kay's classmates in high school, so I'm hoping she can help me as quickly as possible."

Luci waited while a conversation took place on the phone. *So, Linda Kay is still using her maiden name. I wonder if she is divorced or never got married. She was one of the cutest girls in the class, so chances are she's divorced. Looks like I'm not the only one in my class with problems.*

Her train of thought was interrupted as the receptionist hung up the phone and a door simultaneously opened.

"Luci Carlito, I can't believe it's really you. What are you doing back in Summerfield?"

Luci looked over to the source of the voice and discovered that her former classmate was still recognizable. In fact, Linda Kay Spurgeon was looking better than ever.

"Linda Kay, how are you? By the way, the name is Luci Clark now. I've been married for over twelve years."

"Oh, that's right. I can never remember the girls' married names when they don't live in town. Come in. Come in, and let's discuss what I can do for you."

Linda Kay motioned towards her office as she spoke. "I see you've already met my receptionist, Sharon Tidwell. Sharon, Luci and I used to be on the cheerleading squad together way back when."

"Nice to meet you, Luci," said Sharon.

"Yes, way back when, but we won't say how far back," Luci joked as she stepped into Linda Kay's office.

"So, you're looking for space for a law office?" Linda Kay asked as she pulled up information on a computer screen while Luci settled comfortable into a plush chair facing the desk.

"Yes, I've decided to move back to Summerfield and start my own law practice."

"Oh?" the response came as a question.

Well, no use in hiding it. Pretty soon it will be all over town that

Jeremy and I are separated. Might as well 'fess up and get it over with. Luci pondered the situation before she spoke.

"My husband and I are currently separated, but not divorced. We just need some time apart, so I decided that Summerfield is the best place for me and my children right now."

"Children?" Linda Kay sounded almost envious.

Are all my old classmates jealous of the fact that I now have children? Luci wondered.

"I have two children, a boy and a girl—Brian and Jennifer."

"How lovely…Oh, here it is. I knew I had just the right thing for you. A very nice office space just opened up in the downtown area. Would you like to see it today?"

"Yes. The sooner the better. I'm already licensed to practice law in this state, so it shouldn't be too much trouble to set up a practice. The only thing is I am going to need some assistants. Do you have any idea of who might be able to work as a secretary or receptionist for me?"

"Can't think of anyone at the moment, but if I do, I'll let you know."

"I am also looking for a place of my own. Nothing too fancy, but with enough room for me and the two children."

"Hmmm…let me do some more checking. Do you have any idea what part of town you would like to live in?"

"I've already enrolled the children in school, so I need something in that school zone…Summerfield Elementary."

"I see. I remember when that used to be the only school when we were growing up, but the town has expanded since then." Linda Kay suddenly stopped her train of thought and pointed to the computer screen. "Oh, wait! Here's a house that just came on the market a few days ago. Did you have a price in mind?"

Luci named a figure, and Linda Kay frowned slightly, the only indication that money might be a problem.

"Well, this house is a little more than that, but the owners always ask more than they expect to actually get. We can go over right now to both places if you have the time. Then, if you're interested, we can make an offer and see what happens."

"That would be wonderful," Luci responded, resisting the urge to cross her fingers behind her back.

"Great. We'll use my car. There's a parking lot behind the office, so you should have plenty of space for both clients and employees." Linda Kay was already picking up her purse as she spoke.

Luci felt the slightest flutter of butterflies in her stomach. Was she making the right decision? It was a big step, one that would affect, not only her life, but also the lives of her children. Once she started, there would be no turning back. Was her life with Jeremy really over? It was too soon to tell, but she had to start somewhere, and finding a source of income was the first thing she needed to do. After that, she should be able to afford her own house, and she and the children would move out of Mama and Papa's place. After all, she was a grown woman. She should be able to support herself and her children, even without Jeremy's help. But he would never allow that. Even if things got worse and they did actually get a divorce, he was sure to demand his custodial rights. Besides that, he was an honorable man who met his obligations. He would definitely provide child support. One way or another, she wouldn't be penniless or homeless. It might not be the lavish lifestyle she had grown accustomed to, but she had not grown up with riches, so she knew how to be frugal. The children didn't know it, but their lives were going to be a lot different from now on.

⸺ ❖ ⸺

JEREMY CLARK SPENT A BUSY morning on the phone after his brief encounter with Sheba. He could swear the scent of her perfume had penetrated every piece of furniture in his office. Or was it just his imagination? The woman knew how to get to him, and she wanted him to remember she had been there. Evidently, it was working. How had his life become such a mess in just a few days?

His first call had been to Mike Graham, the private investigator he had hired to try to solve the mystery of the tabloid incident. First and foremost, he needed to know who had been responsible for sending that photo to both Luci and Matt. Once he knew that, he could begin his campaign to win Luci back.

"Mike, I think I might have some more information for you regarding the case," he had explained. He had gone on to quickly relate the details of Sheba's visit, along with the history of their relationship. Mike had agreed that the lead had possibilities, and he promised to check into the whereabouts of one Miss Sheba James during the times that the tabloids had appeared in their respective destinations.

After they ended the conversation, Jeremy had one more call to make. He usually had Belinda make the calls for him, but this was something he needed to handle himself. He scanned the numbers stored on the Rolodex on his desk and then dialed the one he had been looking for. It was the number of Frank Gibbons, his business lawyer. He briefly explained the situation to Frank.

"Sure, I know a divorce attorney. He's the best in his field. His name is Jackson Slayter," Frank responded. "I can put in a good word for you with him, if you'd like."

"I'd appreciate any help you can give me," Jeremy exclaimed.

"Sure, I'll get on it right away," Frank promised.

Jeremy had Belinda make him an appointment with Slayter. She knew his schedule better than he did. He could ill afford to take time out off from his work, but this was necessary. He was trying to save his marriage, but at the same time he had to protect his interests. Luci wasn't the type to try to take him to the cleaners, but he needed to take steps to make sure that didn't happen. He wanted to get it all in writing, just in case his plan backfired.

At a meeting later that week, he explained the whole situation to the lawyer. He found himself thinking it sounded almost too melodramatic to be true, even as he was speaking.

Jackson Slayter sat in his chair without saying a word, elbows propped on his desk and his fingertips supporting his chin. His occasional nod was the only indication he even comprehended Jeremy's account of recent events. *It's like a scene out of "Matlock," I swear this guy could pass for Matlock's twin. I just hope he's as good a lawyer as Matlock was,* Jeremy thought.

"So, this whole thing came about as a result of a tabloid picture?" Jackson inquired when Jeremy finished speaking.

"Yes, I'm afraid so. There have been plenty of other pictures of me with other women in the papers, but this one seemed to hit a raw nerve. I swear to you that I'm completely innocent. I never cheated on my wife."

"Men never do," Jackson observed dryly. "And you are having this investigated, you say?"

"I have a detective working on the case. I don't want a divorce, but I want to be prepared, just in case we go to court. My wife is a lawyer, and a good one at that."

"I understand. Suppose you tell me exactly what you would expect, should the divorce actually occur, and we can work from there."

Jeremy began a list of his demands and inquired about his rights in what turned into a two-hour session. He was surprised that Jackson could spare so much time for one client.

Frank must have done a good job of paving the way for me. I wonder just how much he told Jackson I'm worth? Jeremy thought as he pondered the irony of the situation.

He could see that he had his work cut out for him. He still had a business to run. He needed to find out who sent the tabloid pictures, and he had to worry about the possibility of a divorce. Thank goodness Belinda had come back to work. She was a big help in keeping things in the office running smoothly. That should give him more time to work on the other problems. But it was definitely lonely without Luci and the kids around. How much longer was this unthinkable situation going to last?

Luci found the office space to be quite suitable, as promised. It was located near the Summerfield courthouse and was also close enough to Brooksville's courthouse to make it fairly convenient. She was happy that she would be able to stay in her hometown.

The house Linda Kay recommended was in an older section of town in a quiet neighborhood. It had been completely remodeled with all the amenities. It was not as fancy as the apartment in New York, but it was in the right school zone and also not too far from where Mama Rosa and Papa D'Armon lived.

She had her own bank account, and since she had not begun divorce proceedings, she still had access to all her money. All she needed to do was to set up a bank account in Summerfield and arrange to have some of the money transferred. She would need furniture. Then there was transportation. She couldn't keep driving Mama's car forever. She needed a set of wheels. Her mind was almost spinning, just thinking about what she needed to do.

Linda Kay promised to draw up the papers regarding the rental of the office space. She suggested making an offer on the house while waiting for the funds to come through. Luci agreed that seemed to be the best plan. After returning to the real estate office, Luci said goodbye to Linda Kay and drove away, headed for one of the car lots in Summerfield. She didn't know what kind of vehicle she wanted, but she knew she had to have some kind of reliable transportation.

She drove aimlessly at first, unsure of which car dealership to choose until she saw a sign that caught her attention—Milano's Automotive. Could the business possibly belong to Roberto Milano, her old flame from her high school days? He had been the captain of the football team, ruggedly handsome in an unwashed sort of way. Her parents had never approved of her dating the boy, whose dad was rumored to have Mafia ties. His hair had always been a tad too long to suit Papa, and he had sported the hint of several days' growth of beard before such a thing became popular.

"Does the boy ever bathe?" Mama had once asked.

Her curiosity got the best of her, and she couldn't resist turning into the lot that sported the latest models of Japanese vehicles. Whoever owned it seemed to have a monopoly on the business because the billboard advertised every brand of Japanese car imaginable. She had little doubt that she would be able to find suitable transportation at this business.

She parked her vehicle and headed towards the showroom, hoping she would not be accosted by some eager salesperson before she could even make it inside. She needed to go over some details about prices before actually looking at anything within her budget.

She walked into what was a surprisingly clean and appealing

showroom, totally different from what she had expected of Roberto, if this was even his business.

Guess the boy final grew up and decided to conform to society's expectations.

She looked around at the vehicles on display, but before she could walk over to them, a salesman approached.

"May I help you?" he inquired.

"Yes, I am interested in buying a car, preferably a new one," Luci responded.

"Did you have anything in particular in mind?"

Before Luci could answer, their conversation was interrupted by the sounds of a loud argument coming from what appeared to be the main office. It had ceiling-to-floor glass panels facing the showroom, so all persons inside were visible to anyone in the showroom. Luci could see three men who were evidently in a heated disagreement. One of them resembled Roberto. He had aged, and he was wearing a business suit, but there was little mistaking his still-handsome profile. Her old flame must be the owner of this business.

The door burst open as two of the men rushed through it and ended up in the middle of the showroom, standing in front of the new car display. Roberto stood in the office doorway as one of the men raised his fist and began shouting.

"You haven't heard the last of this, Milano. I'm innocent, I tell you! I didn't do anything wrong."

"Sorry, Tom, but the evidence is all there. I'm afraid you'll have to leave, or I'll be forced to have you escorted off the property. The same goes for you, Eric," he addressed his last remark to the second man, who was visibly upset.

"We're going. Keep your shirt on," Eric retorted, as a flush of anger crept up his neck and reddened his cheeks.

The two men pivoted on their heels and left quickly, while Roberto remained in his doorway. Luci turned towards him, unable to stop herself. He was staring straight at her, she discovered.

"Are my eyes deceiving me or is it really Luci Carlito setting foot in my place?" he asked in the rumbling bass tone she remembered so well.

It took Luci a few seconds to find her voice before she could answer him.

"Yes, it's really me," she finally managed to squeak out, despising herself for letting her emotions show. She couldn't believe she still had feelings for the guy.

"Well, I must say, the years have agreed with you. I thought you were beautiful back in high school, but now you're looking better than ever. What brings you back to Summerfield?"

"Could we talk in your office...please?"

"Yes, certainly. Where are my manners?" he asked as his sales staff stood by with their mouths hanging open.

He lowered the blinds and shut the door as Luci sat down.

"No sense in having an audience," he explained. "I wish I had thought of doing that ten minutes ago."

Luci nodded. "Hindsight is twenty-twenty, they say."

"So, why is a New York lady looking for a car in Summerfield? Are you buying something for your parents?"

"No..." She cleared her throat before continuing. "I'm moving back to Summerfield and need some transportation. Right now, I'm driving my mama's car, but I can't keep doing that."

"The last time I saw you, you were leaving town on your honeymoon with that rich dude. What was his name? Parker..."

"Clark...Jeremy Clark. My name is now Luci Carlito Clark. You... you were at my wedding?" she asked incredulously.

"Yes, on the back row of the church. I had to go. I just had to," he admitted.

"I didn't know...I didn't see you," Luci almost whispered her response.

"You know you almost broke my heart when you broke up with me." He actually looked sad as he spoke. Somehow, it was touching, Luci thought regretfully.

"It's been over twelve years, Berto," she replied, addressing Roberto by the nickname that had stuck with him throughout his high school years. "I did what I had to do. Mama and Papa never approved of you. You know that."

"True love can overcome anything."

"Then I guess it wasn't true love, Berto."

"Maybe not for you."

"We were just high school kids."

"Not any longer."

She couldn't stand this conversation. Not one second more.

"So, how did you end up in the car business?" she asked, hoping to change the topic to a less personal level.

"I never got married. After you left town, I threw myself into the business like my dad wanted me to do. We now have the most successful auto dealership in the area."

"I can see that. You have lots of models to choose from," Luci shifted nervously in her seat.

"Top of the line," he responded proudly. "So, if you're interested in a car, we can fix you up. Let me get my best salesman to help you."

"Thank you. That would be great."

He opened the office door and motioned to the salesman who had first approached Luci. She rose from her seat as the salesman entered the office.

"Henry, this is Luci Clark, an old classmate of mine. She is looking for a vehicle, and I want you to take good care of her," he instructed.

"Be glad to, Mr. Milano. Let's go into the showroom and discuss what you have in mind." Henry held the door open for Luci as he spoke.

Several hours later, Luci found herself driving home in Mama's sedan after completing all the necessary paperwork on the car she had picked out. She had settled on a red Honda Civic. It was a step down from the Lexus she was accustomed to driving in New York, but that life was behind her now and she had a budget to consider. She would be able to pick up the car tomorrow. The children would be excited about it, no matter what model it happened to be. Then there was that new car smell that could never be duplicated. It would be kind of fun to drive around and inhale that scent for a few days anyhow. She felt that she had made a good choice.

Well, the next thing on the agenda was to break the news to Mama Rosa and Papa D'Armon that she would no longer be living with them.

They would be sad to see her and the children go, as they had missed so many years of the children's growing up when she and Jeremy were living in New York. But they would understand that she needed her own space. She had been gone from home for over twelve years now. She wasn't their little girl any longer.

— ⬦⬦⬦ —

JEREMY RUBBED THE SPOT BETWEEN his eyes, willing the headache that developed on his flight from London to New York to go away. But it wasn't working. The plane was in mid-flight now and still had quite a way to go before it touched down. Almost a month had passed since his original conversation with Mike Graham regarding the tabloid case. Mike had thoroughly checked out Sheba James, and her alibi for the time frame had held up. So, there was no way she could have personally placed the tabloid at either his or Matt's house. Still, there was a chance she had hired someone else to do the dirty deed. Mike was sniffing around now, trying to find out more details.

In the meantime, Jeremy had also hired a private investigator to keep an eye on Luci and the kids while they were in Summerfield. If she found out, she would probably never forgive him, but he just had to know what was going on. They were over a thousand miles away, and if some emergency came up, he wanted to know about it. They were still his family, and he was going to take care of them, even if Luci didn't want his assistance.

He had learned plenty in the last few days. Evidently, Luci was establishing herself again in her hometown. He knew all about her new law practice, the house she had bought, the new car purchase, and even where the kids were enrolled in school. In fact, there wasn't much he didn't know about his wife's activities. She would be surprised to learn she had been tailed and that her private accounts had been hacked, but that was what he was paying for. He hired only the best, and it was paying off for him.

Belinda had resigned herself to the fact that Matt wasn't coming back. He had a new girlfriend. She wasn't dating anybody yet. She was wrapped up in her work, often spending extra hours at the office. He wished he could do something to help her. She was too young to let a broken heart get the best of her. Maybe there was another man in her future. It was too soon to tell. She still wasn't back to her usual bubbly self, but she was trying. He did appreciate that. He would have to think of some little reward for her.

Sheba had made several appearances to his office on the pretense of checking on her mergers he was working on. She had even asked Jeremy to accompany her to a play, a request he had managed to wriggle out of. How could he have ever found the woman so appealing when now she irritated him to no end? He had to air out his office after each visit to get rid of the lingering perfume scent. He had finally identified the fragrance as one he had bought her when they were dating. Now she was using it as a reminder, just to torment him, he was sure.

He had done all he could regarding the mergers and then bounced the ball back into her lawyer's court, hoping that would be the end of it. But she kept coming up with excuses to drop by his office. It was like a mouse sniffing around a piece of cheese, and he was the cheese. Well, if he had to be cheese, he was going to try his best to be Limburger, and he hoped that would repel the fascinated mouse.

He hated going home to an empty house. All the reminders were still there. Luci had fled in such a hurry that she had left her clothes scattered about. The children's toys were everywhere, reminiscent of the good times he had playing games with them. He wasn't much of a cook, either, so he found himself wishing he could be in his restaurant in Summerfield, sampling some of Mama Rosa's Italian cuisine that he had made famous. No, this was definitely not the best time of his life.

— ◆◆◆ —

LUCI WAS PROUD OF THE progress she made over the next few weeks. All of her finances had been straightened out, paving the way for the loans on her car and house note. The office rental contract had been approved, and she had picked out furniture for both the office and the new home. Finding a competent assistant for the office had been harder than she thought, but after interviewing ten people, she had settled on one she though was suitable—Cynthia Walker, a woman in her late twenties who had some experience in doing legal secretarial work.

The children had settled in school and were making good grades. Getting them into a routine had helped immensely, as she knew it would. They were good kids, and they didn't complain much, but she knew they missed their dad. She was sorry it had to be this way for now, but she couldn't let Jeremy back into her life at this point. She had to make it on her own.

She had scraped up a few clients. The business had been slow in building up, but word was starting to get around. Some of her former classmates had sent people her way, and a few of them were clients themselves. It was almost uncanny that a taxi cab driver's daughter was now advising people about legal matters.

She attended Parents' Night at the school. The teachers were wonderful, and the kids just loved them. Brian, who was in the fourth grade, had Mrs. Jillian Hawthorne, a very pretty and friendly teacher. Jennifer's first-grade teacher was Mrs. Elizabeth Peterman. Principal Noreen Andrews wasn't any more sociable than she was on the first visit. It was kind of sad that somebody so smart and so attractive had ended up such a bitter person, but it wasn't Luci's problem. She had enough to worry about just taking care of her children, running the household, and keeping up with her new law practice. Noreen had every opportunity to interact with the children as the principal of the school. If she wanted to cut off her nose to spite her face, as the old saying went, it was just too bad. Luci still worried that Noreen might do something to harm her children, but Maxine assured her again that her fears were groundless.

"She's been the principal here ever since Mrs. Caroline Stewart retired. As far as I know, there have been no complaints against her," Maxine told Luci. "Besides, I wouldn't worry about it. We have close connections with the police force in this town. Mrs. Jillian Hawthorne is married to Jake Hawthorne, one of our cops."

"Jake Hawthorne. Wasn't he a couple of years ahead of us in school? Seems like I remember him being the captain of the football team before Berto took over his senior year."

"Yes, that's the same one. We had so many good-looking guys in our school." Maxine sighed as she spoke.

"Don't go there, girl. You got a good man, and I found somebody I thought was wonderful. Guess only time will tell if I made the right or wrong choice."

"I'm praying for you every night."

"Thanks, friend. I need that. Well, let me gather my crew and get out of here. I have lots of work to do."

"Okay, and remember, don't worry. Everything's going to be all right."

—◆◇◈◇◆—

THE NEXT FEW WEEKS PASSED uneventfully, although Luci was still on edge regarding Noreen Andrews. Somehow, she just couldn't shake the bad feeling she had about her former classmate and competitor. She was in the kitchen washing dishes after the evening meal and the children were in their rooms doing their homework when the phone rang. Luci glanced at the Caller I. D. before she answered. It was Mama Rosa.

"Luci, did you hear the news report on TV tonight?" Mama asked.

"No, Mama. I have been so busy I didn't even turn the TV on tonight. What happened?"

"There has been a murder in our town. Police found a man named Eric Wiley stuffed into one of the dumpsters behind Jeremy's restaurant.

"Jeremy's restaurant…you mean Rosalena's?" Luci asked, referring to the restaurant he had named after Mama Rosa and Luci's grandmother.

"Yes."

"Oh, my. How terrible! Do they have any idea who did it?"

"Nobody has been arrested yet, but they said they have some suspects in mind."

"Our little town is always so peaceful. I think I can count on one hand the murders that have taken place in my lifetime."

"Yes, but now crime is everywhere, even here."

"Did they say who found the body?"

"It was one of the restaurant employees who went out to empty the trash. They didn't give a name."

Luci sighed. "I guess it will be in the newspaper tomorrow morning. Well, thanks for letting me know, Mama. I had better check on the kids. They're supposed to be doing their homework."

"Okay, tell them 'hello' for me."

Luci's mind was already racing ahead as she hung up the phone. If the body had been found on Jeremy's property, that meant he would be coming to town. They had not talked since the conversation on the first morning when she had arrived in town. She was trying to distance herself from him, but she knew there was no way he would come to town without seeing her and the children. How was she supposed to gain her independence if she couldn't get away from him?

She hung up the dishtowels on the rack and turned out the kitchen light before making her way down the hall to check on the children. She went over their homework assignments with them, but only half-heartedly. She hoped they wouldn't notice her lack of attention. Fortunately, they were eager to finish their assignments so they could watch their favorite TV program before bath time.

She spent another sleepless night after getting the children to bed. It was almost as bad as her first night in town. She plumped her pillow again and peered at the alarm clock. Time was crawling, as it was only fifteen minutes later than the last time she had checked. *How could the thought of seeing Jeremy again stir up such a turmoil?* she wondered. She did love the guy. Maybe she had been too hasty, but now she was back in her hometown, trying to start a new life. She had never had a real chance to prove herself, never really been out on her own. She had married Jeremy before finishing college. She had to know if she was as good a lawyer as she believed she was. This was her time to flourish or fail. Which one would it be? And just how long would it be before Jeremy showed up on her doorstep?

<hr/>

JEREMY SQUINTED AT HIS NEW cell phone as it rang incessantly, waking him from a deep sleep. He made it a habit to keep the phone on at all times because of business calls, but who would be calling so early in the morning? he wondered. The name that appeared on the Caller I. D. caused him to sit up straight in the bed as he picked up the phone. It was Patrick Sherman, the private investigator he had hired to keep an eye on Luci and the kids in Summerfield.

"Hello, Patrick. What's wrong?" he inquired worriedly.

"The police have found a body in one of the dumpsters behind your restaurant in Summerfield," Patrick responded.

"What? You've got to be kidding! What would a body be doing in one of my dumpsters?" Jeremy exclaimed.

"The case is still under investigation, but I thought I had better let you know. I'll send you more details as soon as they are available."

"Well, stay on it, but I'm afraid I can't wait for the details. Since it's my property that's involved, I'm coming to Summerfield to see for myself. I'll book a flight as soon as I can get out of New York."

"Okay, Mr. Clark. Sorry to be the bearer of bad tidings, but you said I should keep you posted on anything that happened."

"You did the right thing, Patrick. Thanks so much."

Jeremy placed the phone back on the nightstand and ran his hands through his hair. Then he rubbed his eyes, willing them to stay open as he planned what needed to be done next. Belinda usually handled most of the booking arrangements for him, but he wasn't about to disturb her so early in the morning. This was one call he was going to make for himself.

He padded into the living room, the chill from the cold tiles seeping into his bare feet as he left the plush carpet of the bedroom behind. Luci had taken her laptop with her when she left and his was still at his office, so he needed a phone directory. *Where did Luci usually keep it?* he wondered. He had not needed it, as he had all his important numbers programmed into his phone. He hadn't thought to program the number for the airline into his phone, but he would do that now, just as soon as he found the directory.

He cursed softly as he stubbed his toe on the foot of an end table when rounding the couch. That's what he got for not wearing slippers, but he wasn't used to jumping out of bed in the middle of the night...

or early morning hours. Most things in his life were carefully planned. Marrying Luci had been one of his few impulsive moves, and it had been the best decision he had ever made.

Moments later, he located the phone book in one of the kitchen drawers. He found the number he needed and made the necessary arrangements using the house phone in the kitchen. Satisfied that he had done the right thing, he headed back to his bedroom to pack for the trip.

He was quite familiar with the town of Summerfield, having spent many weekends there while his restaurant was being remodeled. Finding his way around town would be no problem. The problem would be in how to approach his wife, who was now keeping him at arm's length. How were they supposed to solve their marital problems if she wouldn't even talk to him? He was going to make it a point to see her while he was in town, he vowed. This separation had gone on long enough.

Unable to go back to sleep after packing, he went into the kitchen to make himself a pot of coffee. If he was going to be awake anyhow, he might as well enjoy the full benefits of caffeine, he decided. He puttered around, looking for something to eat. The kitchen cupboard and refrigerator were almost bare, so it appeared that toast with jelly would be the only accompaniment. He had survived on less, so that would just have to do. Maybe he could grab a doughnut or some fast food at the airport. Now he was definitely missing Mama Rosa's cooking.

He readied the table and slid two pieces of bread into the toaster while waiting for the coffee to finish brewing. Then he turned on the under-the-counter TV set and tuned it in to one of the news channels. It was the usual jumble of depressing situations—riots, demonstrations, famine, and murders.

He listened intently to a description of an unsolved murder in another town, which brought him back to his present problems. Why would someone choose to leave a body in one of the dumpsters behind his restaurant? It just didn't make any sense. Was somebody trying to frame him, or had they just been looking for a convenient place to rid themselves of the evidence?

Now he had two mysteries to solve—the case of the tabloid pictures and the murder in Summerfield. Patrick would be a big help, but this was something he wanted to get to the bottom of himself. Anyhow, it gave him an excuse for arriving in town. He could keep an eye on Luci and the kids while looking into the homicide. Just how much information he would be able to get out of the police department was still up in the air, but he was determined. When Jeremy Clark put his mind to something, he never gave up, and this was one of those times. There was too much at stake for him to quit now.

⭑⭑⭑

Luci rose the following morning feeling as if she had been a participant in a boxing match. Every bone and muscle in her body ached, and it was all she could do to drag herself out of bed. Tossing and turning all night had definitely not been good for her health, she reflected as she stuffed her feet into her bedroom slippers and grabbed her robe. She headed towards the kitchen to prepare breakfast for the children before rousing them.

She barely had the table set and was about to scramble some eggs when her phone rang. She sighed as she walked over to the counter to pick it up. She hoped it wasn't Mama calling again. She just didn't feel like getting into a long conversation at this time of morning.

The Caller I. D. showed the number to be that of the Summerfield police department. *Who could be calling her at this hour?* she wondered. Probably another DUI case, typical for the type of clients she had managed to scrape up so far. What she needed was a major case to get some publicity. Maybe then she would be able to get enough business to support herself and her two children. The money coming in had been a slow trickle, not a steady stream.

"Hello, Luci Clark speaking," she said as she answered the call with the most professional voice she could muster so early in the morning.

"Luci, this is Berto. I need your help. I've been arrested, and I'm in the city jail right now."

"Arrested? For what?" She could barely get the words out as she struggled to keep from dropping the phone.

"I don't know if you've heard about this or not, but there was a murder in Summerfield last night. They found the body of one of my salesmen in a dumpster. He was shot with my gun."

"Which salesman? And how do they know it was your gun used for the shooting?"

"It was Eric Wiley, one of the men who was arguing with me when you came into the showroom."

"Okay, but what about the gun?"

"My gun was found in another dumpster not too far from where the body was found."

"Yes, I heard about the body being found behind my husband's restaurant. But are they sure it was your gun? What about fingerprints?"

"The gun was registered to me. Besides that, my fingerprints were on it. But the gun belonged to me, so, of course, I handled it. I kept it in a drawer in my office, but I kept that drawer locked. I don't how anybody could have gotten access to it. We have security cameras in the showroom and in my office. If anybody was in there, it should have been caught by one of the cameras."

"Well, it sounds like we're dealing with somebody who is both a murderer and an electronics specialist. It had to be somebody who was familiar with the business and somebody who wanted to frame you for murder."

"Then you believe me? You believe I didn't kill Eric?"

"Of course, I believe you, Berto. After all, we did date for several years in high school."

"Honey, we did more than date."

"Please, let's not get into all of that now. I know you, Berto. I know you're not capable of murder."

"Thank you. I needed to hear that because I'm pretty down right now. I just need to get out of this place."

"I have to get the children off to school. I'll be there as soon as I can manage it. I promise."

"Don't worry about bail money. I can take care of that as soon as you fill out the paperwork."

"Consider it done."

"Again, thank you, Luci. I knew I could count on you."

Luci turned back to the task of preparing breakfast as soon as she hung up the phone. She went through the motions almost mechanically, her mind racing ahead as she scrambled the eggs, made the toast, and set two glasses of milk onto the table.

The children made their usual protests against getting up, but they were soon sitting at the table eating the food she had prepared. She hurried back to her bedroom to begin dressing for the day. After a quick shower she supervised the children getting dressed and then managed to attire herself in what she considered halfway decent apparel for an attorney. Thank heavens she wasn't having a bad hair day! At least one thing was working in her favor. She just hoped she was up to handling a murder case in her hometown. There was no telling who might be called as a witness. How would her former classmates feel about being grilled on the witness stand by a taxi driver's daughter?

After dropping the children off at school, she made her way to the courthouse to file the necessary papers for Berto's release. She would just have to trust Berto to come up with the bail money, as there was no way she could possibly afford to post it for him.

After completing the necessary paperwork, she drove straight to the jail, which was located just a short distance from the courthouse. She was surprised to see a crowd of people in the parking lot, which was filled with vehicles of all sorts and sizes, including one van from the local TV station. How had word of Berto's arrest spread so quickly?

The mob began to descend on her as she stepped out of her car. The barrage of questions began almost immediately as a TV camera was shoved in front of her face.

"Is it true that Roberto Milano has been arrested for murder?" was the first question hurled at her.

Before she could respond, other questions followed in rapid-fire succession.

"Are you the attorney representing Roberto Milano?"

"Do you think Roberto Milano is guilty of murder?"

She raised her hands to shield her eyes from the blinding lights behind the TV camera and stepped back from the microphones that had been shoved in front of her.

"Please, I am not at liberty to discuss the case at this time."

To her relief, several uniformed policemen moved up in front of the crowd.

"All right, folks. Let's break it up. Let the lady through," one of them stated.

"Are you okay ma'am?" he inquired. "Let's get you inside."

He turned to the other officers, barking instructions. "You guys see what you can do with this crowd."

Luci walked through the jailhouse door and headed for the front desk.

"Can I help you?" inquired a burly uniformed officer sitting behind the desk.

"I have the papers for Roberto Milano's release," she said, placing the papers on his desk as she spoke.

The officer sifted through the papers before he responded.

"Everything seems to be in order. As soon as bail is posted your client is free to go."

"Bail? I understood him to say that he would take care of that."

"Hold on and let me check." The officer scrolled through his computer screen. "No, nothing is showing up here. Evidently, the bail has not been posted. Would you like to confer with your client?"

"Yes, please. I would like to see him now."

"Okay, wait here and I'll have him brought to a conference room."

Luci waited impatiently until another officer came and escorted her down the hall and around the corner to the appropriate room. Glancing through the door's window, she could see Berto sitting at the table. He was wearing handcuffs and shackles. He was a sorry sight.

How the mighty have fallen. Is this the hometown football hero I grew up with? Now he's sitting in jail accused of murder. Am I the only one who believes he's innocent? I don't know how I'm going to prove it, but he's depending on me. I have to come through for him!

She cleared her throat and nodded to the officer to indicate she was ready to enter the conference room. She managed a slight smile as she walked through the door.

"Luci, thank God you're here! What did you find out?" Berto exclaimed.

"I've filed the papers for your release, but you still need to make bail. I thought you were going to take care of the money."

"They won't tell me anything. I made my one phone call to you, and that's all I was allowed. I need you to do something for me."

"What?"

"I need you to call my father and ask him to put up the bail for me. I could post it myself, but I don't have access to my funds right now."

"Okay, give me the information and I'll see what I can do. But before I go, we need to discuss your case. What can you tell me about it?"

"Not much more than I've already told you over the phone. I had an argument with two salesmen on my staff and I had to fire them. It involved some money disappearing from the vehicle sales they made."

"How could that happen? I thought everything these days was done by computer."

"It is, but somebody must have gotten access to my accounts. I guess we were hacked."

"Well, that's not too surprising in this day and age. What else?"

"Like I said, I kept a gun at the business in case of some kind of altercation. But the gun was always locked up. I never took it out of the drawer. Most of the staff knew about it, though. They used to joke about it…a lot. Plus, we had security cameras all over the place. I don't know how anybody could have gotten the gun without being filmed."

"Well, somebody evidently did. What we need to do is figure out who it was and how they did it. Were you tested for gunshot residue?"

"I was awakened in the wee hours of the morning. I had already showered and changed clothes after I got home."

"Did they confiscate the clothes you were wearing?"

"Yes, but they had already been washed. It was laundry day, and my housekeeper grabs the clothes as soon as I change. She can't wait to get them into the washer."

"I can see that this case is getting complicated. I might have to hire a detective to help me."

"Money is no object. Do whatever you have to do."

"Okay, let's start with getting you out of here. Give me your dad's number and I'll see if he will post bail for you."

She shoved a piece of paper across the table and handed Berto her pen. He quickly scribbled a number at the top of the paper.

"Here, but there's something else I need to tell you." he said as he returned the paper.

"What's that?"

"My dad and I aren't exactly on speaking terms. After I agreed to run the auto business for him, he wanted me to broaden my horizons, so to speak. I know what kind of man he is, even though he is my dad, so I refused. He agreed to leave the business with me and we parted ways."

Luci paused. So, the rumors she had heard all her life about the Milano family were more than just rumors. Maybe there were Mafia connections floating around in Summerfield after all.

"I guess you did what you had to do. I'll do what I can, but until I can get the bail posted, you're stuck in here. Just try to stay out of trouble. You'll be hearing from me shortly." She gathered her belongings as she spoke.

"I'll be good, I promise." He smiled at her with the same lopsided grin that had melted her heart so many years ago.

"Goodbye, Berto," she said as she knocked on the door to signal the officer outside she was ready to leave.

She walked down the hall, her mind jumbled with thoughts of her past and present life.

Why has fate played such a cruel trick on me? Here I am, separated from my husband and now thrown together with my first love, who turns out to have Mafia connections. I don't know what to do about my love life, but now I have to try to make Berto's trial my first priority. If I do that, then I will just have to trust in God to guide me through the rest of the crisis.

It was going to be too much for her to handle alone. She could see that now. The first thing she was going to have to do was hire a detective, along with some kind of electronics or computer specialist. It was going to take a lot of digging to get to the bottom of this case.

Why was Eric Wiley killed? Who killed him and why would they want to frame Berto? Besides that, why was money missing from his bank accounts? And to make matters worse, why did they have to pick the dumpster behind Jeremy's restaurant as the place to leave the body? Could it have been someone who knew she used to date Berto and was now married to Jeremy? What was the connection?

She needed advice, and she needed it fast. Who was the one person in town she could trust, the one person who knew everybody and everything that was going on?

She had it! Who else but her old friend Maxine Gates? Surely, Maxine could recommend a good detective, a relative scarcity in these parts. She could talk to Maxine without revealing anything that would violate attorney-client privilege. After all, the murder story was already on TV and would undoubtedly be the top headline in the morning paper. It wouldn't be long before everyone in town knew she was the attorney representing Roberto Milano. She just hoped the news media wouldn't camp outside her house during the trial.

◆◆◆

JEREMY WAITED IMPATIENTLY AS THE plane landed and taxied down the runway of the Brooksville airport. The airport was located in Brooksville rather than Summerfield, as Brooksville was the larger town. He would have to take a taxi to a motel. He didn't want to call one from Papa D'Armon's On Your Way taxi company. He wasn't ready to make his presence known just yet. He had things to do first. As much as he hated it, he would have to summon a cab from one of Papa's competitors.

He traveled light, so there was no waiting in line for baggage claim after he descended from the plane. All he had with him was a carry-on bag with his toiletry items and a change of clothes. He could always buy more clothes if he needed them. Right now, time was of the essence.

He had opted to stay in Brooksville rather than Summerfield for the time being. He would contact his family when he felt it was appropriate, but right now he wanted to gather as much data as he could about the case without calling attention to himself. He would start by talking to his chief employee, James Lovett, who had worked his way up from being the first cook at Rosalena's restaurant to district manager when the restaurant had expanded to several locations. James was a straightforward and plainspoken man, but there was little that escaped his attention, especially where the restaurants were concerned. If anybody had an idea of why a body would be left in one of Jeremy's dumpsters, it would be James.

He lucked out with the cab because the driver didn't recognize him. He checked into the motel where he had made reservations and then wasted no time in making several phone calls. The first call was to his detective, Patrick.

"Have you learned anything new about the case?"

"No, Mr. Clark. I'm digging around, but nothing so far that I haven't already told you. They haven't released any more information to the public, as it's an ongoing case."

"We're not the public, Patrick. That's why I'm paying you the big bucks. See if you can grease a few palms and get some more information."

"Will do, Mr. Clark. I'll be in touch."

Satisfied that his interests were being watched after, he began his personal investigation with a phone call to James.

"James, this is Jeremy. I'm at a motel in Brooksville and I need to talk to you. How soon can you get here?"

"Mr. Jeremy, I can't believe you're in town. It's been ages since I saw you. Did you hear about the body being found in the dumpster behind Rosalena's?"

"Yes, I heard. That's why I'm here. But I don't want anybody to know I'm here just yet, so don't say anything, especially to the Carlitos."

"I understand. I'll be as quiet as a church mouse on Sunday morning."

"See how fast you can scurry over here to the Brooksville Inn. I'm in room three thirty-two."

"I'll be there pronto. You know you can always count on me, Mr. Jeremy. After all, you're the one who believed in me enough to give me a job and a fresh start when I was down on my luck. I can never thank you enough for that."

"Luci was the one who convinced me to hire you, James. I wasn't too crazy about the idea."

"Somehow, I kinda knew that, Mr. Jeremy. Yep, I always kinda knew that. It's the sort of person Miss Luci is, always trying to help people."

"You're right, James, and now I may have lost her. I'm going to do my best to win her back, but I might need your help along those lines too. But first we have to solve the mystery about the body."

"Yes, sir, Mr. Jeremy. I'll do what I can."

He decided to take a quick shower before James arrived. He laid out his clothes and then took the toiletry items into the bathroom. He glanced down at his left hand, looking at the wedding ring still on his finger. He had found Luci's rings locked in their safe in New York, but he had continued to wear his, partly in hopes that they would soon be a couple again. But the main reason for wearing the ring was to serve as a deterrent to Sheba James, a ploy that did not seem to be working. Sheba had continued to throw herself at him at every opportunity. She was getting to be quite a nuisance. Even if he and Luci didn't get back together, there was no way he was ever getting involved with such a cold-hearted woman again. She was still his number one suspect regarding the tabloid mystery. If not Sheba, then who? He hoped his other detective could come up with the answer to that question before too long. He was missing his wife and family. Why had he ever thought being a bachelor was the perfect life? His perfect life was with Luci and the children. If he ever got them back, there was no way he was going to give Luci reason to doubt him again. How had his world been turned so topsy-turvy?

—◈◈◈◈—

LUCI'S INSTINCTS HAD PROVEN RIGHT when it came to consulting Maxine about finding a detective. Just like their high school days, Maxine seemed to know everybody and everything that was going on in Summerfield. A phone call to her had provided valuable information.

"Oh, no doubt about who you want to use," Maxine informed her. "The top-notch detective in these parts is a guy named Patrick Sherman. He's not cheap, but he's good. Real good. If there's anything to be investigated, Patrick is your man."

"If he's that expensive, I might not be able to afford him." Luci signed as she spoke.

"Oh, come on, girlfriend. Want me to put in a good word for you? His boys are on the same tag football team as mine. I see him at all the games."

"No, I think I had best try this on my own, as it does involve one of my cases. It wouldn't look too good for me to be talking to somebody else about the case."

"Okay, I guess you're right. Do you want me to give you his cell phone number? It's not listed in the yellow pages."

"Yes, please. I will contact him ASAP. Maybe I'll mention that we're BFF's. It might get me a discount."

"Whatever you say, darlin'. It's your call."

Moments later Luci found herself talking to the detective himself. He definitely had a good phone voice. In fact, it was downright sexy. She wondered if men ever hired him to spy on their wives or girlfriends. Or vice versa.

Patrick agreed to meet with her and Berto at her office the following morning, which brought her back to another pressing problem. She still had to make that phone call to Mr. Giovanni Milano. Would he come through for his son? There was only one way to find out.

She reluctantly dialed the number Berto had given her, not knowing what to expect.

A male with a heavy Italian accent answered the call. "Milano speaking. Who is this?"

"Mr. Milano, my name is Luci Clark. I used to be Luci Carlito."

"Luci Carlito—the girl Roberto used to date in high school? The girl who almost broke his heart? What are you doing back in Summerfield?"

"I'm a lawyer now, and I'm representing Roberto on a murder case."

"Yes, yes. I heard all about Roberto being arrested. I would have sent my lawyer to help him, but he indicated he wanted nothing to do with me and my business years ago."

"Well, that has changed now. Roberto needs your assistance in posting bail."

"How times have changed. Why doesn't he use his own money that he is so proud of making all by himself?"

"His assets are frozen right now. It's a very complicated situation, Mr. Milano. I can't discuss the details with you due to attorney-client privilege. I'm sure you understand that."

"There's nobody who understands that term better than I do. But my son needs my help, so how can I refuse? What is the amount you need for the bail?"

"His bail has been set at half a million dollars. I think they planned on keeping him in jail."

"Ahh, they did not plan on any help from the family for my boy. But they are wrong. No matter what happens, the family always stands together in the end. I will make the necessary arrangements. But tell me, Mrs. Clark, will you be needing any assistance for my son's defense counsel?"

"It's too early to know that yet, Mr. Milano. I have hired a detective and may have to hire other skilled people to help me solve this case."

"Whatever you need, just let me know. I'm at your disposal. I know my boy is not a murderer. I don't want him to spend one more minute in jail than is necessary. I'm counting on you to prove his innocence."

"I'm going to do my best, Mr. Milano. I promise you that. Thank you so much."

Luci hung up the phone with a feeling of relief. That was one less problem she would have to worry about. Now she could concentrate on finding out who actually shot Eric Sanders and who had been embezzling money from Berto's company.

— ◆◦◆◦◆ —

PATRICK SHERMAN WASTED NO TIME in phoning Jeremy to inform him of his acquisition of a new client. Although it was somewhat unethical, he felt he could work it out. He would not reveal any aspects of two cases to the opposing parties. After all, Jeremy expected him to keep watch on Luci practically twenty-four seven, and what better way than to also work for her? At least that was the way he looked at it. Luck had indeed dealt him the upper hand in this case.

Jeremy agreed that working for Luci and watching her at the same time was almost too good to be true. It was much more than he had hoped for. But having her involved with a client whose family had mob connections was not good. In fact, he was quite concerned about that, and also about the fact that she was representing her old high school sweetheart. Could there still be a spark left after all these years? He had always trusted Luci. She was the one who distrusted his relationships with other women. Now the tables were turned. Maybe he was getting a dose of his own medicine. Life could be cruel sometimes, he reflected.

His meeting with James had provided little insight into why the body was dumped behind his restaurant. He and James had spent several hours reviewing all his contacts in the area, but none had popped out as a potential enemy. Perhaps his dumpster was chosen because it was convenient, or maybe it was the isolated location behind the restaurant. It wasn't visible from the road, so it had to be somebody who knew the dumpster was back there—or somebody who had been instructed to dump the body there.

Now he had to wait for a copy of the police report before he could do anything else. Patrick would get it for him. He was sure of that. He always hired the best person for the job, and Patrick was the best at what he did. Throwing a little extra cash around never hurt anything either. One way or another, he was going to get to the bottom of this case. Of course, he did hope Roberto wasn't guilty of murder. He didn't really know the guy, but how could somebody Luci had dated be capable of murder? It just didn't fit the picture. No, something was definitely amiss with this case.

THE FOLLOWING MORNING LUCI RECEIVED a phone call while dressing for work. It was Berto, who informed her that his bail had been posted and he was out of jail. She arranged for him to meet her at her law office later that morning. They had much to discuss.

After dropping the children off at school, she headed for the office, her mind abuzz with all that needed to be done regarding the case. She still had to find a computer or electronics specialist to see if they could figure out how the surveillance tapes could have been altered. They also had to figure out how somebody managed to get access to Berto's office and steal his gun.

Although she knew in her heart there was no way Berto could have killed anybody, she still had to prove it in court. The question was, did Berto have an alibi for the time of the murder? She sincerely hoped so.

Well, there was only one way to find out, she reasoned as she parked her car and walked into the back door of the office. She knew that Cynthia would already be there with a fresh pot of coffee brewing. Thank heavens for a competent assistant!

"Good morning, Luci," Cynthia greeted her as she entered the reception area.

"Good morning, Cynthia. We have lots of work today. I have taken on a new case as of last night—the Roberto Milano murder case."

"Oh, my. Yes, I heard about that on TV. It will be quite a change from the cases you've been handling, won't it?"

"Yes, quite a change. Mr. Milano should be here any minute. Please show him into my office as soon as he arrives. Now, how about a cup of that coffee? And have a cup yourself while we're waiting."

"Coming right up." Cynthia moved rapidly around the coffee station as she spoke, fixing the coffee just to Luci's liking. It hadn't taken her long to figure out just how to please her boss.

Luci headed for her office door, coffee in hand, when just at that moment Berto walked through the front door. Freshly shaven, along with a change of clothes, he was looking like a totally different man from the one she had seen at the jailhouse. He could still make her heart skip a beat, even though she had been married for twelve years.

Cynthia looked him up and down and nodded her approval to Luci. *How had her boss managed to snag such a good-looking client?* she wondered.

"Berto," Luci exclaimed. "You made it here in record time. Cynthia, this is Mr. Roberto Milano, our new client. We will be in conference for a while, so please hold all my calls. But I'm expecting a detective, Mr. Patrick Sherman, to join us, so please let me know as soon as he arrives."

"Yes, Mrs. Clark," Cynthia replied, addressing her boss in the most formal manner, as was her custom in front of clients.

"Berto, come in and let's get started." Luci motioned to her office as she spoke. "Would you like some coffee?" she added as an afterthought.

"Yes, please. Just black would be fine."

Cynthia again moved quickly and handed him a steaming cup of the brew. He followed Luci into the office, shutting the door behind him.

He sank into a chair facing the desk as Luci took her seat and turned to face him squarely.

"Okay, Berto. The first thing we need to do is establish your alibi for the time of the murder. I picked up a copy of the police report last night while I was at the precinct. The coroner estimated the time of the murder to be approximately 8:00 p.m. two days ago. Where were you at that time? Please tell me you were with somebody else."

"No, I was out driving, all alone. I was upset over having to fire Tom and Eric, and I needed some time to clear my head. I didn't get home until almost 10:00 p.m. that night. My live-in housekeeper was keeping my dinner warm. Like I already told you, I changed clothes, and she threw them in the washer while I was eating."

"Did you stop anywhere or see anybody you knew while you were out driving?"

"No, nobody. I didn't stop anywhere, and I didn't see anybody."

"Well, that's not good. You were out and about all alone at the time of the murder."

Luci paused as the buzzer on her phone notified her that Cynthia was on the line.

"Yes, what is it, Cynthia?"

"Mr. Sherman is here."

"Oh, good." She placed her hand over the phone's mouthpiece. "Patrick Sherman is here. Maybe he will have some idea of where to proceed from here," she told Berto. "Send him in, Cynthia."

The door swung around silently as Cynthia turned the knob and pushed it open. Luci got her first view of the detective who had come so highly recommended. He was definitely easy on the eyes with a muscular build and a height she judged to be at least six feet six inches tall, with piercing blue eyes and a shock of curly red hair, all giving him a striking appearance. She didn't doubt the ladies would have little problem in hiring him to trail their husbands to see if they were cheating on them. *But would men feel the same way?* she wondered. She pushed the thought to the back of her mind, willing the current case to take precedence.

"Mr. Sherman, this is Roberto Milano, my client. Roberto, Patrick Sherman, our detective on the case."

Berto rose and the men shook hands. Berto settled down into his chair, while Patrick sat down in the one beside it.

Patrick had taken in the scene quickly, as he had trained himself to do. He had seen pictures of Luci, but they didn't do her justice. She was quite a looker. No wonder Jeremy was jealous and worried that she might leave him for another man. Her client wasn't a bad-looking chap, either. Patrick had done his homework and learned that they had been high school sweethearts. Was the spark still there? That was what Jeremy was paying him to find out.

He maintained a deadpan expression as he leaned back in his seat, turning his mind back to the present. He couldn't let on that he was already quite familiar with one Mrs. Luci Carlito Clark. Not yet, anyhow.

Luci spent the next half-hour filling Patrick in on the details of the case. Berto added a few insights, some of which surprised her. He suggested that perhaps someone connected with his father had planned the whole thing and framed him as a way to get even with the Milano family. He pointed out that his dad was bound to have made some enemies over the years. The question was, which enemy would be ticked off enough to plan such a scheme?

"I can see that we are going to have to talk to your dad some more about this case. He offered to help in any way he can. Just how much he is willing to reveal about his business affairs remains to be seen," Luci said.

"Oh God! This is so frustrating. I feel so helpless," Berto exclaimed, banging his hands on the desk as he spoke.

"It's okay, Berto. I know you didn't kill anybody, and you know you didn't kill anybody. All we have to do is create reasonable doubt in the minds of the jury." Luci patted his hand as she spoke, a move that did not escape Patrick's attention.

Patrick recommended several electronics specialists who could help analyze the surveillance tapes.

"What we need to do is see if there is any evidence of a gap in the tapes," he said.

"I looked at them earlier. I didn't see anything unusual," Berto informed him.

"Sometimes it takes a trained eye. We need to have the technician look over the tapes, and then maybe we can all look at them together. We might see something out of place. You never can tell what might show up on a surveillance tape."

"Okay, I'll get right on it," Luci decided.

Patrick and Berto took their leave after deciding there was nothing more that could be done at that point. Patrick promised to see if he could dig up more details about the homicide other than what was in the police report. Berto was assigned the job of consulting with his father to see who might be out for revenge. Luci felt his dad might be more forthcoming with the information to his son than to an outsider. She was left with the task of hiring the electronics specialist.

She looked over the list of names Patrick had supplied. *Which one to choose?* she wondered. *I guess it's pretty much eenie-meenie-minie-moe. Think I'll start at the top and work my way down,* she decided.

The first couple of phone calls proved to be of no help. One guy was too busy to take on any new clients and another one was in the process of updating all his equipment. The third call provided some positive result. The technician, Ken DeWitt, turned out to be one of their former schoolmates. He remembered Luci and Berto, but she did not remember him.

"I was one of those nerdy kids a couple of years behind you, but I recall Berto being a football star and you being on the cheerleader squad. I voted for you, by the way. I still remember that," he informed her.

"Well..." Luci was at a loss for words at this point.

"Never mind. That's not important now. What's important is

proving Berto's innocence. I just don't believe he would kill anybody. He's not the type."

"I'm glad you think so, Ken. Please, please try to come up with something that will help him win this case."

"I'll do my best. How soon can you get a copy of the tapes to me?"

"I'll call Berto and have them sent over to you right away. Please let me know if you find anything unusual."

"Will do."

Luci hung up the phone with a sigh of relief. One more thing off her checklist of things to do before the trial. Now she needed to start working on preparing the briefs and deciding on exactly how to present the case.

<hr />

JEREMY WAS RATHER PERTURBED WITH the Summerfield police department. They refused to release any information about the Milano case to him. How was he supposed to help Luci if he couldn't find out anything? He was counting on Patrick to come through with some more information under the table, but so far nothing had emerged. All he knew was what had appeared in the newspapers. He had to admit it wasn't looking too good for Roberto. The guy had no alibi for the time of the murder, and everyone in the showroom had witnessed his argument with the two salesmen. He didn't know how much longer he could keep his presence a secret from Luci and her family. Maybe it was about time he revealed himself to them.

His train of thought was interrupted when his cell phone rang. He glanced at the Caller I. D. as he pulled the phone out of his pocket. It was Mike Graham calling from New York. Hopefully, he would have some more information on the tabloid case.

"Hello, Mike. What's the latest?"

"Well, it definitely wasn't Sheba who sent out those tabloids. Her alibi checks out and I have found no connection whatsoever with her sending them. But I do have another angle for you. It's something rather far out, but it bears investigation."

"Okay, you've got my curiosity up now. What is it?"

"Suppose you and Luci weren't really the intended targets. What if you were a red herring?"

"You mean somebody was trying to throw any investigation off the trail?"

"Yes, that's what I'm thinking now. Why else would both Luci and Matt have gotten a copy of the picture? What if somebody wanted to break up Matt and Belinda?"

"Why would somebody want to do that? They've been engaged since their college days. Belinda never mentioned another girl in Matt's life. She tells me everything. I'm like a father figure to her."

"Maybe Belinda didn't know."

"Maybe Matt didn't know either. He was crazy about Belinda. I never understood why he didn't give her a chance to explain how the picture came about," Jeremy mused.

"Sometimes love makes people do crazy things, Jeremy."

"Tell me about it! You could be right. She said Matt had already found a new girlfriend. That seemed kind of quick to me, like he was picking up a girl on the rebound."

"Yes. I'm going to check out that angle and then I'll get back to you with what I've found out."

"Great. Keep me posted, Mike. Nothing would make me happier than having Belinda and Matt back together again. Well…nothing except that and me getting Luci back."

"Don't give up. Maybe we can make it all happen."

For the first time in months, Jeremy felt a sliver of hope shoot through his heart as he hung up the phone. If he could prove to Luci the real reason someone had sent her that photo, he might still have a chance of getting her back. He would let Mike handle it from that end and concentrate on finding out what he could about the Milano case. Sometimes murder cases could take a really nasty turn. Plus, there might be mob connections associated with the case. No matter what happened, he wanted Luci and the kids to be safe. He would make that his primary goal for now. The place to start was to meet Luci face-to-face and let her know he was in town.

⸻ ◈◈◈ ⸻

LUCI SIGHED AS SHE SLID behind the wheel of her car and cranked up the engine. It had been a long day and an even longer evening. She had phoned Papa D'Armon to send a cab to pick up the children at school and take them to their grandparents' house. Mama Rosa was always glad to see them, and feeding them was no problem, as there was always an abundance of food at the Carlitos' table. It was an arrangement she had made with her parents when she started working. That way, she didn't have to rush to pick up the children when she was in the middle of preparing a case.

In fact, seeing an On Your Way taxi pull up in front of the school had become a common occurrence. She had signed all the necessary papers for someone else to pick up the children. Papa usually came himself, but when he couldn't make it, he always sent Bob Hardy, his most reliable driver. Of course, they could have ridden on a bus, but she preferred to have them picked up by somebody she knew. Besides that, the bus ride was a long one, and this way they had time to make good headway on their homework while waiting for her to come and get them.

She felt a few pangs of hunger as she drove the familiar route to her old home place. She smiled to herself, knowing that Mama would have set a plate aside for her. It was always good to eat some of Mama's cooking. No matter how tired or depressed she might be, she always felt better after eating Mama's scrumptious cuisine. Somehow, Mama seemed to sense that. There was no getting around the fact that Luci was still her little girl in her eyes. Feeding her family was what Mama did best, and she hadn't let them down yet.

She parked the car in her parents' driveway and headed towards the front door, trying her best to muster a smile for the children's sake. There was a strange car parked out by the street. *Who could be visiting at this hour?* she wondered. Before she could insert her key into the lock, the door swung open and she was almost knocked down as the children greeted her enthusiastically.

"Mama, Mama, you're finally home," they yelled in unison.

"What took you so long?" Brian asked.

"It was just a busy day, son."

"We've got a surprise for you," Jennifer announced.

"A surprise, what could that be?"

"Come see, come see," the children urged, tugging at her hands as they pulled her toward the living room.

She walked into the room and then stopped dead in her tracks as a man sitting on the couch rose and turned to face her.

"Hello, Luci," he greeted her calmly.

Luci could hardly believe her eyes. Her worst fear had materialized. *Well, I guess now I know what that car belongs to,* she thought. She struggled to get the words out, willing herself to speak.

"Jeremy, what are you doing here?" she exclaimed.

"I needed to see you, and this seemed like the best place to start. Besides, I was hungry for some of Mama Rosa's cooking," he said, winking at Mama as she walked into the room.

Luci was seething inside but managed to present a cool façade to the audience that had now gathered in the room. *Of all the nerve. He actually has the impudence to show up here. Here in my parents' home, in front of the children! I guess he thinks I won't lambast him in front of my family. Maybe not now, but we're going to have to settle our problems, one way or another.*

"Luci, I saved you a plate." Mama interrupted her train of thought for the moment. "Come into the kitchen and eat, or do you want to take it with you?"

"Thank you, Mama. I'll just eat it here. That way, no dishes to wash when I get home."

Luci walked towards the kitchen as she spoke, leaving Jeremy standing by the couch. Her chin jutted up just a tad as she passed him. *If he thinks he's getting a kiss, he's sadly mistaken,* she vowed.

She settled herself into her usual chair and proceeded to eat the meal Mama sat in front of her, but she had lost her appetite and the food had little appeal. She forced herself to eat, reasoning that she needed the nourishment. Besides that, she didn't want Mama to worry about her lack of appetite. It never escaped Mama's attention when one of her family members failed to eat.

Jeremy strolled into the kitchen just as she finished the last bite of pasta. She was thankful he had stayed in the living room with the children while she was eating. Otherwise, she was sure she wouldn't have been able to swallow a single bite.

"Mama, I think I'll pass on the dessert," she announced as she pushed her plate away.

"All right, Luci. Maybe next time," Mama Rosa replied.

"Luci, we need to talk," Jeremy informed her.

Luci held up her hand to stop him from saying anything else, but he continued to speak.

"Whether here or at your house, it doesn't matter to me. But there are some things we need to sort out. Take your pick, which place will it be?"

Mama rattled the dishes a little more loudly than usual as she finished washing them in the sink. Luci could feel herself weakening. Being around Jeremy always did that to her. Why was she so susceptible to his charms?

"Have it your way. We'll talk at my house. I have to get the children home and into bed," she agreed reluctantly.

"Great. I'll follow you home in my car."

"Your car? So, I guess that was your car I saw parked out by the street!" she exclaimed.

"Yes, I usually take a cab when I'm traveling, but I decided to rent a car since I may be in town a while."

Luci's heart sank upon hearing those words. *Great, he plans on being here a while. That means he'll be coming around to see the children. There will be no way to avoid him. Just when I was getting my life back on track, he had to show up and throw it all out of kilter again.*

She rose from her chair and walked over to the sink where Mama Rosa was standing.

"Mama, thanks so much for the food and for watching the children," she said as she gave her mother a hug.

"Papa and I are always glad to have them…and you also," Mama assured her.

"Well, we'll be going then. I'll see you again soon." Luci headed back towards the living room as she spoke. She pushed open the door and walked into the room where the children were watching TV with Papa.

"Come on, kids. It's time to go home," she informed them.

"Aww, Mom, we're right in the middle of a show," Brian protested.

"Too bad. It's already late and past your bedtime, so let's go. Say goodnight to Papa," she instructed.

The children reluctantly gathered their belongings and headed out the door after dutifully giving Papa D'Armon a goodnight kiss.

Luci drove home with the image of Jeremy's headlights focused in her rearview mirror. Now he would know where she lived, although it wasn't really any big secret. All he had to do was ask somebody in town and they would tell him. There were few secrets in a town the size of Summerfield. She had learned that long ago. The question was had Jeremy been keeping secrets from her? What had possessed him to kiss Belinda? Would he have an answer for that tonight?

Jeremy followed Luci's car, concentrating intently on the path they were taking. Although he already knew the address, he wasn't familiar with the neighborhood. Most of his dealings in the town had been with the restaurant on the other side of town and Luci's family. No reason for letting her know that he already knew where she lived. That would just irk her more. At least she had agreed to speak with him, so that was one thing in his favor. She had to believe that he wasn't having an affair with Belinda. She just had to!

An hour later the two adults found themselves in Luci's living room, facing each other in easy chairs that were stationed on each side of the fireplace where a fire now crackled invitingly. Jeremy had started the fire while Luci supervised the children's bedtime routine. Getting the children to bed had been no easy task, as they were overly excited about seeing their father again. Brian had asked Luci the dreaded question as she tucked him into bed.

"Mom, is Dad going to live with us again?"

"Brian, I don't know. We'll just have to wait and see. Go to sleep now," she had responded.

The question now weighed heavily on her mind as she looked straight into the eyes of her husband for the first time since she had left New York City. *Why am I having such a hard time communicating with him?* she wondered.

Jeremy spoke first. "Luci, why did you leave without waiting for me to explain about that tabloid picture?"

"I…I don't know," she stammered. "It just hit me the wrong way, I suppose. I've been seeing newspaper pictures of you with other women for years. But this time it was a woman you work with, a woman you see almost every day. I just don't know what to think, Jeremy. I don't know if I can trust you anymore."

He sat quietly, listening to her answer. Then he began what he hoped would be a plausible explanation. "Luci, you should know that there is nothing going on between me and Belinda. What was photographed was just a friendly kiss on the cheek after I won the award, nothing more. You know the tabloids always blow things out of proportion, trying to get the latest scoop, trying to lure in more readers."

"What about the fact that you spent the night in Washington, D. C.? How do I know you had separate rooms?"

"You can check the hotel records. We booked two rooms."

"That doesn't mean you used both rooms."

"Luci, Belinda is like a daughter to me. Besides, she's engaged to Matt Collins…or at least she *was* engaged to him."

"Was engaged? What do you mean?"

"It seems that whoever sent you a copy of that tabloid also sent a copy to Matt. Now he and Belinda have broken up…his idea."

"Why would somebody do that? Now I'm totally confused," Luci confessed.

"I have a detective working on the case. He has come up with an interesting theory, but I'm not at liberty to divulge any more information at this point. If it works out, I will be totally in the clear."

"Well…" Luci was at a loss for words, but her mind was racing. *A detective...He said he had hired a detective. Does that mean he would also hire a detective to spy on me... to keep track of all my activities?*

She was drawn back to the present by the sound of Jeremy's voice.

"Luci, I love you so much, and I miss you and the kids. Won't you please forgive me and come back home to New York with me?" He abandoned his chair and quickly covered the distance between them to kneel down in front of her, taking both of her hands in his. "You still love me...I know you do."

Luci felt herself weakening once again. Then she steeled herself, drawing her hands from his grasp.

"Yes, it's true. I will always love you, Jeremy Clark. But I've started a new life for myself in Summerfield. I want to find out if I can make it on my own...without the Clark money or influence. Besides, I've taken on an important case, a murder case involving one of my old high school friends."

Jeremy blinked. He couldn't let on that he already knew about the case. He had already let it slip that he had hired a detective in New York. If Luci found out he had also hired Patrick Sherman...well, he didn't even want to think about what consequences that might incur. Luci was one stubborn woman, and he had just made a little chink in that wall she had erected around herself since leaving him. He wasn't about to backtrack now and give her a chance to shut him out completely again. He stood and then walked over to the front of the fireplace, giving himself time to think.

"A murder case? Are you sure that's what you want to do? Sometimes murder cases can take a nasty turn." He hoped his response would convince her that he was totally surprised.

"I can't discuss the details of the case due to attorney-client privilege. You should know that."

"Yes, I understand. What was I thinking? But I'm just concerned about safety for you and the children."

"The children and I will be just fine. We've been getting along on our own for months now, as you can see. I have my own law practice. They're enrolled in school and have made new friends. Plus, I now have this house and my own car. Besides that, I have my family here. What more could we need?"

She rose from the chair and walked over to the fireplace to face him. There was no way she was going to argue with a man who was looking down at her.

"What about love? You just said you still love me, and I still love you. Can you live without love, Luci?"

"I have the love of my family, the love of my kids."

"That's not enough. Not for a beautiful woman like you, Luci. You need a man in your life. I want to be that man again."

"I'll think about it, Jeremy. That's the only promise I can make right now. It's getting late, so I think it's best if you leave."

Jeremy could see that he wasn't going to win the war tonight. Not by any means. But he was making progress. At least she had talked to him, even let him follow her home. He didn't want to push his luck.

"Very well, Luci. You're right, I suppose. I'll be in town for a few more days checking up on some business."

"Oh? I thought maybe you would be leaving tomorrow."

"No, I can't have everything done by then."

He headed towards the front door as he spoke. Luci followed closely behind him. A blast of cold air shot into the room as he opened the door. Luci thought it wasn't nearly as cold as the chill she'd felt around her heart when she first glimpsed that photo of him kissing Belinda.

"Goodnight, then," she called out as he stepped onto the porch.

She watched as he climbed into the car, started the engine and drove away. Somehow, the cold didn't bother her at all. After stepping back inside, she closed the door and leaned against it, hugging herself as a slight smile crossed her face.

He still loves me. I knew he would. I didn't want to admit it, but I was hoping against all odds that would be true. Now, if we can just solve the tabloid mystery and I can win this case for Berto, maybe things can work out for us somehow. Please, God, let that happen.

RETURN TO SUMMERFIELD

THE NEXT FEW WEEKS FLEW by, with Luci totally engrossed in preparing for Berto's trial. The hearing had been held shortly after her meeting with Berto and Patrick, and the judge had determined there was enough evidence to proceed with a trial. Things were moving along at a more rapid pace than usual for several reasons. First, the case had drawn a lot of publicity, as a murder was a rare thing in a town the size of Summerfield. Second, the judge wanted to get on with it, as the Milano family was well known in the community. Third, there were still those rumors of the Mafia connections, and people of Summerfield wanted nothing to do with the mob, at least according to reports in the local newspaper. The Mafia connections rumors had been circulating for years, ever since Luci could remember. Why they would pick a town the size of Summerfield was a mystery to her, but she supposed in modern times anything was possible.

Jeremy had stayed in town for almost two weeks. He had managed to visit with the children during that time. Luci had agreed to the visits because she knew the kids missed their dad. But he had to be up to something, she reasoned. Why else would an international businessman spend so much time in Summerfield? Surely, he had more pressing business elsewhere. He claimed to be concerned about Eric's body being found in one of his dumpsters, but was that really the reason he stayed so long? How did he expect to find out anything else beyond what was in the police report? What was his real motive for being in Summerfield?

Their contacts during his visits with the children had been casual. He hadn't brought up the subject of getting back together again. She was thankful for that because she needed more time. Although she still loved him, she still had to prove to herself that she could make it on her own. If she went back to Jeremy, it would be on her terms, not his. For the first time in her life, she was exerting her independence, and she loved it.

She was relieved when he finally informed her he had to leave town. It gave her a little extra time to think about her situation, not that she had much free time to do that. She had worked hard to keep up with the usual cases because they were her bread and butter. Berto's case was the jam. Money from that would give her leeway in her budget and make it possible to afford a few extras she and the children had been doing without. She had to admit they had been good sports about it. Oh, there was some complaining at first, but they had soon settled into a routine and didn't seem to miss all their extra luxuries too much. Maybe it was a sign they were growing up, especially Brian. He was becoming a regular little man now, always watching out for his mom and sister.

She held several late-night sessions with Berto after dealing with her other cases. They had gone over all the evidence together, time after time. Nothing new had come to light that would help prove his innocence. She had only his word and her belief in him to go by. She needed something more concrete to present at trial.

Ken Dewitt had been going over the security tapes from the auto sales office, but he hadn't found anything to indicate that the tapes had been tampered with. Luci decided it would be best if she and Berto looked at them together, so she called to ask Ken if that would be possible. Ken informed her that he could bring the tapes to her office. After checking with Berto, they agreed to meet Ken the following night at 8:00 p.m.

Luci hurried back to the office after rushing through a meal at her parents' house. Mama had insisted on cooking a full-fledged Italian feast for her and the children, declaring that she thought Luci might be getting a little too thin. Luci had picked at her food, her mind absorbed in the details of Berto's case. She had reluctantly agreed to leave the children with her parents overnight, as she didn't know how late she would be working.

After parking her car, she walked into the office and turned on the lights, hoping that Berto and Ken would arrive soon. Somehow, she was beginning to have an uneasy feeling about working alone late at night. She couldn't shake the notion that she was being watched, maybe even being followed. It wasn't anything definite she could put her finger on, just something in the back of her mind.

She was relieved when they both walked in together. They got right to work, viewing the tapes several times. Things were beginning to go a bit blurry for her, but she wasn't about to give up. Somehow, there just had to be a clue to prove Berto's innocence. She was sure of it.

"Let's look at them one more time," she instructed as she rubbed her eyes wearily.

"You're the boss," Ken responded as he rewound the tape and began playing it again.

Luci stared intently at the screen, watching for anything unusual in the background of the room. Then she saw it. How could she have missed something so obvious? How could Ken have missed it?

"Wait! Stop the tape there. Can you zoom in on the clock?" she asked.

"Sure thing. Hold on a minute," said Ken.

"There. Right there. Do you see it?" she asked. "The clock jumped five minutes. That means the tape was tampered with."

"You're right!" Berto exclaimed.

"I don't know how I missed that," Ken mused. "Maybe I need to hire you as an assistant," he joked.

"I knew it! I just knew it! Somebody else was in my office the night Eric was killed," Berto declared.

"The question is, why were they in your office? Was that when the gun was stolen?" Luci pondered the situation.

"It must have been. I opened the gun drawer earlier in the day, and the gun was in it," Berto informed her.

"That means somebody had to have gotten the key to the gun drawer and the key to your office. How would they have gotten into the building without setting off an alarm?" Luck inquired.

"Perhaps it was somebody who knew the security code," Ken suggested.

"You're right! Who has access to the code?" Luci asked.

"Well, there's me, the office manager, and some of the salesmen," Berto spoke slowly as he considered the possibilities.

"We know it wasn't you. What about the office manager? Any reason he would want to try to implicate you in a murder?" Luci pressed for an answer.

"It's a she, and no, Mrs. Hodnett is as reliable as they come. She's been working for me for years."

"That leaves the salesmen then," Ken interjected.

"Yes, what about the salesmen? Perhaps we had better go over the list. Ken, I think that about finishes your work here. We have what we need to know from the tapes. Thank you for coming. Berto and I will discuss the case further on our own." Luci rose and extended her hand to Ken as she spoke.

"Yes, of course. I'll be in touch. Let me know if you need anything else." Ken shook her hand and gathered his equipment. He was gone in less than two minutes.

Luci found herself alone with Berto once again. *Was it a good thing?* she wondered. She was still attracted to him, despite the fact that she was a married woman. *A married woman who is separated from her husband,* she reminded herself.

Berto spoke first. "So, here we are. Just the two of us."

"Yes." Luci was unable to get another word out as her voice failed.

"What I wouldn't have given years ago to be alone with you."

Luci cleared her throat, willing herself to speak. "Berto, let's just concentrate on the case. Once we get that solved, we can talk of other things."

"Yes, of course. What would you like to know?" he asked.

"Let's focus on the salesmen. You have one salesman dead. Who would want to kill him?"

"Eric was a likable guy. He didn't have any enemies that I know of."

"Give me a list of the salesmen who had access to the entry code, and I'll have Patrick run a background check on them. Maybe he can dig up something to help us with the case." She shoved a notepad and pen across the desk.

Berto paused and thought a minute and then began writing. It didn't take long for him to complete the list.

"That's everybody I can remember," he told her as he pushed the pad back towards her side of the desk.

"Everybody you can remember? Are you in the habit of giving out the access code to just anybody?" she asked incredulously.

"No, of course not. It's just that we had some salesmen leave. I guess I should have changed the code, but I never got around to it."

"Why do salesmen need the access code anyhow?"

"Sometimes they have to meet potential customers who can't come during regular business hours," he explained.

"Oh, I see. Well, I suggest that from now on you be more careful."

"Don't worry. I will. I've definitely learned my lesson."

"Now we know somebody gained access to the building and in a five-minute span they managed to get into your office and steal the gun. They must have turned off the security tape somehow. The question is, how did they get a key to your office and a key to the gun drawer? Do you recall anything unusual happening regarding your keys in the days before the break in?" She quizzed him.

"No, nothing...but wait. I remember my keys were missing one day. I couldn't find them anywhere. On that particular day I had just laid my keys on my desk when I got a call from the service department. I walked down the hall to check on the problem. When I got back, I couldn't find the keys."

"Are you in the habit of leaving your keys lying around unattended?" Luci asked skeptically.

"No, but after that, I walked to the front lot to talk to a customer. When I got back, the keys were on my desk under some papers. I thought I had just mislaid them."

"If somebody went into your office, it should be on one of the tapes."

Berto shook his head. "The tapes are automatically erased after five days. There would be no record of it."

Luci rolled her eyes and looked towards the ceiling as she took a deep breath and then let it out.

"Berto, you know you're driving me crazy, don't you? Every time I come up with an idea of how to prove your innocence, you throw a boulder into my path."

"I'm sorry. It's just how things have worked out."

"I know. I know. It's not your fault, Berto. It's just that I'm getting so frustrated at coming up with dead ends."

"I wish I had an answer for you, but I don't."

"Think, Berto. Is there anybody who would want to frame you for murder? Anybody at all? Do you have any enemies?"

Berto sat a little straighter in his chair and looked her squarely in the eyes as he responded. "Everybody has enemies, I suppose. You know about my family connection, even though I have separated myself from them. But, no, I can think of nobody offhand. I might have a few unhappy customers, heaven forbid, but hopefully none who would be that vindictive."

Luci drummed her fingers on the desk as she ran ideas through her head. Then she nodded slowly.

"Berto, I think you might be onto something. What if somebody targeted you as a means of getting back at your father for something he did?"

"It's a possibility," he admitted. I don't know my enemies, but my father knows who his are."

"I think this calls for another meeting with Mr. Giovanni Milano," she declared.

"I think you're right, and this time I want to be present."

"Can you make the arrangements? Or shall I?" she asked.

"I'll do it. It's time that my father and I had a reunion." He rose from his chair as he spoke.

"Well, I guess that's about all we can do for now. Let me know when and where your father would like to meet us."

She rose from the table and rounded the desk in preparation for escorting him to the front door. She had learned long ago that keeping the door locked after business hours was both a wise and necessary precaution.

She unlocked the door with her key. They both reached for the handle to open the door at the same time. She quickly withdrew her hand as he took control and pulled the door back. But it was too late for her to avoid that spark that still existed between them, even after all these years.

He paused and turned to face her.

"Luci, there's one more thing."

"What?"

"Thank you for believing in me. Thank you for still caring about me."

He bent down and gently brushed her lips with his.

Luci tried her best not to respond, but she couldn't help but kiss him back. She stepped back, and he turned away without saying another word. She stood in the doorway briefly, watching him walk towards his car. *Where does this leave me?* she wondered. Now she was torn between her first love and her husband. Which one should she choose?

Down the street, inside a car, a camera clicked steadily, recording the kiss and every other move the couple had made since the door had opened. Patrick Sherman was on the job, and he would have some remarkable photos to show his other boss. Jeremy Clark would be interested in what had just transpired. Very interested. That appeared to be all the action for the night. He supposed he might as well head to his office and send the photos to Jeremy via e-mail. He waited until she closed the door and then started the engine and eased the car into the street, careful not to call attention to himself by driving away too fast.

Further down the street the red glow from a car cigarette lighter appeared briefly and then faded away as the occupant of the car lit his third cigarette in the past two hours. He smiled to himself as he took a long drag from it and then exhaled. It took a special talent to tail someone who was already being tailed. He had been hired to keep an eye on one Luci Clark, and that was just what he intended to do. His boss hired only the best, and he was definitely one of the best at his job.

The other private eye appeared to be leaving. Evidently, he had found out what he needed to know.

Let's see if we can liven things up a little for Mrs. Clark, he thought as he reached for his throwaway cell phone.

Luci jumped nervously as the phone rang shrilly in the empty office. She wasn't in the habit of answering the work phone, as Cynthia screened the calls for her. But Cynthia wasn't around. *Who knows I'm here now?* she wondered. *Mama or Papa would call me on my cell phone.*

She hesitated before walking over to the phone and picking up the receiver.

"Hello," she spoke tentatively.

"It would be in your best interest to drop the Milano murder case," a muffled voice responded.

"Who is this?" she demanded to know.

"Somebody who is looking out for you and your family," the voice continued.

Luci glanced at the Caller I. D., but it displayed the number as "unknown."

"My family," she stammered. "What does this have to do with the trial?"

"Keep representing Roberto Milano and you'll find out."

"You stay away from my family! You stay away from my kids," she shouted and then she realized she had lost the connection.

Her hand shook as she hung up the phone. She rushed to the door and flung it open, peering into the darkness. But there was no one in sight. The street was completely deserted. Where could the caller be, and how had he known she was working late?

What should I do? Should I call the police or just wait it out? I don't want to upset Mama and Papa. Plus, I don't want the children to know about this phone call. If only Jeremy were here. He would know what to do! Jeremy always knows what to do.

She hastily gathered up her belongings and closed the office. She glanced around nervously as she headed for her car. Was the caller watching her right now? She was already under enough stress from the trial. Now there was one more thing to worry about. Who could she confide in? She drove home, carefully scanning the side streets and rearview mirror for any hint that someone might be following her. Her mind raced as she tried to focus on what course of action to take.

Berto...Jeremy's not around, so Berto is the logical choice. After all, he's the one who's on trial. He will want me to drop the case, of course, but I can't do that. Everybody else thinks he's guilty. Everybody except me and his father. Speaking of that, I need to talk to Mr. Milano again. He probably won't be too happy to learn that someone is interfering with his son's trial. Well, Berto said he would make the arrangements for us to meet. I hope it's tomorrow. I won't rest easy until this matter is settled.

She spent a sleepless night, as she had expected. Her only consolation was that she had left the children at her parents' house. Mama Rosa would see that they were fed and ready for school. As for herself, she had little appetite for breakfast. She put on the coffeepot and dropped a piece of toast into the toaster, doubting if she could choke it down.

Good thing Mama isn't here. She'd be trying to stuff me with cinnamon rolls or some other treat. Luci smiled at the thought.

Her cell phone rang just as the toast popped up. She ignored the toast and reached for the phone.

"Hello," she said.

"Luci, it's Berto. My father has agreed to a meeting this morning. Could you be at his home by 9:00 a.m.?"

"Yes. I'll be there."

"Great. See you then...but are you sure everything's okay? Your voice sounds different. Has something happened? Tell me, please, Luci."

She hesitated before responding. "Yes, Berto. Something did happen last night after you left. I had rather tell you about it in person, though. I think it's something your father might want to hear also."

"Okay, meet me at his house and we'll talk about it then."

"I'll be there," she replied before hanging up the phone as a dozen reasons not to go flashed through her mind.

Oh, stop it! You made a commitment to see Berto through this, and that's exactly what you are going to do, she chided herself silently.

She managed to consume the cold piece of toast with the aid of a cup of hot coffee to wash it down, reasoning that the meeting with the eldest Milano on an empty stomach would not bode well with her nerves.

She grabbed her purse and car keys and headed out the front door. She looked around apprehensively, surveying all the side streets as she walked to her car. *Is someone watching me now?* she wondered.

Moments later, she followed the maid down the hall to the immense den of Mr. Giovanni Milano. She scanned the surroundings, taking in every detail as she walked into the room for the second time. Apparently, nothing had changed since their first meeting. It was still obvious that the Milano family had more money than they could ever spend.

It must be nice, but maybe the way he got the money was not so nice.

Maybe that's why somebody is now trying to get even with him by framing his son for murder, she mused.

Mr. Milano rose to meet her. "Well, well, Mrs. Clark. Welcome back to my home."

Luci nodded curtly. "Thank you, Mr. Milano."

Berto spoke, breaking the tension that hung over the room like a heavy blanket.

"Luci has called to my attention some information regarding the case that we feel you should be aware of. You might even be able to help with a problem."

"Yes, please continue," Mr. Milano responded.

"Luci, suppose you explain since you know more of the details than I do," Berto suggested.

"Very well. I'll get right to the point. I received a very strange phone call last night. Someone wants me to drop the case. In fact, the caller threatened me and my family if I continue as Roberto's lawyer," she informed him.

"What? This happened last night, and you're just now telling me about it?" Berto rose halfway out of his chair as he spoke.

"I...I had to think about it first," Luci spoke hesitantly. "This involves my family also, not just me. I have to be sure that my kids are safe."

Mr. Milano raised his hand. "Stop. Stop this bickering, you two. We must think now. We must all act together as a team. Tell us exactly what the caller said."

Luci shook her head and looked down at the floor before looking up again. She sighed as she responded.

"For the past few days I've been having an eerie feeling...like I was being followed. Like somebody was watching me all the time. Last night, after our meeting, Berto, I got a phone call. It was a voice I didn't recognize and an unknown male caller. He threatened to harm my family and me if I continue to represent you in this case. I'm sorry I didn't call you, but I had to sort things out in my mind. I didn't know what to do."

"Still, you should have let me know," Berto complained.

"Well, we know all about it now," Mr. Milano interjected. "We won't let anything happen to you or your children. Don't worry. I will send somebody to watch your house whenever you're at home."

"But what about when the kids are in school? Who will watch out for them then?" Luci asked.

"I'm sure they'll be fine at school. They have the entire faculty and the teachers' aides watching the students at all times," Berto assured her.

"I suppose you're right," Luci replied. "But that brings us right back to the heart of the problem. Who would want me to drop the case? And why would they want it dropped?"

"Have you reached a conclusion about that?" Mr. Bruno inquired.

"Do you want to tell him about our discovery last night, or shall I?" Luci tossed the question to Berto.

"One of my security tapes was tampered with. Somebody was in my office for five minutes that are not accounted for on the tape," Berto informed his father.

Mr. Milano sat silently, assessing the situation, his fingertips tapping together. Then he spoke, weighing his words carefully.

"And exactly what was supposed to have happened during those five missing minutes?" he inquired.

"We think that's when my gun was stolen...the gun used to frame me," Berto told him.

"Ah, it is becoming clearer to me now. They are framing you, but the person they really want to hurt is me. Sending my son to jail for life would be my greatest punishment," Mr. Milano pondered as he spoke.

"That's about the size of it. So, now here we are. We're stuck trying to prove that I'm innocent. Otherwise, I *will* go to jail, no matter what happens," Berto spoke ruefully.

"So, Mr. Milano, what we need from you is a list of who might be enough of an enemy to want to do this sort of thing," Luci said.

"You want a list of my enemies...and we have how many days before the trial?"

"Dad, please, this is no joking matter."

"I know. I'm so sorry, son. I was just trying to ease the tension a little. Of course, I know it's serious. Let me think. Let me think. How many years should I go back?" he wondered.

"Just tell us the first person who pops into your mind. Sometimes the first instinct is right," Luci suggested.

Mr. Milano rose and began pacing the floor. "Sorry, but I can think clearer sometimes if I'm moving," he explained.

"Whatever works for you, Dad," said Berto.

"It's good to hear you call me 'Dad' again. I've missed that."

"And I've missed you also, but now we need you to stay focused," Berto reminded him.

"Of course, of course." Mr. Milano continued to pace as he spoke.

Luci and Berto exchanged glances, wordlessly communicating their hopes that Mr. Milano would provide some kind of answer to the puzzle.

"Well…" He stopped in his tracks as Luci and Berto leaned forward in anticipation of an answer to the puzzle.

"No, no, not that one," he half muttered to himself as he began pacing again.

They settled back in their chairs, perfectly willing to give him time to think. The only sound in the room was the ticking of a grandfather clock that sat in a corner near the fireplace.

Luci stared at the clock's pendulum swinging back and forth and felt her eyelids start to grow heavy from lack of sleep the previous night. She blinked and drew a deep breath, willing herself to stay awake. She was jolted back to reality when Mr. Milano began to speak.

"There are several possibilities," he informed them. "A man in my position does not get where he is without acquiring some liabilities along the way."

"Do you have any names for us?" Berto asked impatiently.

"Names? No, not at this time. I will do my own investigation into the matter. It will be handled, I assure you. What I'm most concerned with at this time is having my son well represented at his trial. I had my doubts about you at first, Mrs. Clark. I admit that. But I can see my Roberto is in very capable hands. Rest assured that I will do my best to see that you and your family are protected, should you choose to remain the lead attorney on the case. So, what will it be? Will you continue to act as my son's lawyer?"

"I have never quit a case before, and I'm not about to start now. We won't let the bad guys win," Luci declared.

"Thank you, Luci, from the bottom of my heart," Berto told her.

"Well, if that's all the information you can give us for now, I must be going. I have a full day's work ahead of me," Luci stated.

"Me, too, Dad. The cars are calling me. I have to go to work." Berto echoed her lead.

They both stood as Luci reached into her purse for the keys and then hitched her purse strap over her shoulder.

"I'll walk you to your car," Berto told her. "Don't worry, Dad, I know the way out," he added.

"Very well. I will attend to the details on my end and you two prepare for the trial. Don't fear for your safety, Mrs. Clark," said Mr. Milano.

"Thank you, Mr. Milano. I'm feeling somewhat relieved after sharing my burden with someone. Please don't let anything happen to my children."

— ◄◙◙► —

ACROSS TOWN THINGS WERE MOVING along at the usual brisk pace at Summerfield Elementary. Principal Noreen Andrews had just finished making her rounds, popping into classrooms unannounced to briefly observe activities.

The first graders had been reading a story about frogs in coordination with their science experiment on tadpoles. *They are so inquisitive at that age,* she reflected. But the one child who had caught her eye was Jennifer Clark, the daughter of her old nemesis. *She is definitely a beauty, like her mom,* Noreen admitted reluctantly.

If only I had a little girl. I just know she would be a beauty, too. Maybe they would even be competitors, just like Luci and I were in our high school days, she thought. *Oh, well, wishful thinking. Too late for that now. There will be no children for me, at least none of my own.*

Plus, that son of Luci's was no slacker, either. The little booger had won first place in the social studies fair. Most of the kids depended on their parents to help them with their projects. *When had Luci, Miss High and Mighty Lawyer, had time to do that?* she wondered. *Isn't Luci supposed to be wrapped up in a murder case now...a murder case that involved her old high school sweetheart?*

Noreen jumped as her cell phone rang shrilly, echoing off the walls of the empty hall. She glanced irritably at the Caller I. D., noting that it was her husband, Charles. He didn't usually call her while she was at work. What could he want that was so important he had to interrupt her daily routine?

Well, the call would just have to wait until she got back to her office. She let it go to voice mail. She wasn't about to discuss personal business within earshot of anyone who happened to be passing by. Charles would be annoyed, of course, but that was just how it had to be. She could straighten out things with him later. After ten years of marriage, she certainly knew how to smooth his ruffled feathers.

She had made only a few steps down the hall when the phone rang again. She didn't even bother to check the Caller I. D. She knew it would be Charles, and he would most definitely be upset that she had not answered the call. She began to walk briskly to her office.

The phone rang a third time just as she entered the office and closed the door. Feeling safe within the walls of the room that had become her sanctuary, she drummed up her courage and managed to answer the call in a normal tone of voice as she sat down behind her desk.

"Noreen, where have you been? I have called you three times," Charles chided with a telltale trace of annoyance in his voice.

"I'm sorry, darling. I was observing some classes and couldn't answer right away."

She hoped he bought it. Charles Andrews was not used to being ignored, and there were usually dire consequences for anyone who chose that course of action.

"I have an assignment for you. A very important assignment. I want you to follow my instructions to the letter. This is something only you can do. I'm depending on you to help me with a difficult situation."

"Exactly what do you want me to do, Charles?"

She listened intently as he described his elaborate plan in detail. As the purpose of the scheme became clear to her, she began to feel alarmed. She waited for him to finish before she responded.

"No, I won't do that, Charles. I can't! I could never do anything that might cause harm to any of my students," she protested.

"You can, and you will," he responded. "I know our marriage is basically a marriage of convenience. Haven't I always given you everything you wanted? You wanted riches. You got them. You wanted more education. I paid for it. You wanted a position of power and recognition in the community. I made that happen, too."

"What...what are you talking about?" she stammered.

"Do you think you got that job as principal all by yourself? Oh, you were so happy and so proud when you were appointed. I didn't tell you, but it was my influence that put you over the top when it came down to the voting by the school board members."

"You're lying!"

"No, my dearest wife. I am not. There was another person up for the position. It was someone who was favored by the majority of the board members...until someone began to question his character. Rumors of that got back to the board, and his name was dropped from the list of candidates for the job...your current job."

"I...I knew he left town suddenly, but I never knew why. You! You were the one behind all of that? Charles, Charles, what have you done? Do you know how serious it is to defame a teacher's character?" She began to sob as she spoke, barely able to get the words out.

"Oh, good grief! Get control of yourself, woman. Do you want your staff to know you've been crying? Noreen Andrews, the Ice Princess! That's what they call you. Or did you know that? Somehow, I think you did."

"Must you always be so cold?"

His laugh reverberated through the phone into her ear. "I seem to remember quite a few nights when you didn't find me cold at all."

"That was at the beginning of our marriage. I was happy. I thought we were going to be happy," she lamented.

"Perhaps things would have turned out differently if I could have given you the one thing you wanted the most—a child of your own. But that's one thing I couldn't make happen."

"We could have adopted."

"I told you, I refuse to raise a child who is not my biological heir. We couldn't have a child, but now you have two hundred children to watch over."

"It's not the same. I wanted a baby to hold in my arms, a baby of my own…a baby of our own."

"It's all in the past now. You know the score on that. No more crying. Dry your eyes and make yourself presentable. Everything is set, and the plan will go into effect this afternoon. Do I make myself clear on that?"

"Yes, Charles. Crystal clear."

She hung up the phone and sat up straighter in her chair, reaching for a tissue from the box that was always sitting on the corner of her desk.

LUCI COULDN'T OVERCOME THE FEELING that something was wrong. She had been restless all day, hardly able to concentrate on the cases she was handling. She had met with several clients to update them on the work on their cases. However, she had to admit that she had not given them her full attention. In the back of her mind was that niggling feeling that something was about to happen—something big involving Berto's case. Despite Mr. Giovanni Milano's promise to watch over her children, she couldn't help but worry.

She jumped as the buzzer on her phone sounded, alerting her that she had a message from Cynthia. She picked up the phone and pushed the button to Cynthia's office.

"Yes, Cynthia. What is it?"

"There's a phone call for you, Luci. The Caller I. D. shows it as an unknown number. Shall I put the caller though?"

Luci felt a stab of fear in the pit of her stomach. What if it was the same caller she had heard from last night? Well, there was only one way to find out. She had to take the call.

"Yes, put the call through, please," she instructed. "Hello, this is Luci Clark speaking. How may I help you?"

She waited as she was greeted by silence on the line. Then the same muffled, raspy voice came through.

"Are you going to drop the Roberto Milano case?"

"Who is this?" she demanded to know.

"Who I am is not important," was the response.

"I am not in the habit of discussing my cases with anyone," she countered.

"I'll take that as a 'no.'"

"What do you want?"

"If you don't drop the case, you will find out shortly. It would be in your best interest to forget about Roberto Milano."

"I'm not dropping the case. Stay away from me and my family!" she exclaimed as she slammed the phone back on its base.

She burst into tears as she sat in her chair, stunned at her reaction to the unknown caller.

The office door opened just a crack as Cynthia poked her head in.

"Luci, is everything all right? I thought I heard shouting. Oh, my. You're crying. Something is wrong!" Cynthia walked into the room as she was speaking.

Luci reached for some tissues and wiped her eyes before replying.

"I can't tell you about it, Cynthia. I just can't."

"Luci, I'm your legal secretary. Anything you tell me will remain confidential. What is it? Is it your family? A client? What happened?" Cynthia spoke softly.

Luci blew her nose and took a deep breath.

"Very well. I'll tell you. But you have to promise not to tell anybody else. That was a threatening phone call. Somebody wants me to drop Berto's case."

"Threatening in what way?"

"The caller hinted if I don't drop the case, harm could come to me and my family. I can handle myself, but I can't let anything happen to my babies."

"Of course, you can handle yourself. I remember all those classes you took on self-defense," Cynthia soothed her. "But if you're being threatened, we need to call the police," she continued.

"No, not the police," Luci protested. "Berto doesn't need any more negative publicity regarding his trial. Besides, I already told him and his dad about it this morning. Mr. Milano is supposed to send somebody to watch the school."

"It's not the same as having the police watching out for you."

"I know, but that's the way it is for now. I just don't know of anything else to do."

"Put your trust in the Lord, and I'll say a prayer for you," Cynthia told her.

— ❧❧❧ —

THE BELL FOR FINAL DISMISSAL rang at Summerfield Elementary. Noreen Andrews walked towards the bus stop, glancing around nervously as she tried her best to look composed. It was time to carry out the mission she had been assigned. When Charles gave an order, one did not dare refuse.

She spotted the familiar sight of the On Your Way taxi driving into the lane for car pickups. After checking to make sure the other teachers on bus duty were busy loading students into the buses, she walked over to the line of students waiting their turn.

She assisted several of the students as their cars stopped at the designated spot to pick them up. Then it was Brian and Jennifer's turn as the taxi pulled into place. She opened the door and smiled cheerfully.

"Well, children, looks like your ride is here," she announced unnecessarily.

Jennifer climbed into the back seat first with Brian close behind. He hesitated with one foot in the door as he stared intently at the driver.

"That's not Mr. Bob!" he exclaimed.

"Oh, I'm sure it will be fine. After all, it's your grandpa's cab. He wouldn't send anybody he didn't trust to pick you up," Noreen reassured him as she gave him a gentle, but firm boost into the cab.

"But it's not Mr. Bob. We're not supposed to ride with anybody except Mr. Bob or Papa D'Armon," Brian protested as Noreen quickly closed the door.

She breathed a sigh of relief as the taxi pulled out of the driveway and sped away. She watched intently as it headed into traffic. She halfway expected the back door to open and Brian to come tumbling out.

She quickly turned her attention to getting the other riders loaded into their respective cars. Good thing she had redirected the usual duty teacher to another assignment at the last minute. There were some advantages to being principal, no matter how she got the job, she contemplated.

Twenty minutes later, with the parking lot cleared and all the children gone, she walked back to her office. The school was quiet now. Almost too quiet. It gave her an eerie feeling.

She closed the door as she walked into the office, digging her cell phone out of her pocket before sitting down behind her desk.

"It's done," she said. "I did what you wanted, Charles. Now please promise me that no harm will come to those children."

"I've already told you that they are just pawns. I am not interested in them. I'm interested only in the results of our mission. Now we wait."

— ◆◆◆◆◆ —

Bob Hardy moaned softly as he opened his eyes and tried to make out his surroundings. His head felt like it was about to split open. He touched the back gingerly and felt a large lump that was covered with something sticky. He drew his hand away and brought it around into his line of vision. Blood. He had a bloody wound on the back of his head.

What the Sam Hill? he thought. *Where am I and how did I get here?*

He tried to stand and then everything went blurry. He sank back down to the ground wearily. It was obvious he wasn't going anywhere. Not yet, anyhow. He peered towards the end of the alley and spotted a dumpster. It had a name on the side. If he could just make that out, he would know where he was.

He squeezed his eyes shut and then opened them again. Things were becoming a little clearer to him now. He could just read the letters on the dumpster.

D'Amico's Grocery. Ah, that was it. He was in the alley by a grocery store, but how did he get there?

It began to come back to him slowly. He had been flagged down on his way to pick up the Clark children. A man whose car was stranded by the road had asked him for a ride to the nearest garage. He had agreed, and the guy had climbed into the back seat. That was the last thing he could remember until he woke up in the alley.

There was no sign of the guy now, and, even worse, no sign of the taxi. What would anybody want with a taxi? It wasn't like stealing a regular car. A taxi would be hard to get rid of unless they stripped it down and sold it for parts.

Unless…unless it wasn't the taxi they wanted. What if they were going to use the taxi as a means of getting their hands on the children? He had been cautioned to be extra careful, as their mom was a lawyer who dealt with all sorts of people. Maybe it was the children they were after. He had to warn the family. He managed to pull himself upright and began a long and painful journey to the front of the alley. It wasn't that far to walk. He could make it. He had to make it!

⟶•❈❈❈•⟵

MAMA ROSA LOOKED AT THE clock. It was five minutes later than the last time she had checked. The snacks were ready for the children, but they were nowhere in sight. It was thirty minutes past their usual arrival time. What could be keeping them? They had never been late before. Maybe she should call Luci to see if she had picked them up.

She walked over to the kitchen counter and picked up the phone, but it rang before she could dial. The Caller I. D. showed Luci's number. She punched the *talk* button.

"Hello," she said hesitantly.

"Mama, are the children with you?" Luci asked worriedly.

"No, they're not here. I was just about to call you to ask if you had picked them up."

"I called the school and asked them to keep the children there until

I could pick them up, but the secretary said they had already left. One of the teachers saw them leaving in one of Papa's taxis. Where could they be?

"Well, if Bob picked them up, they might have stopped to get an ice cream cone on the way home. You know he likes to treat them sometimes, even though he knows he's not supposed to," Mama informed her.

Luci laughed nervously. "Yes, I had a sneaky feeling that was what was spoiling their appetites for dinner. He means well."

"But even if they stopped, they should be here by now," Mama said.

"Maybe they had engine trouble." Luci mulled the situation, hoping for the best.

"Possibly, but the taxis are fairly new. Papa trades them in every three years now."

"Okay, thanks, Mama. I'll check some more and get back to you. Please call me if they arrive at your house."

"I will do just that, Luci. I just hope nothing has happened to our babies," Mama was beginning to cry as she spoke.

"Everything will be fine, Mama. Try not to worry."

Luci hung up the phone feeling fearful for her children's safety. It was time to alert Berto and his dad. True, they didn't want the police involved, but if someone had kidnapped her children, she was going to have to go against their wishes. It was not a showdown she looked forward to.

Who to call first? she wondered. Berto was the logical choice. He would be better at handling his dad than she ever could. She made the call quickly and explained the situation to him. He assured her that he would come over to her office right away.

Cynthia was still on hand for moral support. She offered to make a new pot of coffee.

"Thank you, Cynthia. I could use a cup of coffee about now," Luci told her. "You really don't have to stay. Berto will be here soon."

"I'm not going anywhere until those children are found!" Cynthia declared.

"Thank you so much. You're the best."

They both looked towards the door as they heard the sound of tires squealing in the parking lot.

"That must be Berto," Luci exclaimed. "I'll let him in."

Luci pushed aside the blind covering the glass panel on the back door and spotted Berto hurrying up the walkway. She opened the door and he entered quickly, his large frame easily filling the space she had created.

"Berto, thank heavens you're here. I don't know what to do," she sobbed as she spoke.

"Luci, I promise you, we will find the children." He reached out and hugged her tightly. "It's going to be okay. Trust me."

"I hope so, Berto, but right now we have no idea of where they might be. I thought your father was going to have somebody watching the school." Her tone was almost accusatory.

"He did. We did have somebody there. Let me phone my dad and find out what happened. Excuse me for a moment."

He disappeared into a conference room with his cell phone plastered to his ear, closing the door behind himself. Luci and Cynthia exchanged glances, each trying not to let the other one see how worried she was.

Berto was back in the main office in less than two minutes. He was shaking his head as he walked into the room.

Luci's heart sank when she saw the grim expression on his face.

"They put one over on us," he admitted. "Our man saw the taxi picking up the children and the principal was helping them into the cab, so he thought everything was normal. It never occurred to him that anything was wrong."

Luci felt icy fingers creeping around her heart as his words sank in. Noreen, her nemesis, had been in on it. But she had no proof...at least not at the moment. Why would Noreen want to hurt her children, or any child, for that matter? Noreen was supposed to be an educator, someone who loved children and looked out for their welfare.

Would she stoop so far as to harm my children just to get even with me for some grudge left over from our high school days? Luci wondered.

"I think we have to call the police. It's really serious now," Berto announced.

"Yes, I think you're right," Luci agreed.

"Do you want to make the call or shall I?" he inquired.

"I have to do it. They're my children. I should be the one to report them as missing."

Luci barely got the words out before she began sobbing hysterically. Berto walked over and gathered her into his arms again.

"Shh. There now. Don't cry. It'll be all right." He patted her gently as he spoke.

She rested against him, reassured by his strength and feeling safe in his arms. But despite it all, she couldn't overcome her feeling of dread.

"Berto, Berto, what have I done? If anything happens to my children, it will be my fault. I should have dropped the case, but I wanted to help you. I know you're innocent."

"No, Luci. It's nobody's fault. If there's anybody to blame, put the blame on my family and their lifestyle. Little did I know when I was growing up that it would all lead to this. I'm accused of being a murderer, and now your children are missing."

"It's time to call the police now," Cynthia reminded them.

"Yes, you're right," Luci agreed.

Moments later she was on the phone with the police department explaining the situation. The desk sergeant assured her that someone would be over to her office immediately.

"Well, now all we have to do now is wait," Luci announced as she hung up the phone.

In what seemed like only seconds later, two unmarked police cars screeched into the parking lot behind the office. Cynthia let them in quickly, shutting and locking the door behind them. After introductions all around, the officers settled down to the business of getting all the facts. They excused themselves into a conference room to discuss the situation. When they emerged, it was evident they had formulated a plan.

"What we need to do, Mrs. Clark, is to agree to drop the case once the children are handed safely over to you. But be sure to stress that you won't agree to do that until you get them back safely," the lead officer instructed. "In the meantime, we are going to set up a wire to try to trace the next call. Try to keep the caller on the line as long as possible."

"Yes, of course," Luci agreed. "Jeremy...I must let Jeremy know about the children. Please excuse me while I make a call to him."

She walked into her office, shutting the door behind her and then picking up her cell phone, which was sitting on the desk. Making the call was going to be one of the hardest things she had ever done. Jeremy would like nothing better than to get custody of the children if she went through with the divorce. This would give him added ammunition. But he was their father and he had a right to know that his children were in danger, so she had no choice in the matter.

Reluctantly, she dialed the number.

—◆◄◙◘◙◘◙►◆—

Patrick Sherman sat in his car, which was parked just down the street from Luci's law office. He had been watching all the activities in the parking lot. Evidently, something was up…something big. First the Milano character had come racing into the parking lot like he was being chased by demons. Then two more cars had arrived. He recognized the detectives who had emerged from the two unmarked police cars. What could be happening that could have caused Luci to summon help? He couldn't just barge in without an excuse. Why didn't she call on him for help? That was definitely one stubborn woman!

He racked his brain. Surely, he could contrive some excuse to make an appearance at her office. He had to find out what was going on. He knew there was nobody better at pulling off a bluff than Patrick Sherman. He would just play it by ear and come up with some reason for dropping by her office after hours. He started the car and drove slowly down the street, parking beside the unmarked police cars. He exited his car and hit the lock button on his key chain, subconsciously straightening his tie as he headed towards the door.

He knocked on the door and was admitted by Cynthia, who looked surprised to see him.

"Mr. Sherman, we weren't expecting you!" she exclaimed.

"Oh, I saw the cars in the parking lot and just thought I would drop by to see if there are any new developments in the case," he replied, mentally kicking himself for not coming up with something more original.

"Oh, my. Oh, my, yes. There are definitely some more developments," she responded.

"So, what's happening?" he asked.

"Luci's kids have been kidnapped. They are threatening to hold them until she agrees to drop me as a client," Berto explained.

"Kidnapped? This is getting to be serious!" said Patrick. He wondered if Jeremy had been notified. He didn't have to wait long for an answer.

"Luci's in her office calling her husband right now," Berto told him.

"I see. So, what's the plan? Or is there a plan?" Patrick inquired.

Luci emerged from her office before Berto could reply.

"Jeremy is catching the next plane out of New York. He'll be here in a few hours," she announced.

"Okay, Mrs. Clark. What we need you to do is remain calm and wait for another phone call. Since the last call was to your office, the best thing is for you to wait here until you hear from the kidnappers again," said one of the detectives.

"Of course. I'm not going anywhere...not until I know my babies are safe," Luci declared.

They didn't have to wait long. Just when Luci thought she couldn't wait another minute to know if her children were unharmed, the phone rang. Everything had been set up to trace the phone call. She looked at the detectives, who nodded to her as a signal to answer the call.

"Hello," she said.

"This is your last chance. Drop the case if you want to see your children again," the same raspy voice instructed.

"I won't drop the case until I know my children are safe," she protested.

"That won't happen until the trial is over. It's the only guarantee that you won't be the lead counsel," was the response.

"That could take weeks! What will happen to my children in the meantime?" Luci demanded to know.

"The children are unharmed. You will just have to take my word for that."

"Let me talk to them. How do I know you really have them and that they are safe?"

Luci glanced in the direction of the detectives, who were motioning for her to try to keep the caller on the line.

"Not now. You will hear from the later, after the trial starts."

"Wait…" Luci pleaded, but the line went dead.

The detectives shook their heads. "Sorry, not enough time," one of them informed her.

"Berto, I'm so sorry," she said. "I don't know how another lawyer is going to be ready for the trial by Monday."

"That's the whole idea. They know you're the best and they want me to lose. They want to see me go to jail," he replied.

"We haven't given up," said the main detective. "We have people questioning all the teachers at the school and the principal, who put them in the taxi. Maybe one of them will give us a lead."

"I'll send for some sandwiches. Looks like it's going to be a long night," Cynthia announced.

⸺◈◈◈⸺

BRIAN CLARK LOOKED AROUND, TAKING in the drab surroundings of the room he and Jennifer had been escorted to after a bumpy cab ride. It wasn't a very pleasant place, and besides that, it smelled like cigarette smoke. His mom had always told him to watch out for his sister, and that was what he intended to do. He didn't know why the bad man had taken them away and shoved them into this room. Jennifer was beginning to cry. He felt like crying, too, but he was a boy, and boys were supposed to be brave. At least that's what his dad always said.

Jennifer stopped crying long enough to ask a question.

"Why are we here, Brian? Why aren't we home with Grandma Rosa?"

"I don't know, Jen. I don't know why the bad man brought us here, but you have to stop crying. We don't want to make him mad."

"But I'm hungry!"

He was starting to get hungry, too. It was way past the time when they would have already eaten their afternoon snack at Grandma Rosa's house. Maybe there was something to eat somewhere in the room.

He climbed out of the chair they were both huddled in and began to plunder through the drawers of a table that held a pot of stale coffee and the remnants of several half-smoked cigarettes. He found two packages of crackers in one of the drawers.

"Here. Eat these," he instructed, holding out one of the packages to Jennifer.

"What is that?" she asked.

"It's crackers, silly."

"But I don't like crackers very much."

"Well, that's all we have for now, so you'll just have to eat them," he said in his best imitation of a grown-up voice.

"Oh...okay."

They tore open the packages of crackers and began to nibble on them.

"Brian, I'm thirsty. Can I have some water?" Jennifer asked.

"I don't see any water in here. Maybe there's a cup in the bathroom," he told her.

He had his doubts about the cleanliness of the cup, but he was willing to give it a try. To his relief, he did find a cup that looked halfway presentable. He rinsed it out under the faucet and then ran some water into it.

"Here's your water," he announced as he walked back into the room, holding the cup carefully.

"Don't drink it too fast. We don't have any more clothes if you get your shirt wet," he cautioned.

"Okay, Brian. I'll be careful." Brian shook his head, suddenly feeling very grown up. *Kids!* he thought.

Jennifer sipped on the water and then took another bite of her cracker before posing another question.

"Brian, when can we go home? I want to go home."

"I don't know. Maybe in a little while. Just do what I say and try not to cry anymore, okay?"

"Okay, Brian. I'll try."

He walked over to the door and tried the knob. It was locked from the outside. *No big surprise there,* he thought. There was a curtain over the window. Did he dare look out? *No, probably not a good idea,* he decided. *No telling who might be watching the room.* At least there was a TV set in the room. Maybe he could find a show to watch, something to keep Jennifer entertained. As for himself, he wasn't in a very cheerful mood. He really didn't care one way or the other.

"Hey, want to watch some TV? Maybe we can find some cartoons," he suggested.

"Okay, I like cartoons," Jennifer agreed.

He switched on the TV and flipped through the channels until he found the one with cartoons.

"How's this?" he asked.

"That's a good one. I like that one!" Jennifer exclaimed.

He felt a little relieved at being able to distract his sister so easily. She didn't realize the seriousness of the situation, but he was old enough to know that they were in a lot of trouble. A man they had never seen before had taken them to a place they didn't want to be. Now they were locked in a room. He didn't know why, but he was positive nothing good would come of it. He wondered if their mom was looking for them. Somebody should have missed them by now. He didn't even know what time it was, but he knew it had been a long time since they left school.

He wished his dad would come and get them. Dad was big and strong and wasn't afraid of anything. If only Dad were around, everything would be okay. His dad always protected them.

—◈◈◈◈◈—

It was almost midnight and no more calls had come in. Luci was getting restless.

"Why haven't they called again?"

"Perhaps they're waiting until after the trial, just like they said they would do," Berto replied.

"Yes, I don't think there are going to be any more calls tonight," the lead detective informed her.

"But we don't know that. I can't go home. What if they call and I'm not here? What would happen to the children?" Luci wondered.

"There's a couch in the spare conference room. It can be used as a bed," Cynthia suggested.

"Why didn't I think of that?" Luci exclaimed.

"Nobody's blaming you for not thinking straight," said Berto. "Why don't you lie down and try to get some sleep? We'll man the phones and if a call comes, we'll wake you."

"I don't think I can sleep," Luci protested.

"My dear, you should try. This may turn into a long ordeal. You have to keep up your strength," Cynthia said.

"I guess you're right. I'll lie down, but just for a few minutes. What about the rest of you?"

"We'll be fine. Don't worry about us. I can nap in a chair," Berto assured her.

"And we have some relief people coming in to replace us," said one of the detectives as the other one nodded in agreement.

"Sure, we'll be fine," added the second detective.

"We need to let my parents know what's going on. I haven't called Mama for several hours," Luci mused.

"They're probably asleep by now," said Berto.

"Oh, you don't know my parents! When anybody in the family is in trouble, it's their problem, too. It was all I could do from keeping them from rushing over here," Luci exclaimed.

"Well, it was best for them to stay home in case a call should happen to come there," said Berto.

"Yes, they know that. It's the only reason they aren't here with us now. But what about Jeremy? His plane should be arriving this morning. Somebody needs to meet him at the airport."

"I can do that," Patrick said quickly, seeing his chance to meet with Jeremy and fill him in on everything. "I need to go home and shower and change clothes anyhow."

"Oh, great. I have a picture of him on my phone. Here's what he looks like," Luci told him as she passed the phone to him.

"No problem," Patrick responded.

"That leaves just you, Cynthia. I insist you go home for a little while and try to get some rest," said Luci.

"Oh, I'm not leaving," Cynthia protested.

"You won't be much good to me if you're exhausted. I need somebody to answer my regular business calls in the morning," Luci told her.

"I guess you're right. We can't shut down the phones, and we might be hearing from other clients," Cynthia admitted.

"Then I guess everything is settled. I'll try to get some rest on the couch and everybody else has their assignment," Luci decided.

JEREMY CLARK WAS SO MAD he could almost spit ten-penny nails. How had his life gotten to be such a mess? First, his wife had left him and taken the two kids. Then he was being accosted by a woman he could barely tolerate, much less stay in the same room with. Finally, his secretary had all but quit on him when her fiancé broke off their engagement. Now, to top it all off, his kids were missing and had most likely been kidnapped. Would it ever end?

And to think it had all started with that blasted tabloid picture somebody had sent to Luci. That was the beginning of the whole thing...the rock that had started the waves in motion in his sea of life. Luci and the kids would still be in New York, safe and sound, if not for that picture. Well, they could mess with him all they wanted, but when they started messing with his kids, that was different. He had been on the airplane for over two hours. Normally, he didn't mind flying, and he usually occupied himself with business matters when in flight. Not this time. This time all he could think about was his family.

How is Luci holding out without me there to reassure her? he wondered. *Or is she finding comfort in the arms of her client Roberto Milano?* He had gotten the e-mail reports of their late-night conferences, complete with pictures...pictures of Luci kissing another man. He never thought she would go that far. Maybe he didn't know his wife as well as he had envisioned.

Patrick Sherman wasn't the only detective under contract who had been busy. There had been new developments in the tabloid case, thanks to the persistence of Mike Graham, his New York detective. Mike had dug around and found what appeared to be the answer to the tabloid mystery. Jeremy now had the evidence he needed to convince Luci that he was innocent, if only she would hear him out. Well, she was a lawyer, so, hopefully, she would be willing to listen to both sides of the argument. But he would take care of that problem after the children were found and back home with their parents.

He was relieved when the "Fasten Seat Belts" sign came on and the pilot made the announcement for passengers to prepare for the landing. He had to switch to a smaller plane for the last leg of the flight to Brooksville. Patrick Sherman had phoned and said he would meet his plane in Brooksville, so he wouldn't have to catch a cab to Summerfield. It wouldn't be long before he would see Luci again. He was more than ready to be reunited with his family...all of them.

— ◆◆◆◆ —

LUCI AWAKENED AFTER A BRIEF nap on the couch in her conference room. She had spent most of the night tossing and turning, and when she finally did doze off, she had a nightmare about the kidnapping. She dreamed that the children didn't make it home safely and all their efforts to save them had been in vain. The dream had seemed so real that it took her a moment or two to recognize her surroundings and realize that only a few hours had passed since she had spoken to the kidnapper.

She rolled off the couch and hurried to the door. Pulling it open, through another door she spotted Berto sitting behind her desk with his eyes closed. Evidently, he had been there all night. If there had been a phone call, he would have awakened her.

Her attention was diverted by the sound of the coffeepot spitting out the last few drops of hot coffee into a fresh decanter. She looked over to the other side of the office and saw one detective sitting at Cynthia's desk while the other one was manning the coffeepot.

"Good morning, Mrs. Clark," one of them said to her.

"Good morning," she replied. She was certain she must look a fright...rumpled clothes, smudged makeup, and hair all a mess. *Nothing like sleeping in your clothes,* she thought.

"Well, now what? There have been no more calls, so what's our next step?" she inquired.

"We wait," one of the detectives replied.

"We have detectives watching the house of the school principal because she was the one who put the kids in the taxi. It seems rather suspicious, even though she denies knowing that anything was wrong. We think she knows more than she's letting on," the other detective added.

"Oh…" Luci was at a loss for words as the reality of Noreen's possible involvement sank in. She sat down in one of the chairs in the reception area.

"Cynthia's not back yet?" she inquired, after realizing that her trusty secretary was nowhere to be seen.

"Doug here finally convinced her to take your advice and go home after you went to sleep," the first detective responded, motioning to the other detective as he spoke.

"Yes, no sense in her wasting energy. We need her in full strength today," Doug noted.

"I'm so sorry, but I didn't catch your names last night," Luci told them.

"I'm Joe and this ugly guy is Doug," the first detective informed her.

They all chuckled, but it didn't relieve the tension in the room. Luci's stomach was still tied in knots. She couldn't remember how long it had been since she had eaten, and the coffee was beginning to get a little repetitive. What she wouldn't give for some of Mama Rosa's cinnamon rolls!

There was a knock on the door, and Joe walked over and unlocked it. He opened it slightly and then held it wide as Mama Rosa entered carrying a tray that was giving off a familiar and delicious odor.

"Mama, what are you doing here?" Luci exclaimed.

"I couldn't stay away any longer. I had to do something, so I baked my special cinnamon rolls for everyone," Mama explained.

"Bless you! I was about to starve," Luci exclaimed as she peeked under the napkin covering the tray. "Sausages, too! Mama, you're a lifesaver!"

"I'll second that one," said Doug.

"And I'll second his second," said Berto as he rose from his chair and took the tray from Mama.

"Well, what are we waiting for? Everybody, please help yourselves. I brought paper plates and napkins also," Mama informed them as she deposited a plastic bag on the table.

"But what about the phone at home?" Luci asked.

"Papa is there at the house. He will answer if anybody calls," Mama assured her. "Luci, I brought fresh clothes for you also."

"Mama, thank you so much. You think of everything."

They ate quickly without conversing. They all had their own agenda and their own worries. Luci gathered the clothes Mama had brought and then excused herself into the bathroom to change and freshen up as best she could. She kept a spare toothbrush and toothpaste for emergencies, as she often had meetings with her clients after eating. She brushed her teeth, splashed water on her face, and dabbed it dry with a paper towel. She changed clothes and ran a comb through her hair and then looked into the mirror and evaluated the results of her efforts.

Well, not the best job of grooming I've ever done, but at least I look halfway presentable now. But I really don't care about my looks. All I want to do is find my children. She tacked on a silent prayer as thoughts flitted through her mind. *Please, God, watch over them and keep them safe for me.*

She picked up the dirty clothes and folded them. After stashing them in the bag that had held the clean clothing, she opened the bathroom door and walked back into her office. But before she got to the reception area, her cell phone rang. The Caller I. D. showed Jeremy's cell phone number.

"Hello," she said.

"Hello, Luci. Patrick picked me up at the airport in Brooksville. We're on our way to Summerfield now and should be there shortly. Where do I need to meet you?"

"We're all gathered in my office. That's where the calls from the kidnapper have been coming in."

"Okay, that's where we will come then. See you soon."

"All right, Jeremy. Goodbye."

She walked into the other room, cell phone in hand.

"I just heard from Jeremy. He's on his way," she announced. "He's... my...husband, the children's father," she explained to the detectives.

"Oh, good. Jeremy's coming. Everything is going to be all right. Jeremy always knows what to do," Mama exclaimed.

Luci took a deep breath and willed herself to hold her tongue. Evidently, her family was still enthralled with Jeremy, just as she had been when they were first married. He was wonderful in many ways, but could he save the children?

Before she could respond, Joe's phone rang. Everyone stopped talking and listened to his side of the conversation. He hung up and turned to face the crowd.

"Okay, we have official orders. We wait here. They'll let us know about further developments," he informed them.

Luci tried to stifle a sob, but to no avail. She wanted to be strong for Mama Rosa's sake, but her nerves were on edge. The sobs just wouldn't stop coming. Berto rushed over and wrapped his arms around her, holding her tightly.

"Shh...there now. It'll be okay, Luci. You'll see. Be strong now, like the girl I've always known," he said.

"I'll try," she blubbered.

As the others stood by nervously, a knock sounded on the door. Joe walked over and unlocked it and then opened the door wide to admit the person on the other side. A silence fell over the room as the visitor entered.

Jeremy Clark walked into the room and spotted his wife in another man's arms. Just how far had things progressed between Luci and her high school sweetheart? *Is it too late to save my marriage?* he wondered.

—◆◄◊►◊◄◊►◆—

NOREEN ANDREWS WAS WORRIED ABOUT those two children she had so insistently shoved into the taxi. The police had questioned her for hours, but she had stuck to her story that she knew nothing about the kidnapping. She insisted that she did not realize the driver was not one of the regular company drivers. They finally seemed to believe her because they let her leave the police station. She was now at home awaiting the arrival of her husband. He had been gone all night, and it wasn't like him at all. Where could he be?

She heard the front door open and she walked into the foyer to see Charles stepping through the door.

"Where have you been?" she asked.

"I was taking care of some business, my dear. That's all I have to say about the matter at this time."

"Charles, so help me, if you do anything to hurt those children…"

"The children are perfectly fine. I told you, nothing to worry about."

"And I'm supposed to just take your word for that? Charles, those are my students you are talking about. I'm responsible for them. I should never have let myself be talked into helping you with this scheme of yours, whatever it might be."

"It's more than a scheme, Noreen. Much more. It's bigger than either one of us, something I can't stop, even if I wanted to. Anyhow, it's too late now."

"I have to see them, Charles. I have to know that they are okay. Please, I'm begging you to take me to them."

"Noreen, you know you ask the impossible. The less you know about this, the better for you."

"I'm your wife, Charles. If you can't trust me, then who can you trust? I've stood by you all these years. Please grant me this one request."

He stared at her with eyes that seemed to bore right through her. She felt a chill sweep over her body, something that had never happened before with her husband, despite his sometimes-questionable schemes.

"No, it just won't work! I can't do it, I tell you," he declared.

"Please, Charles. I never asked you for much. Please, I'm asking for the sake of the children."

He sighed, his demeanor changing slightly as he responded, "Very well. I can see that you're determined to get your way. Let me shower and change. Do you have anything for me to eat?"

"I can fix you some bacon, eggs, toast, and coffee. It will be ready by the time you're through dressing."

She found herself talking to his back, as he was already climbing the stairs to their master bedroom suite. She walked into the kitchen and took out the ingredients and utensils she needed to prepare the meal. She knew Charles would keep his word about taking her to see the children. Despite his faults, he wasn't a liar. She had never known him to lie in all their years of marriage.

She busied herself preparing the food she had promised him. She had no doubt he would eat it, although she couldn't possibly swallow a bite of food herself. She wished now she had never gotten mixed up in his business. She should have followed her gut instinct and refused to go along with the plan. But he was her husband, and he was definitely the dominant force in the relationship, despite rumors to the contrary. Outwardly, the world knew Noreen Andrews as a cold-hearted, calculating person who always got what she wanted. Inwardly, she still had a heart buried somewhere deep inside. That heart had been battered and bruised, but it was still there, and right now it was tugging at her conscience.

Charles reappeared by the time she was dishing up the food. He slid into a chair at the kitchen table, and she silently sat the plate in front of him.

"Smells good. I'm really hungry," he said.

She dropped into a chair across the table from him and propped her elbows on the table, resting her chin on her hands.

He glanced up as he put a forkful of eggs into his mouth, chewing slowly and deliberately.

"What? I said I would take you to the kids. What more do you want?" he exclaimed.

"Charles, why did you have to involve those children? Whatever your scheme is, couldn't you have accomplished it without putting young lives in danger?"

"I told you, the kids are safe. They'll be just fine. There's nothing to worry about."

"How can you say that? There's always something to worry about if kidnapping is involved, especially with kids."

He polished off the last piece of toast and swallowed the last of the coffee before dabbing his mouth with the napkin. He stood and wiped his hands slowly before responding.

"Thank you for the breakfast, Noreen. It's time now. If you want to see those children, grab your purse and we'll be on our way. Just remember this—you are sworn to secrecy, no matter what happens. You can't tell anybody where they are."

The walked out to his car and climbed in. As they fastened their seatbelts, Noreen posed a question.

"You're not going to blindfold me?"

"There's not much point. You know this town like the back of your hand. Even if I blindfolded you, you'd figure out where you were about ten seconds after the blindfold was removed. That's why it would have been best for you to leave well enough alone."

"I'm sorry, Charles. I just can't help it."

"I understand, Noreen. I really do. And remember, no matter what happens, I do love you. I always have."

"Thank you for that, Charles," she whispered as he put the car into gear and backed into the street. *Yes, we are both cold-hearted, but I know he really does care for me in his own way, and I do love him, even though we've grown apart,* she reflected. *A baby. That's what we both needed to make this marriage complete.*

❖

ACROSS TOWN IN LUCI'S OFFICE, Joe's cell phone rang. He listened intently and then responded. "Right, got it. I will relay the information."

After disconnecting the call, he looked around the room at the expectant faces staring at him.

"That was headquarters. A car with principal Noreen Andrews and her husband just left their house. We've got a tail on them, so now we have to wait and see where they're headed," he informed the crowd.

"Oh, please, dear God, let them help us find my children," Luci exclaimed.

"Our children," Jeremy corrected her.

"Yes, of course, our children. Jeremy, I'm so sorry this all happened. I'll never forgive myself if anything happens to them."

"Don't go blaming yourself. When this is all over we have a lot to discuss," he responded.

"Yes, we do. But right now, our main concern is the children. I just can't help wondering where they are and if they are scared. Jennifer is so young. I hope Brian is looking after her," Luci lamented.

"Brian's more mature than you give him credit for. I know he'll do everything he can to keep his sister safe," Jeremy assured her.

Joe's phone rang again. He spoke briefly and then told them what he had learned.

"That was headquarters again. They told me we can follow the progress of the vehicles if I log into the official website. We can follow the GPS on the unmarked police vehicle."

"Great! Let's do it," Jeremy exclaimed.

"You can use the computer at my desk," Cynthia offered. She had slipped in quietly while Joe was talking.

"I'll bring up the website," Doug offered.

"Yeah, you're a lot better with computers than I am," Joe admitted.

The crowd moved around Cynthia's desk and began to stare intently at the screen as Doug logged onto the site and entered his password. As the screen focused to reveal a moving red dot, the street names came into view.

"I know that area," Berto announced.

"You do?" Luci asked anxiously.

"Yes, I used to play there when I was a kid. It's run down now, but there are still a lot of older houses and one seedy motel."

"A motel? If there's a motel there, maybe that's where they took the kids," Joe mused.

"Good thinking. I was about to say the same thing," Doug told him.

"That's got to be it! I'll bet they are holding the kids in one of those motel rooms," said Berto.

"It's best to wait and see if that's where the Andrews couple is really headed. We don't think he's picked up the tail, but he could be trying to throw us off the track," Joe cautioned.

"I can't stand it! I just can't stand not knowing if they are okay," Luci exclaimed.

NOREEN GLANCED AROUND AS SHE and Charles exited the car he had just parked in front of what had to be the seediest joint in town. It almost made her skin crawl just to look at the place.

"Are the children here?" she asked.

"Yes. Just follow me and there won't be any trouble," he told her as he walked up to a door and knocked three times.

"Yeah? Who is it?" came a faint voice from the other side.

"It's me. Open the door," Charles instructed.

The door opened slowly to reveal a tall, muscular man in what appeared to be yesterday's clothes. Noreen recognized him as the man who had been driving the taxi that had picked up the children.

They walked into the room, and Charles shut the door quickly.

"Well, how's it going, Larry?" he asked.

"I'd say things are right on schedule. The kids are in the room on the other side of the suite. Don't worry. They can't get out. Everything is locked up right and tight, and there's no phone in there," was the response.

"So, Mrs. Clark agreed to drop the case?" Charles inquired.

"Yep, just as you said. Her kids come first. She's dropping it right away."

"Splendid. This is my wife, Noreen."

"Ma'am, you shouldn't have come here," Larry responded.

"Charles, what about the children? You said I could see them." Noreen brushed him off and turned to her husband.

"Excuse me for saying so, but, ma'am, that ain't really a good idea," Larry protested.

"It's not your decision to make," Noreen informed him.

"Yes, I have agreed to let her see the children," said Charles.

"But, Boss, right now they don't know who we are. If they see your wife, they will put two and two together. I thought you wanted to keep your name out of this," Larry continued with his protests.

"As my wife told you, it's not your decision to make," Charles cut him short with a terse reply.

"Okay, okay. You're right. Not my call," Larry agreed.

"Perhaps I could check on them while they're sleeping. That way, they wouldn't see me, and they wouldn't make the connection," Noreen suggested.

"Brilliant thinking, my love, as always," Charles told her. "Larry, why don't you slip in and check on the little dears and see if they're asleep."

"Sure thing, Boss."

Larry unlocked the bathroom door quietly and made his way over to the adjoining room. Noreen sank into one of the chairs while Charles began to pace around the confines of the small room, which had obviously seen better days.

Larry returned shortly, closing and locking the door behind him.

"Well?" Noreen inquired.

"Both sound asleep in the middle of the bed. Dead to the world," Larry reported.

Noreen looked at her husband.

"Charles, please," she pleaded.

He nodded. "Make it quick, Noreen, before they wake up."

Larry unlocked the door again, and Noreen slipped through the bathroom. She opened the door to the bedroom suite quietly and peered into the dimly lit room. She could just make out the outline of two forms lying in the middle of the king-sized bed, huddled together beneath the covers.

She tiptoed into the room, her heart beating so fast she was sure they would hear it and awaken. She approached the bed and bent down to get a closer look. As things came into focus, she saw two angelic faces, eyes closed in sleep. She breathed a sigh of relief and brushed back the stray hairs that had fallen over Jennifer's face. It was obvious the girl had been crying because traces of dried-up tears were streaked down her face.

"Poor little hearts. Don't worry. I'll keep you safe," she whispered.

She slipped back out of the room just as quickly as she had entered. She re-entered the sitting room to find Charles still pacing the floor, while Larry was sitting by the phone, smoking a cigarette.

Disgusting, she thought. The place smelled bad enough without his adding to the stench.

"Must you smoke?" she asked as she sank into the chair she had vacated.

"Sorry, ma'am," Larry apologized as he ground out the cigarette in an ashtray that was already overflowing with cigarette butts.

"I need some air," she announced as she rose from the chair and headed towards the door.

"Hold on. You can't go outside. No telling who might be out there," Charles warned her.

"Oh, of all the...Very well, have it your way," she gave in and returned to her seat.

Larry walked over to the window and pulled the curtain back slightly. He scanned the parking lot and then began cursing softly.

"What's wrong?" Charles inquired.

"Some people out there. Lots of people and what appears to be police cars," Larry informed him.

"What? They followed us. They put a tail on you, Noreen. I knew bringing you here was a bad idea," Charles glared at her, his eyes blazing as he spoke.

"I'm so sorry," Noreen whispered.

"Too late for that. What are we going to do now?" Larry asked.

Before Charles could respond, a tiny voice interrupted their conversation.

"Who are you?" the voice inquired.

They all turned to look at the source of the query.

"How did those children get in here? Noreen, you didn't lock the door behind yourself," Charles scolded.

"Well, they've seen us all now, so the jig's up," Larry observed.

"Not quite. We still have some leverage. The police aren't going to do anything that might harm the children," Charles calculated as he spoke.

"Mrs. Andrews, what are you doing here? Did the bad men kidnap you, too?" Brian asked.

Noreen rushed over to the children and hugged them both, keeping her arm around Jennifer as she responded. "No, Brian, I'm just here to keep you and Jennifer safe."

"I want my mama," Jennifer said as she began to cry again.

"There, there. It's okay. I'll get you back to your mom, all safe and sound. Don't you worry," Noreen reassured her.

The crowd looked expectantly at Charles, awaiting his next move. Before anybody could speak, the phone rang.

"Aren't you going to get that?" Noreen asked after the fifth ring.

"Why should I? We all know who it is," Charles retorted.

"All I can say is you got yourself into this mess, and now you are the only one who can get yourself out of it," Noreen told him.

"All right, I suppose I'll have to see what they have to say," Charles replied as he picked up the phone. "Hello," he spoke into the receiver, his voice echoing in the otherwise quiet room.

ON THE OTHER END OF the line things were anything but silent. Police cars swarmed into what had been an almost deserted, sleepy parking lot. A vehicle carrying Luci and Jeremy wasn't far behind. Luci had been successful in her efforts to convince the two detectives that she had to be on the scene when her children were found.

Luci and Jeremy were escorted to the motel office, where one of the police negotiators was on the phone with the kidnappers. He motioned them in and indicated that they should be quiet while he tried to convince the kidnappers to let the children go.

"I understand, sir. We're all on the same team here. Our main goal is to get the children returned safe and sound. So, tell me, what would it take in order to accomplish that?" The negotiator was speaking into the phone as the worried parents entered the room.

"Yes. Yes. I understand. I will see what I can do. Give me about ten minutes," he said as he hung up the phone.

He turned to Luci and Jeremy, who had both taken a seat in some hastily arranged chairs that now lined one of the walls.

"Our hunch was right. Your children are here in this motel. The kidnappers do have possession of them at this time. We are doing everything we can to get them back to you as quickly and as safely as possible."

"Oh, God," Luci said as she began sobbing.

Jeremy gathered her in his arms. "Shh, don't cry. The police know what they're doing." He hoped he sounded more confident than he felt.

"Excuse me a minute while I confer with the captain," the negotiator told them as he headed towards the door.

—◆◇◆◇◆—

INSIDE THE CROWDED MOTEL ROOM things were growing more tense by the minute. Charles, always the calm, cool, and collected one, was beginning to sweat. Larry was pacing the floor nervously as he lit one cigarette after another, ignoring the scathing looks from Noreen each time he dragged out his lighter.

Brian looked over at Jennifer, who sobbed softly. He knew she was scared, but he was determined to put up a brave front and protect his sister to the end. He just wished his dad would come and get them. He didn't understand why Principal Andrews was here, but she seemed to know the men who had kidnapped them. Maybe she could help them get away somehow. He sat silently, lost in thought as he pondered the situation.

Noreen sat in one of the armchairs, while the two children huddled together in the other one. She didn't know how much longer she could keep Charles and Larry at bay and away from the children. She must protect them at all costs. It was her fault they were in this situation. She had put them in harm's way. Her career was over now, and she was most likely facing a jail term as an accomplice to the kidnapping. It was not the way she had envisioned her life headed just a few short weeks ago. Why hadn't God seen fit to bless her with a child of her own? That was all she ever really wanted—a loving husband, a successful career, and a child to dote on and spoil. Instead, she had turned into a shrew, one of the most hated women in town. *Where exactly did my life taken a wrong turn?* she wondered. *Why do people like Luci Carlito Clark seem to get all the lucky breaks?*

She looked at Charles and decided it was time to make a move.

"Charles, why don't you let the children go? There's really not much point to the whole kidnapping scheme now. I don't understand why you did this in the first place."

Charles turned to his wife with a pained look on his face. "You don't understand. You don't understand. Well, let me tell you the whole sordid story. I had a brother once, an older brother who was my idol. He was smart, handsome, had any woman he wanted…everything I wanted to be."

"A brother? I never knew…" Noreen interjected, but he waved her off.

"I never talked about him because it was too painful. But he's gone now, dead, thanks to Mr. Giovanni Milano."

"I don't understand," Noreen responded.

"Let me finish. My brother got what he thought was the ideal job, working for Mr. Milano. Like I said, he was smart, so he moved up the corporate ladder pretty fast. Then something happened. There was some kind of scandal about illegal betting. My brother was the bookkeeper. So, what did Milano do? He fixed it so the whole thing fell on my brother's shoulders. My brother went to jail, while Milano stayed free, going about his everyday business. He hadn't been in jail very long when he was killed in a knife fight. Somebody stabbed him with a shiv. I think Milano arranged that, too, in order to make sure my brother's actions could never be traced to him."

"So, just how does this tie into the children and the kidnapping?"

"I'm getting to that. One of Roberto's car salesmen, Tom Downing, has a gambling problem. He lost way more than he ever made and got deeply in debt. He started siphoning money off his car sales accounts. He even managed to hack into the system and took money from another salesman's account, a guy named Eric Wiley. When that wasn't enough, he started borrowing money all over town from anybody he could. Finally, he ended up at my loan organization. I did a little checking into his background and found out about his illegal activities. So, I offered to make all the debts go away for him if he would do something for me."

"Charles, no…what did you do?" Noreen whispered.

"I told him to bump off Eric Wiley and make sure that Roberto

Milano was framed for it. That way, Roberto would spend the rest of his life in jail, payback for what his dad did to my brother."

"My God, Charles, how could you be so cold-hearted? Murder? I never thought you would be involved in something like that," Noreen exclaimed.

"Well, now you've done it for sure. You shouldn't have said all that in front of the kids. I'm not going to jail for somebody else's murder," Larry announced as he pulled out a gun.

Noreen screamed, a high, piercing scream that penetrated through the windows and into the parking lot, where a crowd of police personnel had gathered.

"What do you think you're doing?" Charles demanded to know as Larry began waving the gun around.

"I ain't going down for this, I tell you. Not for murder," Larry shouted.

"Put that gun away before somebody gets hurt," Charles exclaimed.

Noreen rushed over to the chair where the children sat as Charles and Larry began struggling over the gun. She gathered them into her arms and they crouched together, watching helplessly as the two men tussled.

Then a shot rang out, and Noreen slumped to the floor, blood oozing from a gunshot wound.

"You stupid fool, what have you done?" Charles exclaimed as he wrestled the gun from Larry's grip and aimed it at Larry's chest. Charles pulled the trigger. Larry staggered briefly and then dropped to the floor, moaning as he fell.

Charles rushed to Noreen's side, the gun still in his hand. The children sat frozen into place, unable to comprehend what had just happened. They were both crying.

"Noreen, I never meant for this to happen. Nobody was supposed to get hurt," he exclaimed as he lifted her into his arms, dropping the gun in the process.

"Charles...too late...don't hurt the children," Noreen whispered as she took her last labored breath.

He sat rocking her body as silent sobs racked through him. "No…no…no. Why? Why?" he asked.

Before anyone could move, the door burst open, and the room was suddenly filled with smoke and blinding lights as the police launched their grenades. They descended on the room quickly.

"Get on the floor, hands above your head," a voice ordered through the smoke and haze.

Charles put up no resistance and was immediately taken into custody and handcuffed as the gun was kicked away from him. The children continued to cower in the chair, covering their eyes from the blinding lights.

Someone raised both windows and the smoke began to dissipate. One of the officers rushed over to the children and began to comfort them.

"Hey, kids, it's okay now. You're safe, and your parents are waiting outside. Come on, I'll take you to them," he said.

He picked up Jennifer, while a policewoman walked over and took Brian's hand.

"It's all right, son," she said as she began to lead him out of the room.

Luci and Jeremy were waiting in the parking lot, having been given the all clear by the police captain.

"There they are," Luci exclaimed as she spotted the children being escorted from the motel.

"My babies! Are you all right?" she asked as officers handed the children over to her and Jeremy.

Jennifer wrapped her arms around her daddy's neck as if she would never let go, while Brian stood to the side after giving his mom a hug.

"What's wrong, Brian?" Luci asked.

"Mom, I have something to tell you," he began hesitantly.

"Go on, son. You know you can tell me anything," said Luci.

"Principal Andrews was there. She's…she's dead now."

"Oh, no! Dead? Do you want to talk about it? Please tell me what happened."

"One of the bad men was going to shoot me and Jennifer, but Principal Andrews saved us. She was trying to keep us from getting shot and a bullet hit her. Mom, there was so much blood. It was really scary. I didn't know real blood would look like that. It was nothing like my video games."

"So, Noreen had a heart after all," Luci mused.

"What? What did you say, Mom?" Brian asked.

"Nothing, son. I was just thinking out loud. I'm just glad you and Jennifer are safe now," Luci responded as she reached out and gave Brian a gigantic hug.

"I don't know about the rest of you, but I've had enough of this scene. Let's go home now," Jeremy suggested.

"Good idea," Lucy agreed.

The police captain walked up as they finished their conversation.

"Is this nightmare really over?" Luci asked.

"Yes, we have arrested Charles Andrews, and he's given a full confession. He couldn't stop talking. We have a warrant out for the arrest of Tom Downing, who was responsible for killing the other car salesman. Andrews didn't hold anything back when he told us what happened. We have an ambulance on hand, so why don't you get the children checked out and then we will give you an escort home," he told them.

"Good idea," Luci told him.

"I'm okay. I don't need to be checked out," Brian protested.

"Brian, do as the officer says. We'll have you both checked out, and then we're going home because your mom and I have a lot to talk about," Jeremy instructed.

"Aww, Dad, okay," Brian agreed reluctantly.

Luci spotted two stretchers hauling black body bags being wheeled out of the motel room. She quickly turned the children so that they faced in the other direction as the family headed towards the ambulance. They had been traumatized enough for one night, she reasoned.

❖

SEVERAL HOURS LATER, WITH THE children fed, bathed, and tucked into bed, Luci found herself alone with Jeremy as they sat in her living room drinking coffee.

"I'll never get to sleep tonight after drinking the coffee you made," she told him.

"I'll never get to sleep with or without the coffee," said Jeremy.

"I just hope the children don't have nightmares," Luci spoke worriedly.

"I'm sure they'll be fine. However, we might want to have them talk to a psychologist as the police suggested," Jeremy told her.

"Yes, I think that would be a good idea. Children are so impressionable."

"Luci, there is something else we need to discuss. I have some news about the tabloid incident. I'm hoping this changes your mind about suing me for divorce."

"What is it, Jeremy? What can you tell me that I don't already know?"

"Remember, I told you I hired a private investigator to look into the tabloid case. He's one of the best private eyes I know. I love you so much, Luci. I had to do something. I can't let you go. I can't lose you and the children."

"Go on," she told him.

"As I told you, somebody sent a copy of that picture to you and to the fiancé of my secretary, Belinda. Somebody had a motive, but I just couldn't figure out what it was. Mike did a lot of digging, and he finally found the connection."

"So, what was it?" Luci asked curiously.

"Seems that you were a distraction in the case, something to throw everybody off track. The real target was Belinda. There was another girl who was in love with Belinda's fiancé, Matt Collins, and she wanted to break him and Belinda up. I noticed that he seemed to find another girlfriend very quickly, a girl named Tammy Risinger. Pretty girl, but nothing like Belinda. No heart, just out for her own selfish motives."

"Oh? I'm speechless. I really don't know what to say, Jeremy." Luci blinked back tears as she spoke.

"Matt and Belinda are back together now, and the wedding's back on. Looks like I'll be escorting the bride down the aisle, after all."

"I'm so glad for her and Matt!" Luci exclaimed, sniffing slightly as she spoke.

"So am I. But where does that leave us, Luci? What about the divorce? Would you be willing to drop the lawsuit and give our marriage a second chance? I'll do anything you want, anything at all. Just name it," he pleaded.

Unable to stop herself, Luci burst into tears, feeling a full crying jag coming on again. She tried to speak between sobs, her voice coming out in jerky sentences. "Jeremy, I'm so torn. I love you so much, but I don't think I can go back to the life we had."

Jeremy gathered her into his arms and began kissing the tears away. "Baby, baby, we'll work this out. I promise you."

"I have my law practice here now. Plus, Mama and Papa aren't getting any younger. They need to see their grandchildren grow up," she told him.

"Then you can stay here. *We* can stay here. I'll set up a satellite branch of the New York office here in Summerfield," he continued to plead his case.

"You'd do that for me?" she asked hesitantly.

"I told you—anything you want."

She flung her arms around his neck and kissed him soundly.

"Jeremy, I love you so much. You know I could never say 'no' to you."

"Then you'll drop the divorce proceedings?"

She smiled sheepishly. "I never followed through. I filled out the papers, but I never took any action after that."

He laughed. "Then I have a confession to make also. I talked to a lawyer, but only to protect my interests involving custody of the children. Nothing was ever filed on my behalf."

"Then I guess we're still good," Luci commented.

"Oh, yes, we're still very good, as good as ever—no, better than ever," he corrected himself. "But there's just one thing we need to clear up."

"What's that?" Luci asked.

"What about Roberto Milano? Exactly how does he fit into the picture?"

"Berto was my first love, but now he's just a friend. I could never love him the way I love you."

"Does he know that?"

"I'll...I'll talk to him. I'll make him understand that he was my past, but you are my future. I wasn't sure, but now I know what I want."

"You don't know how glad I am to hear you say that," Jeremy exclaimed as he took her into his arms again.

Their kiss was interrupted as Brian and Jennifer walked into the room.

"Mama, I couldn't sleep," Jennifer announced.

"Me either," Brian added.

"Oh, you two, come here," Luci instructed, opening her arms wide as she spoke.

They rushed over, and soon all four people were hugging in a gigantic embrace.

"So, kids, do you know what I want to do next?" Jeremy asked.

"No, what, Dad?" Brian inquired.

"I'm going to throw the biggest party ever at our Rosalena's restaurant. I just might invite the whole town of Summerfield!"

"Summerfield, my hometown. Definitely the best place to be," Luci declared.

Part III

"Smooth Sailing"
Regenia's Story

Smooth Sailing

"No, no, no!" The words sprang involuntarily from Regenia Whitworth's lips as her car began to sputter and almost stalled in the middle of a busy street. It hiccupped as it jumped several times, giving her fair warning that it was about to quit. She grasped the steering wheel tightly and did her best to guide it to the side of the road as traffic rushed by on the driver's side, horns blaring as apparently irritated drivers showed no concern for her distressed state of affairs.

The car belched loudly and let out a stream of smoke as the steering wheel locked and the dashboard panel lit up, indicating the engine had completely died. She could only hope that she was safely pulled off by the side of the road. She glanced in the side mirror, watching for a break in the traffic, although she didn't know what she could do to remedy the problem.

"Why me? Why now?" she asked as she pushed the button to unlock the door. She released the hood lock and climbed out slowly, careful not to muss her clothes. She was on the way to an important job interview, one of many during the past few weeks. This one had sounded promising, and she really needed a job. The money was almost gone, and she didn't know how she would stretch it out to last many more days.

She struggled to open the hood, but finally managed to pry it loose and raise it to an upright position. She looked at the maze of parts that were crammed into a space that appeared to be almost too small for them. She had no idea what to do or which part might not be working. She had spent seven hundred of her precious few dollars on the vehicle just a few days ago when her other car had quit running. The salesman at the used car dealership had assured her that everything was in working order. That's what she got for trusting people!

Maybe I should have majored in mechanics instead of business administration, she pondered as she tried desperately to blink away the tears that threatened to spill down her cheeks at any moment. Just when she thought things couldn't get any worse, she caught a glimpse of flashing red lights as a police car pulled up behind her vehicle.

Oh, great! I hope I'm not going to get a ticket for blocking traffic or something equally as bad. She tried her best to look composed as an officer exited the car and began walking towards her.

"Good morning, ma'am. Having car trouble, are you?" the officer inquired.

"Yes, officer. It just died on me. I barely managed to pull off the road."

"I see. Well, let's take a look and see what we have here." The officer joined her at the front of the car and peered at the engine. He then bent down and looked underneath the vehicle.

"I don't see anything leaking, so it's not your water pump. No apparent oil leak, either. You didn't notice any warning lights coming on before it stopped?"

"No, sir. It just sputtered and died. No warning lights whatsoever. I just bought the car a few days ago, so I'm not that familiar with it."

"Well..." the officer pushed on the back of his cap as he scratched his head. "I believe the best thing to do is to call a tow truck. We can't leave it here beside the road. Do you have towing insurance?"

"No, I have just liability."

"That's too bad. I'll try to find you the least expensive tow operator I can. Hold on and I'll be right back."

She watched as he made his way back to the patrol car, relieved that she was receiving help rather than a traffic ticket. Rush hour seemed to be over, as the traffic had slowed, and cars were moving at a more leisurely pace. Of course, that was not a good sign, as it also meant the time for her job interview was fast approaching. She really didn't see how she was ever going to make the interview now.

She smoothed her black tailored skirt nervously. Her hands then flitted towards her immaculate white blouse. Not a fancy outfit, but it was all she had. Most of her other clothes consisted of jeans and casual tops. She traveled light and had ever since she and her little family had left their hometown and headed as far as their meager funds would take them. It was just by chance they had ended up in Summerfield. She had seen an ad in the paper for a secretarial position in a doctor's office when they had stopped for a meal at a local restaurant.

Her family—funny, but that's exactly what they were, the only family she had left. Her sister, Marlene, was five years younger. Then there was Timmy, her son, her wonderful, lovable two-year-old son. Her whole world revolved around him now. She had to keep him safe, no matter what. Everything had been fine as long as they had money. But now their funds were running low. Protecting Timmy was her number one priority. But keeping him away from the public wasn't going to be so easy. What if he got sick? What if she got sick and couldn't work, even if she found a job? Just thinking about it made her head hurt.

Her train of thought was interrupted as the officer approached her vehicle again. She hoped he had some good news about the towing.

"I found a tow truck for you that's not too expensive. We're supposed to rotate among the calls, but I can personally recommend this fellow. He'll do right by you and not overcharge. He's on his way now. He should be here shortly," the officer informed her.

"Oh, thank you so much. I'm new in town. I just got here yesterday and I'm looking for a job. I was on my way to a job interview when the car broke down."

"Aw, gee, that's too bad. I would give you a ride, but we're not allowed to use the patrol cars to carry people on personal errands." The officer looked truly regretful as he spoke.

"Oh, that's okay. I understand." she assured him.

Yeah, I understand, all right. I understand that my luck is getting even worse. I'm almost out of money and now I have a car that's broken down. Plus, I left my sister and my son in a motel room that we could barely afford. I've just got to find a job somehow, or else we have to keep on moving until I do. Somehow, somewhere, there has to be a job for me. There just has to!

She spotted the tow truck coming down the street. It certainly didn't take him long to get here. Of course, she didn't know how she was going to pay for the tow, much less get the vehicle repaired.

The tow truck pulled up in front of the car and then backed up and the operator jumped out. "Good morning. How are you doing today?" he asked.

Before she could respond, the officer took charge. "Good morning to you, Bart. The little lady here needs a tow, and I told her you would fix her up just fine. I'm going to leave it with you now. Looks like you've got everything under control."

"Sure thing, Officer O'Neal. No problem at all."

Regenia had remained quiet during the exchange, but the fact that the tow truck driver was a handsome, muscular man had not escaped her notice. His blue eyes twinkled as he spoke, and the sun shining on his shock of red, wavy hair gave it an even more intense color. Not that she was interested in men. Not anymore. Not after what she had been through the last two years, ever since Timmy had been born. She sighed, willing herself to remain calm during a crisis.

"Okay, ma'am. I'm going to get this car loaded onto the tow truck. Where do you want me to haul it?" the driver asked. "Oh, by the way, my name is Bart Murphy."

"Regenia Whitworth. Pleased to meet you," she responded, dragging out the manners drilled into her since childhood.

She watched as the car was slowly lifted onto the back of the truck, almost holding her breath for fear that it would somehow fall from the truck and end up a total loss. Bart evidently knew what he was doing because the job was finished in no time.

"Well, any decision about where you want to drop her?" he asked as he secured the chain onto the back of the truck.

"No, I'm new in town, and I don't know any shops here," she admitted. "I...I was on my way to a job interview."

"Well, tell you what. I'll be glad to drop you off wherever you want to go, and then I can take the car on to my shop. My kid brother, Jim, is a pretty fair mechanic. I'm letting him help me out in the shop, and he'd be glad to check it out for you. We can hook it up to a diagnostic computer and see what's wrong with it."

"Oh, I don't want to put you to any trouble."

"No trouble at all. Just tell me where you were headed. I know this town like the back of my hand. I have to, being a tow truck driver." He chuckled as he spoke, and she noticed he had dimples when he smiled.

Now why did you have to go and notice something like that? You don't have time for a man in your life, she chided herself silently.

"I was applying for a job at a doctor's office." She pulled out a notepad from her purse to check the address. "It's the office of Doctor George Halley."

"I know where that is. Everybody in town knows Doc Halley. He's been here since the Dinosaur Age. What kind of job are you applying for?"

"It's a secretarial position," she told him.

"Secretary, huh? Wonder what happened to the other secretary. She's been with him a long time."

"I have no idea. I just saw the ad in the paper and made an appointment for the interview."

"Well, hop into my cab and I'll drop you right off."

She stepped onto the rung beneath the door of the cab and heard a loud snap as she put her weight onto her right foot. She looked down and discovered that she had lost the heel off her shoe. She stooped down and scooped it up, depositing it into her purse.

Oh, great! As if things weren't bad enough. Now I have to hobble into the interview room. She barely restrained from moaning as she slid into the cab and shut the door.

"What was that pop I heard?" Bart inquired before he started the engine.

"I'm afraid I broke the heel off my show," she lamented, pulling it out of her purse to show him.

"Oh." He stared at the heel, trying his best to keep a straight face.

She looked so sad. He didn't want to upset her any further by laughing. She was a pretty little thing with long, soft curly black hair and the bluest eyes he had ever seen. A bit on the skinny side, though. It looked as if she hadn't eaten a decent meal in quite a while. Or maybe she was one of those girls who wanted to be pencil thin. Well, he didn't have time to think about that. The last thing he needed was to get involved with another woman. His heart had already been broken twice, and he wasn't about to let his guard down again.

He turned the key and started the engine without saying another word. They rode in silence until they reached the street where the doctor's office was located. When he brought the truck to a stop, she reached for the handle.

"Hold on a minute. I have a solution to your problem," he announced.

"What? You carry a humongous tube of Superglue in your glove compartment?"

"Nope, but I know what we can do."

He jumped out of the cab and hurried to the passenger side, arriving just as she swung the door open.

"Hand me your other shoe," he instructed.

"I beg your pardon?"

"Hand me your other shoe."

She stuck out her left foot and he removed the shoe swiftly. Before she could even utter another word, he hit the shoe heel on the pavement and it broke off. He picked up the heel and handed it to her, along with the shoe that now matched its mate in height and style.

She opened her mouth to speak, but no words came to mind.

"You're welcome," he said, bowing gallantly as he spoke. "I'm sorry, but the shoes are ruined anyhow and now you won't have to hobble."

"I guess you're right," she admitted. "Maybe they won't be looking at my feet."

Not if they have any sense, they won't, he thought.

He extended his hand and helped her down from the cab. Before he could say anything else, she gave a cry of dismay.

"Oh, no!"

"What now?" he asked.

"I've got a grease spot on my blouse. It must have happened when I opened the hood. Why did I think I knew anything about engines?"

He could see that she was close to tears now. She had been holding up pretty well, despite the circumstances, but a body could stand only so much in one day.

"I don't suppose you have any club soda in that cab of yours," she asked half-jokingly, her voice almost cracking.

He noticed that she blinked rapidly as she spoke, a sure sign that tears were just about to fall.

"No, sorry. I can't oblige you on that count. Maybe there's a restroom where you can repair the damage."

Now he was feeling really sorry for her.

"I'm afraid water would just make it worse. Well, I'm already late. I might as well go and get it over with."

"Wait...before you go, here's my card. Give me a call when you get through with the interview, and I'll let you know if we've found out anything about your car."

"Okay, I'll do that. Thanks."

He watched he walk towards the entrance of the building. She was going to be all right. He could see that now. She might be down, but she wasn't out. She had courage; he had to give her that. He didn't know what kind of trouble she was in, but he could sense there was a lot going on in her life. A person didn't just drive into town looking for a job when they didn't know anybody, especially not a town the size of Summerfield. No, she was hiding something...or hiding from somebody. He didn't know which. Oh, well, not his problem, he decided as he hopped into his cab and headed the tow truck towards his shop.

He pulled into the shop's yard a few minutes later with the car in tow. He exited the cab and headed into the garage, where Jim was tackling his latest project.

"Hey, brother, what's up?" Jim asked.

"Oh, not much. Brought in another clunker. Thought you might take a look at it and see what you can do to fix it up."

"And just why would I want to do that? Car belong to somebody we know?" Jim continued his inquiry.

"Uh, no. Nobody we know. Just somebody who needs a hand. I told her we would see what we could do to get her car fixed."

"Her car...hmm...I think there's more to the story than you're letting on, big brother."

"No, not really. Just trying to help somebody who's in trouble."

"So, where's the lady now?"

"I...uh, I dropped her off for a job interview."

"Dropped her off for a..." Jim let out a hearty laugh that echoed off the shop walls.

"Oh, stop it," Bart protested.

"Okay, okay, brother. I guess you can drop somebody off it you want to. After all, it's your company."

"Well, the car's out in the back lot. Let me know when you've got a place for it, and I'll bring it inside. Preferably today."

"Right. I'm about to finish up here and then I can take a look at it. Any idea what the problem might be?"

"Nope. I told her we would run a diagnostic check on it and go from there."

"Sounds like a plan."

Bart smiled to himself. There was nothing Jim liked more than a challenge, and if he was any judge of cars, this one might just prove to be a challenge to repair. He hoped for Regenia's sake the repairs wouldn't be too expensive. He would do what he could to help her out on the cost, but they might have to buy some parts. He whistled a familiar tune as he headed to his office.

⸺◈◈◈⸺

REGENIA WALKED INTO THE BUILDING slowly, trying to calm her nerves as she searched for the office suite with the number listed in the ad. She was late, and her clothes were a mess, but she had to give it a try. The job sounded the most promising of any she had investigated in weeks.

She opened the glass door and walked into the doctor's office, finding herself facing a room full of patients. A receptionist who was manning the phones motioned her to the desk and held up one finger as a signal she should wait.

"May I help you?" the receptionist inquired after she had finished the conversation and hung up the phone.

"I'm here to apply for the secretarial position that was advertised in the paper," Regenia responded.

"Oh, I'm so sorry, but I think that position was just filled. There was an applicant who came in just a few minutes ago, and from what I understand, she was hired. Just a moment. Let me check with the doctor to be sure."

Regenia's heart dropped when she heard the news, and she had a hard time keeping her shoulders from slumping as well. She had been counting on getting this job. *What was she going to do now?* she wondered. She managed to keep a smile on her face, but just barely.

The receptionist headed out the back door of the office area, leaving Regenia to study her surroundings. There seemed to be a lot of patients, which was a good sign. If she could get the job, she would be plenty busy with paperwork and records. All she could do was hope, but she hadn't made the appointment in time, so she couldn't really blame the doctor for hiring somebody else.

The receptionist was gone just a few minutes. Regenia looked at her expectantly as she re-entered the office and began to speak.

"I'm so sorry, but the doctor had to conduct the interviews during his lunch break. When you didn't show up at the appointed time, he went on to the next applicant. She had all the necessary qualifications, so he decided to hire her, as we are in desperate need of help here."

"Oh, I see. I understand, but I was unavoidably detained with car trouble," Regenia responded.

The phone rang, interrupting their conversation. Regenia realized there was no point in continuing, so she waved at the receptionist, who had already resumed her responsibilities, and took her leave. She was somewhat relieved to walk out of a roomful of sick people. She just hoped she hadn't caught anything contagious from her brief visit.

There was nothing left to do except call the tow truck driver and see if his mechanic had found out what was wrong with her car. She fished through her purse looking for the business card he had given her. Why did the item a woman needed always seem to be in the bottom of her purse? Finally, she found it and she punched in the number on her cell phone. *Can't wait to see how much these repairs are going to cost,* she lamented silently.

"Bart's Towing and Repair Service," a voice answered after the first ring. She recognized the voice as that of the tow truck driver.

"This is Regenia Whitworth. Have you found out what the problem is with my car?" she inquired.

"No, my brother hasn't quite finished his other job yet, but he's going to look at your car as soon as he can," Bart replied.

"Oh, I see. I just finished the job interview, and I was wondering how extensive the repairs were going to be."

"Did you get the job?" Bart asked.

"Actually, I didn't even get an interview. By the time I got there, the position had been filled because I was late."

"What are you going to do now?"

"I suppose I'll just take a taxi back to my motel and call you tomorrow about the car and then make a decision."

"Tell you what. Let me call the taxi for you. I've got special connections with one of the companies in this town, and I can probably get you a discount on the fare."

"Really? I didn't know they did that."

"Cross my heart and hope to die." Bart regretted the words as soon as they left his mouth. *Stupid, stupid, stupid. Is that all you can think of to say?* He chided himself silently. Why was he having so much trouble conversing with this woman?

"Well, I could use all the help I can get financially," she responded, breaking his train of thought.

"Sure, no problem. Let me call the On Your Way taxi service, and they'll have a cab there in no time. Are you still at Doc Halley's office?"

"Yes, I'm in the lobby."

"Okay, hang tight. Just watch out the front door for a cab to pull up. No sense in waiting outside."

"Thank you so much, and I'll call you first thing tomorrow to find out about my car."

"Okay. Talk to you later then," Bart replied as he hung up the phone. He didn't have to look up the number. He knew it by heart.

Regenia waited impatiently for the cab to arrive. Why was the tow truck driver being so nice? Most people nowadays wouldn't have bothered to help a stranger. Well, with her financial situation, she would take all the help she could get, and then some. What was she going to do now? Furthermore, how was she going to break the news to Marlene that she didn't get the job? It wasn't going to be a very happy reunion when she got back to the motel room.

She spotted the cab as it pulled up to the curb, and then she hurried outside. The cab driver saw her approaching and hopped out to open the door for her. She was surprised at the unusual gesture.

"On Your Way Taxi at your service, ma'am," he said.

"Thank you," she replied as she climbed into the back seat of the cab.

He shut the door and hurried around to the driver's seat. "Where to?" he inquired as he started the engine.

"I'm staying at the Four Star Motel on Oak Hill Street," she told him.

"Have you there in a jiffy. By the way, I'm Tony Carlito, the son of the owner of this company. Bart's a special friend of ours, and he told me to take good care of you."

"Regenia Whitworth. Pleased to meet you," she responded as he pulled out into the street. She hoped he wasn't going to be the chatty type because she was not in the mood to make small talk. All she wanted to do was make it back to the motel room, kick off her now-dilapidated shoes, and try to get some rest. To her relief, he began to concentrate on the driving, leaving her to her own thoughts. She leaned her head back against the seat and watched the scenery.

Not a bad little town. Somewhere in this town there just might be a job for me yet, she thought. *If ever there was a town to be stuck in, this just might be the best place to be. The people seem friendly enough, and the scenery is pleasant to look at with clean streets, well-kept yards, flowers growing everywhere, and a downtown street that's bustling with business.*

In what seemed like no time at all, the taxi pulled up in front of the motel. She shook her head slightly, willing herself out of the trance she had been in for most of the ride.

"How much do I owe you?" she inquired.

"No charge. The fare has already been paid," Tony informed her.

"Already paid? What do you mean?" she asked incredulously.

"I told you, Bart is a special friend of mine. He took care of the fare. Said it was a gift to welcome you to the town."

"Oh, well…I don't know what to say, but I'm truly grateful for that gesture. I'll be sure to thank him tomorrow."

"Okay, ma'am. Have a good night."

She climbed out of the taxi and headed towards the front of the motel and then turned to go down a walkway that led to her room. She dreaded telling Marlene about not getting the job, but she might as well just come right out with it and get it over with. Then there was the matter of the car breaking down. It was not going to be a good night for her family, but she had to put on a brave front for Timmy's sake.

As she approached the door to their room, she heard what sounded like faint screams coming from the other side of the door. Fighting the urge to panic, she hurriedly opened the door and peered inside. Timmy was running around the room with a pillowcase on his head, screaming at the top of his lungs. Marlene was sitting in the middle of the bed, doubled over with laughter.

She quickly stepped into the room and closed the door behind her, breathing a sigh of relief. Evidently it wasn't an emergency after all.

"Hey, you guys need to tone it down a little," she admonished, giving Marlene her best grown-up, big sister look.

"Sorry, sorry, but we were just burning off a little cabin fever," Marlene apologized.

"I can see that, but remember Timmy needs to be able to sleep tonight. If you get him too keyed up, he'll stay awake for ages."

"Mommy, Mommy," Timmy exclaimed, pulling the pillowcase off his head when he heard Regenia's voice.

"Hi, baby. I'm back," she said, bending over to give him a hug as he wrapped himself around her legs, nearly knocking her off-balance.

"How did the interview go?" Marlene inquired.

"No sale," Regenia responded. "Even worse, now we have no car."

"No car? What happened? Did you get into a wreck?" Marlene asked anxiously.

"No, no, nothing like that. The darn thing went out on me. I managed to get it off the road, and then a nice policeman called a tow truck for me. The car has been towed to a garage."

"Did you make it to the interview?"

"Yes, but by the time I got there, I was late, and the position had already been filled. So, now we have to start all over again from square one with the job search."

Marlene rolled over on the bed and groaned. "Oh, God. Why did we have to have such bad luck? Everything was just peachy until a few months ago. I was a happy, carefree teenager, and you were in your last semester of college. Now we're just drifting from one town to another. I want my old life back!"

"You know that's not possible right now. You know why we have to keep moving." Regenia nodded her head towards Timmy as she spoke.

"Mommy, hungwy," Timmy announced.

"Oh, baby, I'm so sorry. Mommy will see if she can find you something to eat." She gave him another hug. "Did you find the vending machines yet?" she inquired of Marlene.

"Yeah, yeah, there's a little room down the hall with all kinds of snacks and drinks. But when are we going to get some real food again? Timmy's not the only one who's hungry in this family," Marlene grumbled.

"Let me get a little snack for Timmy and we'll assess the situation. I have to see how much money we have left. We can't stay in this room too long or our money will run out. Then we'll be living out of the car...if we still have a car."

She kicked off her shoes and headed towards the suitcases to look for another pair.

"Oh, no, what happened to the shoes?" Marlene burst out laughing again.

"Long story. Tell you later. Much later," Regenia responded as she pulled out another pair of shoes from the suitcase and slipped them on.

Regenia rummaged through her purse searching for loose change. Every penny counted now. She managed to find what she thought would be enough for at least some kind of snack from the vending machine.

"You stay with Timmy, and I'll run down the hall and see if I can get him some crackers and juice. Then we'll figure out where we can go for some hot food that doesn't cost too much. In the meantime, see if you can find some cartoons for him to watch," she instructed.

"Okay, okay, cartoons, my favorite," Marlene drawled as she picked up the TV control and began to flip through the channels. "Hey, buddy, want to watch some cartoons with your Aunt Mimi?"

"Yay!" Timmy yelled enthusiastically as he plopped down in front of the TV set.

"You know, you're good with kids when you want to be," Regenia observed. "Hang on and I'll be right back."

Marlene gave her a salute and a half-hearted smile as she slipped out the door. She had no trouble spotting the vending machines, and she made her selections quickly. She felt as if the weight of the world was on her shoulders with a younger sister and a son to care for. Money was the main problem right now. If she could just find a job and lay a little money aside, everything would work out.

She mentally calculated how much cash she had on hand. There was no way she was about to sit down and count it at one of the tables in the snack room. No telling who might walk in at any minute. If memory served her correctly, there was still about five hundred dollars in their little stash. That might sound like a lot to some people, but compared to what they had started out with, it wasn't much. Besides that, if they had to live in a motel, it wasn't going to last very long.

She walked back to the room and let herself in. Timmy was engrossed in the cartoon that was playing, and Marlene was thumbing through a magazine that had been left in the room.

"Hey, Timmy. I brought you a snack," she announced.

"Juice!" he exclaimed.

She smiled and kissed his head as he ran over to claim the food. She opened the juice and handed it to him, then unwrapped the package of crackers.

"Want one, sis?" she asked, holding out a cracker to Marlene after giving one to Timmy.

"Thanks, I'm starving. So, what are we going to do for food?" Marlene inquired.

"Well…why don't you check the paper and see if there are any coupons for discounts on fast food?" Regenia suggested. "I need to take a shower and change out of these dirty clothes."

"Mmm…okay, I can do that," Marlene agreed as she chewed slowly. "Hold on, stomach, help is on the way!" She picked up the paper and began to turn through the pages while Regenia picked up a change of clothes and headed towards the bathroom.

"Don't take too long," she yelled as Regenia closed the bathroom door.

<hr />

Less than thirty minutes later, they were sitting at a table in a McDonald's restaurant that was located just a few blocks from the motel. Regenia was thankful for that because they didn't have to call a taxi and use any more of their rapidly shrinking funds for transportation. Even better, Marlene had found several coupons in the paper, and that allowed them to get the food at a discount. *At least there has been one lucky break in an otherwise bad day,* Regenia reflected as she bit into her hamburger.

Marlene looked around the crowded restaurant, eyeing all the young men who were within her age group. Regenia sighed inwardly as she watched her sister look longingly at a group of friends who were obviously enjoying themselves. It hadn't been that long ago when it would have been Marlene right in the center of such a group, laughing and joking without a care in the world. Regenia was sorry that her sister was going through such a hard time, but it just couldn't be helped. If only she could get a job, then maybe things would begin to look up again for their little family.

They finished their meal and deposited the trash into the trash receptacle as they exited the restaurant a few minutes later. Regenia had to admit that she felt better after getting some solid food into her stomach, and she was sure the same would apply to Marlene and Timmy. Problem was, she didn't know how many more meals she could afford if a job didn't materialize soon, preferably tomorrow. Plus, there was the problem with the car. She would have to call Bart tomorrow and find out what was wrong with it and how much the repairs were going to cost.

Regenia managed to get Timmy settled and bedded for the night in the rollaway bed that had been provided by the motel management. She and Marlene would share the king-sized bed that took up most of the space in the crowded room. It wasn't a fancy room, but it was all that could be expected for the price. She just hoped there weren't any bedbugs or some other unknown insects crawling about.

She sat in a chair that was located by a reading lamp, looking through the "Help Wanted" ads in hopes of finding another job she might apply for. The TV was playing softly in the background as the local station came on with the news.

Marlene exited the bathroom after taking her shower and washing her hair. She fluffed her hair with both hands as she headed towards the bed, and then she let out an ear-piercing scream. Regenia looked up as Marlene danced about the room, frantically swatting at her head.

"Oh, make it stop! Make it stop!" Marlene screamed.

"What's the problem?" Regenia inquired anxiously, jumping out of her chair and dropping the paper to the floor.

"A roach! A flying roach! It's in my hair. Get it out!" Marlene was almost crying as she spoke.

"A roach? Are you sure? I didn't know they could fly." Regenia responded in disbelief.

Timmy woke up and began to cry. "Mommy, Mommy!"

"Oh, baby, it's okay. Your Aunt Mimi just thought she saw a big bug. It's gone now. You can go back to sleep," Regenia reassured him, tucking his covers back in and giving him a hug. To her relief, Timmy sniffled and dozed off.

"Gone? That thing is still in here somewhere," Marlene exclaimed, swatting as she spoke.

"Well, just open the door and maybe it'll fly out. Try to be quiet, can't you? You woke Timmy up," Regenia scolded her.

"I can't help it! We never had to deal with roaches or any other kind of bugs. Dorcas kept the house in perfect order. Never a speck of dust anywhere, and now we have flying roaches and probably bedbugs, too."

"Hopefully, we won't be here long. If I can just find a job, we can look for a better place to stay. Until then, you'll just have to deal with it," Regenia observed.

"I'm sorry, sis. I know you have it harder than I do, but it's just so hard for me. I had to give up all my friends and all the parties and good times when we left our hometown. I was going to college. I was going to be a happy co-ed. Now we're just two nobodies on the run with a little boy to watch out for."

"It won't last forever. I'll make things right. You just have to trust me," Regenia said.

"Can you? Can you ever make things right again? We had everything we wanted—plenty of money, parents who loved us, a beautiful home, and great clothes. It's all gone. Now we have nothing, just a few hundred dollars standing between us and the 'wolf at the door.'"

"I said I would handle it," Regenia retorted sharply, her patience drawing to an end. "Let's turn in and get some sleep."

"Sure. Whatever you say. You're the boss, as usual." Marlene sighed as she flounced down onto the bed.

Regenia picked the paper up off the floor and laid it onto the table. She turned off the reading lamp and TV and walked over to the other side of the room. After crawling under the covers, she turned off the bedside lamp and prepared to settle in for the night. She just hoped she would be able to sleep.

After what seemed like only minutes, she was awakened by an alarm ringing close to her ear. She had set the trusty little clock to go off at 6:45 a.m. It had been with her since her college days, and it hadn't let her down yet. She turned on the bedside lamp and peered at the clock, barely able to comprehend that it was yet another day. Her brain was definitely foggy.

The first order of business was to get everybody up and dressed and then head to the motel's dining room for the complimentary breakfast. At least that wouldn't deplete their meager money stash. She roused Timmy and Marlene and told them it was time to get up if they wanted to eat. Marlene grumbled, as usual, but she didn't protest too much, as she was eager begin eating the free food. Timmy didn't eat a lot, but he loved cereal and milk, and Regenia was sure that would be among the selections.

Thirty minutes later when they walked into the dining room and made their way to the buffet table, Regenia got a bowl of cornflakes and milk and some toast for Timmy and sat him at one of the empty tables. Marlene had loaded a plate with everything she could grab, and she sat down beside Timmy while Regenia went back to get her food. She decided on bacon and eggs, as she felt she needed something solid to tide her over until lunch. Besides, it was free and there was no telling when they would be able to get another substantial meal. She didn't blame Marlene for taking advantage of the free food. She wouldn't be surprised to find a bagel or two stashed away in one of Marlene's pockets.

Now we're living like we're in a scene from "Oliver Twist," she thought wryly. *I just hope we don't turn into pickpockets!*

After they finished the meal they headed back to the motel room. Regenia didn't know much about roaches, but she was pretty sure they came out at night, so maybe there wouldn't be another incident with the flying "critters" during the morning hours. She had to make that phone call to the garage to find out how much the repair work on the car was going to be. Somehow, she had the feeling it wasn't going to be good news.

⚊ ⟡ ⚊

BART SHUFFLED THE PAPERS ON his desk, looking for a bill he needed so he could call a customer back about a repair job. He was positive he had just seen the bill last night before he closed up, but now it was missing. *How did things just seem to walk off his desk all the time?* he wondered.

"Hey, bro, Bill Sandifer called again about the work on his Chevy truck. Did you have that bill for him?" Jim yelled over the noise in the shop.

"I'm working on it. I'll give him a call as soon as I find the bill," Bart yelled back.

"Why don't you just give it up and get a secretary or something? You know you can't keep things straight in the office and run out on calls all at the same time."

"Been thinking about that, little brother. I guess the right person just hasn't come along. I need somebody who will work cheap, but who also does good work."

"Yeah, that will be a hard combination to find. Most people who are good workers don't work cheap," Jim agreed.

Their conversation was interrupted by the shrill ringing of the phone in Bart's office. He peered at the Caller I. D., noting it was from the Four Star Motel. It had to be Regenia, asking for an estimate on the car repairs. He hoped Jim had followed his instructions and checked it out when he opened this morning.

"Hello, Bart's Towing and Repair Service," he spoke into the receiver in his best businesslike voice.

"Hello, this is Regenia Whitworth. I was wondering if you had gotten an estimate on the repairs on my car yet."

"Well, yes, I do have that somewhere. My brother looked it over this morning. Hang on and let me check with him to see what he found," Bart told her, punching the "hold" button.

"Hey, Jim, what did you find out about that car I brought in yesterday morning?" he called out through the office door.

"I wrote it all down for you. What did you do with the paper I put on your desk?"

"Paper? I haven't seen any paper from you since I walked in this morning. Are you sure you put it on my desk?"

"As sure as my name is James Devon Murphy." Jim walked into the office, wiping his hands on the side of his work pants, shaking his head as he spoke. "Brother, I believe you are getting addled in your old age. I'm telling you, what you need is a woman around here to keep you straight." He poked through the papers on the desk and held up a pink piece of paper triumphantly. "Here it is. Told you so."

Bart glanced at the paper before picking the phone back up. "Thanks, that will be all for now."

"Sure thing. Anytime," Jim chuckled as he backed out of the office and closed the door.

"All right, I have the estimate right here. It looks like we will have to do some major work on the car, but it can be fixed. My brother is still learning, so I'll throw in the labor free, but you will have to pay for the parts. We can do a complete repair job for you for about six hundred dollars. I know that sounds like a lot for an older car, but I promise you if my brother fixes it, everything will be fixed right and you shouldn't have any more trouble with it."

"Oh, my." Regenia was at a loss for words. She had only five hundred dollars, so the six hundred was totally out of the question. What was she going to do without a car and without a job? She couldn't even go job hunting without transportation. "I'm afraid that's a little steep for me at this time," she admitted.

"Say, did you find a job yet?" Bart asked as an idea began to formulate in his head.

"No, I haven't had time to look anymore after yesterday's complete washout."

"You said you were looking for a secretarial position. Have you had any experience in that kind of work?"

"I took three and one-half years of business courses in college. I was just a semester away from graduating when I had to drop out," she told him. "I used to work in my dad's office in the summertime. That's what got me interested in business and bookkeeping."

"I see. Well, it just so happens that I need a secretary or receptionist or bookkeeper, or maybe all three. Would you be interested in the job? It wouldn't pay much, but we could go ahead and fix your car, and you could work off the debt and make some money on the side."

Regenia hesitated. It seemed almost too good to be true. But there was still the problem of finding a place to live. They wouldn't be able to get much of a place with just five hundred dollars, and anywhere she rented was sure to require a security deposit and most likely some kind of deposit on the utilities.

"I'd like that, but we also have a housing problem at the moment," she admitted.

"Well, I just might have a solution for you with that, too," he informed her. "It just so happens that there's a small apartment in the back of the garage. I used to live there when I first started out, but now I've moved to a bigger place. It's just been sitting there empty for the past year or so, but it's still in a livable condition. All it needs is a little cleaning, and everything will be as good as new."

"How much would it cost me to rent it from you?" she asked.

"Tell you what. I'll throw in the first month's rent free while you try out the job. If you decide to stay, then we can negotiate a price. If not, it's no big loss to either one of us."

"I...I don't know what to say!" Regenia exclaimed breathlessly.

"Say 'yes.' You'll be doing both of us a big favor."

"Yes, yes! I'll take the job," she agreed, hoping she wasn't sounding overly enthusiastic.

"Great. How soon can you be here?"

"I can be there as soon as I can get a taxi. I'm already dressed, and we just got through with breakfast. My sister took my son for a walk."

"Your son...I didn't know you were married."

"I'm not."

"Oh, I'm sorry. I didn't mean to pry. It's just that you look so young."

"Well, sometimes looks can be deceiving. Sometimes I feel like I'm a hundred years old." She sighed as she spoke.

"Who doesn't? Sometimes I feel the same way myself. At least that's what my kid brother keeps telling me. He thinks I came in on Noah's Ark."

"I know what you mean. My younger sister thinks the same thing about me."

They both laughed.

"I can see we have a few things in common. Well, get over here as soon as you can, and I'll get you started and show you the apartment at lunchtime," he instructed.

"Sure thing. I'll be there shortly," she responded as she hung up the phone.

Marlene and Timmy walked into the room just as the conversation ended.

"Who were you talking to?" Marlene asked.

"It was the guy who owns the garage where my car was towed yesterday, and you won't believe what just happened," Regenia exclaimed, her eyes sparkling as she spoke.

"I don't know what it was, but if it can bring a smile to your face, it must be good," Marlene observed.

"He offered me a job," Regenia told her. "A real, honest-to-goodness job. Can you believe it? After all this time, we might actually have some money coming in again!"

"What kind of job? I know you can't fix cars," Marlene joked.

"No, silly. It's a secretarial/bookkeeping type of job. Plus, there's an added bonus."

"What? A job for me, too?" Marlene wiggled her eyebrows.

"No, something better—a place to live. He has a small apartment in back of the garage, and it's ours if we want to move in."

"Really? Are you kidding? Anything to get out of this Roach Motel! It can't be any worse than this room," Marlene declared.

"I have to look the place over first at lunch. Maybe we can go over and clean it tonight and move in tomorrow. The place has been unoccupied for a while, so I have a feeling we might have to do some heavy cleaning," Regenia informed her.

"Well, at least it will be clean dirt," Marlene grumbled.

"We're already going to have to pay for another night at the motel, so we might as well sleep here. Plus, we have to buy some sheets and towels and other supplies. You and Timmy hang tight here, and I'll let you know. But keep your fingers crossed and pray hard that it will work out for us."

"Already praying as you speak," said Marlene.

Regenia leaned down to face Timmy, who had been listening in on the conversation.

"Hey, little buddy. Mommy has to go to work now. I got a new job. I want you to stay here today with Aunt Mimi and watch TV and stay out of trouble. I'll call you at lunch and see how things are going. Do you think you can do that and be a good boy for your mommy?"

"Uh-huh." Timmy responded, pointing towards the TV set.

"I'm going to leave Aunt Mimi some money, so you can go back to McDonald's for lunch. How would you like some chicken nuggets and fries and fruit for lunch?"

"Yay!" he exclaimed.

"So, here's enough money for lunch, and be sure that he gets some milk to drink. Do you think you can manage?" she asked as she handed the money over to Marlene.

"Of course. I know I act dumb sometimes, but I know how to handle kids. Just leave everything to me. Be sure to call and let me know about the apartment. I can't wait to get out of this place," Marlene told her.

"Look on the bright side. We made it through the night here, even with the flying roaches, and I didn't see a sign of bedbugs."

Marlene changed the subject, "Thank the Lord for small favors. How are you going to get to work?"

"Looks like I'll have to spend a little more of our money on a cab. It's too far to walk. but if I get the job, it'll be worth it. Oh, did I mention that we get the first month rent-free?"

"No, but the apartment is sounding better and better all the time. Hurry up and get there, and let me know when we can move in."

"Will do. Why don't you call that On Your Way taxi company for me while I freshen up my makeup and then I'll head out," Regenia instructed as she walked into the bathroom.

"Sure, I'll be glad to," Marlene responded as she walked over to the TV set, turned it on and flipped through the channels again until she came to a cartoon for Timmy.

⚬

MOMENTS LATER REGENIA FOUND HERSELF walking into Bart's garage. She looked around, uncertain of what to do amid the usual chaos that transpires in a garage setting.

She spotted Bart near the back of the garage, standing with his head bent over as he and a mechanic peered under the hood of one of the vehicles.

"That sounds about right, Justin," he advised the mechanic, his voice rising above the noise and the clanking of tools against metal.

He looked in her direction and grinned as he saw her standing in the entrance. He headed towards her, walking at a brisk pace as he maneuvered around various obstacles in his path.

"Hi, glad to see you could make it," he told her.

"Well, I'm here, so show me the office and tell me what you want me to do."

"Sure, right this way," he instructed, motioning to an office on the left side of the garage. "Sorry things are such a mess, but every time I think I'm going to get my papers straight, I get another call for a tow truck. That's why I need somebody in the office full-time. I'm hoping you're the answer to my prayers."

"I don't know about that, but I'll do my best. Do you have any kind of special filing system or any method of keeping up with your records and your customers?" she asked.

"Well, kind of. I call it 'Bart's Bewilderment,'" he joked. "Nobody can find anything if I'm out of the office."

"I see. Okay, let's look at what you have, and maybe then I can devise something that will be easy for both of us to keep up with."

They walked into the office, and she gazed at the mound of papers scattered on top of his desk.

"So, you can actually find something amid all this stuff?" she teased.

Bart looked rather sheepish. "I never was much on organizing. Ask my mom. She always thought my room was a mess."

"Let's start at the top of the pile and work our way down. What kind of invoices do you use?" she inquired as she hung her purse on the back of the chair and sat down.

After thirty minutes of discussion and looking over papers, Regenia felt she could handle the job. Their session had been interrupted by several phone calls, the last one being a request for a tow. Bart had sprung from the room like a caged animal let loose. Regenia could see that office work was not his forte. She just hoped he would be back in time to give her the promised tour of the apartment during her lunch break.

She soon found herself engrossed in the work as she sorted through the various forms, receipts, and orders for parts. She pulled out a pad that she found in one of the drawers and began making a list of supplies that would be needed. She planned to ask Bart about ordering them when he came back from his towing run. It felt good to be working again after being on the road for several weeks and spending the night in less than desirable motel settings. Maybe she had finally found a place where she and her little family could settle down, at least for a little while.

She was amused as the men found excuses to pop into the office as soon as Bart left, the first one being his brother, Jim, who introduced himself to her. She could see the family resemblance immediately, although Jim's hair was black, rather than red. After Jim came George, the oldest of the mechanics, a friendly chap with a kindly way about him. Following George, she met Darren, who was an obvious flirt, and Justin, the most serious of the bunch. They were apparently checking her out, most likely viewing her as a prospective match for their boss, she reasoned, as she exchanged friendly banter with them. Too bad, as she wasn't in the market for a new beau at the moment. Things in her life were just too complicated, and she didn't want to drag anybody else into the mix.

Almost before she knew it, several hours had passed. She was surprised to see the hands of the office clock approaching noon. Bart still hadn't returned from the tow job. She hoped he hadn't run into some kind of problem. She hadn't brought any food with her, so she wasn't quite sure of what to do about lunch. Maybe she could call in an order for delivery. She began to look for a phone directory. She knew there had to be one somewhere in the office.

"Eureka!" she exclaimed as she spied the phone book under a pile of mechanics' magazines and dragged it out. To her embarrassment, Bart chose that particular moment to enter the office. She paused as she clutched the book to her chest, her cheeks reddening slightly.

"Oh, you're back," she said.

"Yes, finally. There was a problem with the tow, and we had to call in extra trucks from another service, but we finally got it all straight. It was a wreck on the highway headed into town."

"I hope nobody was injured," she remarked.

"Well, some injuries, but nothing fatal. Some guy with an out-of-state license tried to pass in a no-passing zone. I was the lucky chap who got to tow his convertible after pulling it from a ditch. He wasn't wearing a seat belt and was partly ejected from the vehicle. His vehicle is fine, but he has a broken arm and leg and also some head injuries, I think. He also caused some other people to be injured, including a little boy and his mom. People who hurt kids deserve whatever they get. That's all I can say about that."

"Yes, nobody should hurt a kid," Regenia said softly, her voice cracking on the last word.

He looked at her sharply, wondering what might be causing her to have so much pain. *Time to change the subject,* he decided. "So, what have you been up to while I've been gone?"

She cleared her throat before speaking. "I've pretty much gotten the files organized. but we're going to need some filing materials. I wasn't sure how much you want to store on the computer and how much you want to store in actual paperwork. I was just looking for a place to order some food for lunch."

"Why not just look on the computer?" he asked.

"We didn't go over that before you left, and I didn't want to use it before checking with you first."

"No worries. We close an hour for lunch or nobody would get anything to eat. I just put the answering machine on in case somebody calls for a tow. Plus, I have my calls forwarded to my cell. Why don't I take you out for a quick bite?"

"You promised to show me the apartment at lunchtime, remember?" she reminded him.

"Yes, I did. Say, let's order a pizza. I can show you the apartment while we wait for it to arrive."

"Sounds good to me," she agreed. "I can't wait to see it."

"Hang on and I'll call the closest pizza place. We order from them all the time." He picked up the phone as he spoke and dialed the number without looking it up. She listened as he put in the order. "There. That's taken care of. Now on to the tour," he announced. "Step this way, my lady."

She followed him out the back of the shop, which was now quiet with all the mechanics taking their lunch break. Even the entrance door had been closed, blocking out all sounds from the street.

They walked towards a small frame house behind the shop. Regenia looked at it hopefully. It didn't look too bad from the outside, but there was no telling what the inside was like with just a bachelor occupying it last. She didn't know how neat Bart was, but if his desk was any indication of his habits, the apartment might not be in good shape. Still, he didn't appear to be a slob. Maybe he had just been too overwhelmed with his workload.

They climbed the stairs to the apartment, which was located over a double carport. Bart jiggled the key in the front door and opened it for her. "The lock's a little tricky," he explained. "I've been meaning to get that fixed. If you decide to stay here, I'll have it taken care of first thing tomorrow."

He flipped the light switch in the front room, and Regenia looked around. *It isn't half bad,* she decided. The walls were painted a soft blue, and the floor was covered with a light beige vinyl material. The room was bare except for a couch covered with a plaid throw cover and an armchair that was flanked by an end table and a lamp.

"I'm sorry, but there's not a lot of furniture here. I moved most of my stuff out when I moved to a bigger place," he apologized.

"As long as we have a place to sit, somewhere to eat, and a bed to sleep in, we'll be okay," she assured him.

"There's a queen-sized bed and dresser in the only bedroom. I'm afraid there's no dining table, but there's a breakfast counter with a few stools. I usually took my meals on the couch, so no need for a table."

"I'm sure we can manage," she murmured as she looked around, taking in the blinds that covered the windows and the empty spot that once held a TV.

"Oh, you do get all the kitchen appliances. I bought all new ones when I moved to my new place. I never got around to selling them. I figured they just might come in handy someday if I decided to rent the place."

"Why haven't you?" she asked.

"It's a little too close to the garage for comfort. We have a lot of valuable tools and equipment in there, and I just don't want a lot of people coming and going so close to all of that. But you're going to work for me, so that's a different story."

"I see that all the utilities are still connected."

"Yes. It didn't cost much because I wasn't using the place. It would have been more trouble to disconnect and then reconnect them, so I just left everything on."

"How did you happen to acquire this property?" she asked.

"I started working for an older guy. He and his wife lived in the apartment. They didn't have any kids, so they never needed a bigger place. When he got too old to work, he sold the business to me. They both became disabled and had to move to a nursing home. That's when I moved into the apartment. It was so handy and close to the job. After the business became more profitable, I decided to get a bigger place. I kind of miss it, though. I could just walk out back and be home when the day was over. Now I have to drive all the way across town."

"Oh, that's so sad…about the couple, I mean. I guess you were pretty important to them."

"Yes, I was kind of like the son they never had. They were really good to me. That's why I like to try to help people out when I can. It's my way of paying society back."

"So, you look on me as a charity case?" she teased.

"Not exactly. If you can straighten out my office, it will be anything but charity. Anybody's who's ever tried to find anything on my desk can tell you that. You'll earn your keep, believe me. Things can really get to hopping on a good day."

"I look forward to the challenge then. Now, about the apartment— how soon can we move in?"

"As soon as you like. Tonight…tomorrow, makes no difference to me."

"Well…" she hesitated. "My sister would like nothing better than to move in tonight, but we've already paid for the motel for another night. I think we might need to do some cleaning and get some supplies." She walked over and opened the blinds, looking across the parking lot.

"Sure, whatever you want. So, do you want the key?" He dangled it temptingly as he spoke.

"Yes, of course. I'll take it." She held out her hand, and he dropped the key into it.

"Holy smokes, there's the pizza delivery guy," he exclaimed as he glanced out the window. "Let me run and catch him before he gives up and takes the pizza back."

She watched as he rapidly descended the stairs, smiling as she observed his athleticism. He obviously kept in shape. She wondered if he worked out. He turned and waved at her as he accepted the pizza from the delivery man. *Lunch is going to be interesting,* she thought as she closed and locked the door and began walking down the stairs. She couldn't wait to put her office skills to use again. She walked back to the office, where Bart had already cleared a spot on the desk and had the pizza box open and waiting.

They dug into the pizza with relish, savoring every bite. Bart had gotten a couple of Cokes from the soft drink machine near the office. She couldn't believe she had worked up such an appetite. It was the first time she had felt really hungry in days.

"Oh, I almost forgot. I promised to call my sister about the apartment during lunch," she exclaimed. "I'm sure she's on pins and needles waiting to hear from me. She can't wait to get out of that motel." She went on to describe the incident with the flying roaches the previous night and soon found herself laughing along with Bart as she ended the story.

"Please don't judge our town by that incident. We have lots of quality motels and businesses, even though it's a small town," he told her as they finished the pizza, and he picked up the box to deposit in the trash.

"Oh, I won't," she promised.

"Here come the guys now. Time to go back to work," he noted as the men began to file in. Someone let the door back up, and the phone began to ring immediately,

"I guess you're right," she agreed as she picked up the phone. She would call Marlene as soon as she got a chance. Right now, it was time to take care of business.

⚬⚬⚬

AFTER PUTTING IN A FULL day of work, Regenia was ready to head back to the motel. Bart offered to drop her off, and she was grateful, knowing it would save her another cab fare. He seemed to sense that she was trying to make every penny count, although she knew he would never embarrass her by saying so. Well, at least she would be staying right behind the garage, so she wouldn't need a ride to work once they moved in.

She had conferred with Marlene between phone calls, and they had agreed to pick up cleaning supplies and anything else they could afford after they ate supper. She couldn't wait to start cleaning and sprucing up the apartment. It would be the first place they could call home since they had left their parents' former home on the East Coast weeks ago. *Was it only weeks ago? Somehow, it seems like years ago,* she reflected.

They dined at McDonald's again, taking advantage of the dollar menu. She hoped that they would be preparing their own meals by suppertime tomorrow night. After the meal they headed to Wal-Mart, reasoning that it was probably the cheapest place in town to find the supplies they needed.

Fortunately for their budget, they managed to catch a bus not too far from McDonald's. That saved them a little money on cab fare. They took their time going around the store, picking up everything they thought they would need for cleaning, sleeping, and bathing. They would get most of the food supplies after the refrigerator had been thoroughly cleaned out, but Regenia grabbed a few sandwich materials, along with some bananas, chips, soft drinks, and a gallon of milk.

They had to take a cab to the apartment because there were too many bags to carry on the bus. But Regenia felt the money was well spent, as they would be living rent-free for the next month. She was sorry there was no TV set to entertain Timmy, but she had picked up some inexpensive books and coloring materials. He wasn't very good at coloring, but he had fun trying.

The cab pulled up in front of the apartment, and Regenia almost held her breath, hoping Marlene wouldn't complain too much about it. After all, it was a garage apartment in the back of a garage, a really low-brow type of life compared to what they had been used to when they were growing up. But it would be a roof over their heads-- their own roof--at least for the time being.

Marlene sat in silence, taking in the scene as she gazed at the surroundings. "So, this is the fabulous apartment you've been telling me about?" she asked incredulously.

"I never said it was fabulous. I said it was an apartment."

"Uh-huh. Well, let's go and see what you've gotten us into. I just hope there won't be any flying roaches."

The cab driver assisted them with getting their bags to the top of the stairs, and Regenia handed him the fare. He bade them goodnight and departed quickly, the tail lights of the cab fading into the distance.

"What are we waiting for? Let's get inside before we get mugged or something," Marlene said.

"Oh, sure. Sorry. Guess I was just lost in thought for a moment," Regenia apologized as she unlocked the door and flipped on the light. "Well, this is it—our little home for the next few months, or at least until we have to move again."

Marlene looked around, but to Regenia's surprise, she didn't complain. "Okay, let's get the bags inside," she said, suddenly businesslike in her attitude. "Where do you want to put this stuff?"

They spent the next few hours cleaning and polishing everything in the place. When the shelves had been cleaned to Regenia's satisfaction, she gave Marlene the go-ahead to start putting things away. They didn't have many supplies yet, but just getting what they had onto the shelves made the place seem more homelike. She hoped she would be able to afford a small TV before too long. Until then, they would just have to make do.

"Could we spend the night here instead of going back to the motel?" Marlene asked as she stored the last of the towels in the bathroom.

"I don't know. All of our clothes and other things are back at the motel. We don't even have our toothbrushes with us," Regenia pointed out.

Marlene sighed. "I guess you're right, but I just don't know if I can take another night of the flying roaches."

They both started laughing and couldn't stop. Marlene doubled over, holding onto the kitchen counter, and Regenia laughed so hard she almost cried.

"Stop, you're making my sides hurt," Regenia protested, wiping her eyes with a clean dish towel. "Remind me to buy some tissues tomorrow."

The laugh session was interrupted by a knock on the door. They looked at each other.

"Were you expecting anyone?" Marlene asked.

"No, I have no idea who it could be at this time of night," Regenia replied.

"Don't answer it. Maybe it's a burglar."

"Burglars don't knock, silly," Regenia responded as she walked over to the door and peered through the peephole.

She was relieved to see it was Bart. She opened the door quickly.

"Come in, Bart. What are you doing here at this time of night?"

"I was just checking on you. I remembered that you said you might do some cleaning tonight, and I just wanted to see if there was anything you needed," he explained, nodding at Marlene as he spoke.

"Oh, I'm so sorry. Bart, this is my sister, Marlene. Marlene, my boss," Regenia made the introductions.

Before they could say anything, a cry came from the bedroom. "Mommy, Mommy."

"Excuse me," Regenia exclaimed as she headed for the bedroom.

Bart looked at Marlene with an unspoken question in his eyes.

"That's Timmy, Regenia's son," Marlene told him.

"Yes, she mentioned that she has a son."

Regenia exited the bedroom with Timmy in her arms. Timmy was still sniffling from his crying jag.

"Bart, this is my son, Timmy. He's usually pretty good, but all this moving around has him confused. Sometimes he wakes up and doesn't know where he is, and he gets scared. We bought a sleeping bag for him. Marlene and I will share the bed."

"I'm sorry there isn't another bed for him. Maybe I could scrounge up a small bed from one of my friends. Some of them have kids who have probably outgrown their beds."

"That would be nice, but don't go to any trouble on our account."

"I'll see what I can do first thing tomorrow. I promise. So, are you sleeping here tonight? I thought you said you were staying at the motel."

"Well…" Regenia hesitated. "Marlene is all for staying here, but we left all of our clothes and belongings at the motel."

"Tell you what. I could run you back over there to get them."

"I guess that would be all right if you're sure it's not too much bother. Timmy can stay here with Marlene."

"No problem," Marlene interjected. "Timmy, do you want to stay with Aunt Mimi while your mommy goes to get your pajamas and teddy bear?"

"Teddy. Want teddy!" he exclaimed.

"Sure thing, little buddy. And Mommy will bring your toothbrush, too. Would you like that?" Regenia asked.

"Uh-huh," Timmy responded, wiggling as he spoke.

"I can see you want to get down now," Regenia observed as she lowered him to the floor. "I just hope he's not too wide awake to go back to sleep in a little while. Let me get my purse and we'll be off to the motel. I can settle the fee and check out tonight, although I'll miss their Continental breakfast."

"I've eaten a few of those myself," Bart told them.

"You two can keep the Continental breakfast, along with the bugs in that place," Marlene declared.

⸺◦❈◦⸺

THE NEXT FEW DAYS WENT by peacefully, with Regenia adjusting to the routine at work and Marlene watching Timmy and doing her best to keep him entertained. They had managed to buy a few more groceries and were preparing some fairly nutritious meals, but nothing fancy. Timmy would have been happy with just peanut butter and jelly sandwiches, but grownups needed something else more substantial, Regenia reflected as she heated a pot of spaghetti sauce and boiled some pasta one night after work. The bread was in the oven, and she had started making a tossed salad to go with the meal.

Marlene walked into the kitchen, surveying the progress on the meal. She took some plates and silverware from the dishwasher and began to set the places for them to eat. "Sorry, sis. You know my cooking isn't up to par. I never learned much about it because we always had a cook. I can make a great batch of chocolate chip cookies, but preparing a whole meal is beyond my job description."

Regenia sighed. "Yes, I suppose you're right, but I think it's about time you started to learn your way around the kitchen. I had to learn the hard way after Timmy was born. We had quite a few burned meals before I got the hang of it."

"By 'we' I assume you are referring to your ex-husband, Ross Cambridge."

"Yes, who else would I be talking about? You know I didn't date anybody else after I met him in college."

"And what a fateful day that was! It would have been better if you two had never met," Marlene bemoaned.

"You're right, but he was so handsome and charming," Regenia admitted.

"And so rich. He charmed the pants right off you—literally."

"I know. I should have had better sense. But when you're young and in love, anything can happen. It was a mistake. The whole thing was a mistake—everything except for Timmy. I wouldn't take any of it back now because of him," Regenia spoke more softly now so Timmy wouldn't hear them talking.

"Yeah, that's one great little boy we've got," Marlene agreed.

Their conversation was interrupted as Timmy ran into the kitchen, waving his latest art project. "Mommy, draw," he announced.

"Oh, what do you have there, Timmy?" Regenia asked. "Let me see. My, that's so pretty. Look at those colors."

Timmy smiled proudly as Regenia examined the indeterminate scribbles on the sheet of paper he was holding.

"You know, I think we might just have a spot for this on the refrigerator," she told him.

He handed her the paper and she placed it under one of the refrigerator magnets. The whole door was covered with his artwork. Timmy beamed as he watched her secure the magnet.

"If you keep drawing, we might have to find another place to put your pictures," she said.

His face fell slightly and then brightened again. He pointed to the kitchen wall. "There," he said.

"Well, maybe. Let Mommy think about it. Now go and wash your hands for supper. Aunt Mimi will help you," Regenia instructed.

Moments later, they sat down to the meal, which they all consumed heartily, topping it off with a dessert of chilled canned peaches. Marlene offered to do the dishes while Regenia gave Timmy a bath and got him into his pajamas.

Bart, true to his word, had seen to having the lock repaired, and he had also found a small roll-away bed for Timmy. Regenia was grateful that Timmy didn't have to sleep on the floor, as it could get somewhat drafty and she didn't want him to catch a cold. That might mean taking him to see a doctor, and then they would want his medical records. *No, it's best for us to try to stay healthy*, she thought, as she went through their nightly routine. The less exposure they had to the public, the better for them.

❦

BART WAS PLEASED WITH THE way things were working out at his shop. He had to admit it—hiring Regenia was one of the best decisions he had ever made. Under her skilled guidance the office was now running smoothly, with a place for everything and everything in its place. She could put her hands on anything at a moment's notice. Plus, she wasn't bad to look at, either. In fact, he had been doing more looking than he wanted to acknowledge, even to himself. Somehow, he couldn't get her out of his mind, even after working hours were over.

Her car had been repaired, so she now had transportation. Earlier, he had volunteered to drive her on errands after work several times, and he had thoroughly enjoyed himself on every trip. Now, he missed the camaraderie they had shared in his truck cab while tooling around town. She was usually serious, but he always found a way to make her laugh. Still, there was always sadness in her eyes and he wondered what caused that. She didn't say much about her previous life, and he didn't press her on the point. But someday he hoped she would open up and tell him what had happened to make her so sad.

Then there was Timmy. He had grown quite fond of the little boy. Marlene often walked down to the shop with him for a few minutes. The kid couldn't be still for a second, and he was usually bouncing off the walls. Too bad Timmy wasn't older, and then he could teach him something about auto repair. If they stayed long enough, that was still possible, but somehow, he had an idea that they might leave at a moment's notice.

Well, the last thing he needed was to fall in love with another woman who would desert him. He had spent years dreaming of Luci Carlito, who hadn't given him a second look in high school. He had thought she was the most beautiful girl he had ever known, but she had eyes for her high school sweetheart, Roberto Milano. They had broken up after graduation when she started college. Bart then thought he might still have a chance, but Luci had fallen for the new kid on the block when Jeremy Clark had breezed into town and opened a new restaurant. He knew then there was no point in trying to win her heart.

He was crushed, but he got over it on the night of the grand opening of the restaurant when he met Jeremy's sister, Judith. Luci was beautiful, but Judith was exquisite. They seemed to hit it off right away, much to his surprise, because they were from two different worlds. Judith said he made her laugh, and he did have to admit he could be a pretty funny guy when he wanted to be. But she was a New Yorker, and he was just a Summerfield kid who had grown up in a simpler lifestyle. They had a few dates, but she had gone back to New York and the life she was accustomed to, taking a large chunk of his heart with her. *Why can't I find the right woman, one who loves me just the way I am?* he wondered.

He shook his head, trying to erase the image of Regenia from his mind. The last thing he needed was to get mixed up with a woman who came with so much baggage. Regenia was evidently hiding something, and it must be something serious. But she did good work, and that was all he needed right now—somebody who could manage his office. He had to get over any romantic notions he might have involving her. He could do it if he just put his mind to it.

His thoughts were interrupted as Regenia breezed into the office, bringing with her the scent of jasmine and the glow of sunshine. Even though her eyes always held a hint of sadness, she had a way about her that could brighten his day. It was hard to remember what things had been like before she started working in the office.

"Good morning, Bart," she said as she walked over to the desk.

"Good morning. I was just looking over some of the jobs we got yesterday. Have all of the parts been ordered?"

"Yes. I took care of that already. They should be arriving any time now."

"Great. Let me get out to the garage and see what the men are up to. Here's your chair."

He rose awkwardly and motioned to the chair as he spoke, mentally cursing himself for being such a klutz when he was around Regenia. *Why can't I be a smooth operator like, say, Jeremy Clark, who won Luci's heart with little apparent effort? Why do my relationships with women always have to be so difficult?* The thought flitted through his head as he walked around the desk.

Regenia didn't seem to notice his discomfort, or if she did, to his relief she overlooked it. She just smiled and said, "Thanks. Guess it's about time I got to work."

She watched as he walked through the door and back into the shop. She could see that he was uncomfortable and wondered what had brought about the change. He had always been so jovial and so kind to her. What was going through his mind now that made him see her in a different light? She certainly hadn't done anything to encourage any kind of relationship, although she did have to admit she thoroughly enjoyed herself whenever he was around. Somehow, he always seemed to have the knack for making things better whenever she felt down. No other man had ever made her feel that way, not even Ross. In fact, now that she thought about it, she realized that the relationship with Ross had been basically one-sided. It had always been doing it Ross's way or not at all. Too bad she hadn't realized that before she got so involved with him. How could she have fallen for somebody so self-centered?

She snapped back to reality when the phone rang, signaling that the day at the office had officially begun. She soon found herself engrossed in the work of answering the phone, ordering parts, and scheduling repair jobs, along with several requests for tows. If this pace continued, Bart might have to buy another tow truck and hire another driver.

She worked until it was almost time for her lunch break. As she was about to gather up her belongings and head back to the apartment for lunch, she saw a woman walking into the garage. She had no idea who it might be, as she had never seen the woman before, but she was beautiful and obviously rich, judging from the clothes she wore. Regenia wondered if the woman was having car problems. It was odd that she hadn't called before coming in.

The woman, whoever she was, wasted no time. She made a beeline for Bart as soon as she spotted him. Regenia wondered how she knew he was the head honcho. Bart glanced up from the vehicle he was evaluating, and a look of total surprise came over his face. He walked quickly towards the woman. Regenia, who had already walked out of the office, overheard their entire conversation.

"Judith, what are you doing here?" he exclaimed, wiping his hands on a rag that hung from the back pocket of his work suit.

"Bart, darling. I just had to see you again."

"Are you having car problems?"

"Of course not, silly. You know I have my own mechanic, and he keeps my car in excellent condition. No, it's been a while, and you've been on my mind, so I just wanted to see how you're doing."

"Well, you were the one who left town, remember?" he responded quietly.

"I know," she sighed as she spoke. "I'm sorry, but I just missed the big city too much. All those parties and the night life—that's what I'm used to. I couldn't get it out of my system."

Bart looked around and realized that everyone had stopped what they were doing, and the conversation was no longer private. The usual clang and buzz of the shop had come to a complete stop.

"Why don't we step into the office?" he suggested. He regretted it as soon as the words left his mouth because he noticed Regenia standing there with her purse in her hand. He was caught between a rock and a hard place, as his dad used to say.

"Of course. Anything to get out of this grime," Judith agreed readily. Almost too readily to suit Bart's taste.

They walked towards the office, where Regenia was still standing, apparently frozen into place. *She's looking a little pale*, Bart observed. *How am I going to get out of this one?* he wondered. *If I ever had a chance with her, it's probably blown now.*

"Judith, this is my secretary, Regenia Whitworth. Regenia, meet Judith, my..." he paused for lack of words.

"His friend," Judith finished the sentence for him.

"How do you do?" Regenia extended her hand, her voice a little shaky. She wondered why it bothered her so much. Why should she care about any of Bart's lady friends?

Judith took her hand reluctantly. Regenia noticed the slight hesitation but noted the handshake was firm. The lady obviously had self-confidence. Just what made her so self-assured? Was it her money or her relationship with Bart—or both?

"I was just headed for my lunch break," Regenia announced unnecessarily.

"Oh, sure. Go ahead. It's about that time," Bart told her, noting that the crew had left quietly, shutting the garage door on their way out. He watched as Regenia made her way to the back door, and then he turned his attention back to Judith. He opened the office door for her.

"Always the gentleman," she commented as she walked in.

"Judith, why are you really here?" She had already broken his heart once. He didn't think he could take it again.

"Oh, I don't know. You just popped into my head, and I had to see you again. Like I said, you can always make me laugh, and I'm feeling a little down right now."

"And why is that? Problems with your latest beau?"

She smiled, but the smile didn't reach here eyes, which held the slightest hint of sadness. *Maybe the Ice Queen has a heart, after all,* he thought. *But the last thing I need is a blubbering female on my hands in the shop. I have to find out what's wrong and then get rid of her somehow before the crew comes back from lunch.*

He couldn't believe that thought had just flitted through his brain. A few months ago he would have given anything for her to stay, and now he wanted nothing more than for her to go. He hadn't dated anybody else since she had left town. Could it be that he was really over her? Somehow, it felt as if his heart had been released from a gigantic chain that had been wrapped around it tightly. The chain had broken, and his heart was free again.

"I...I don't know where to start," she told him.

"Start at the beginning. That's always the best place," he responded gently.

"I met somebody—somebody wonderful. At least that's what I thought. I know I've been playing the field for years, just having a good time and breaking young men's hearts. It was all a game to me. I never took any of it seriously. Then I met Chad at a cocktail party. He was handsome and charming and rich and smart—everything I could ask for in a man. He zeroed in on me right away. I was flattered. We dated for several months, and I thought I was in love with him. I've never felt like that before, not with any man. No offense to present company."

"No offense taken."

"Turns out he wasn't quite as rich as he appeared to be. He was more interested in my money than in me. He has a gambling problem. He had already run through his inheritance, and he needed somebody with lots of money to support his habit. He was in love with my money, but he wasn't in love with me."

"So, I think there's more to the story than you're telling me. What else is going on? Why didn't you just get rid of the guy?"

She sat down heavily in one of the chairs by the wall. She bowed her head and then looked up again as she spoke. "I'm pregnant. I just found out a couple of days ago. My family will have a fit if they find out. You know Jeremy. He might kill the guy."

Bart sat down in the chair beside her and took her hand before responding. "No, Jeremy won't kill him. You know that. He might want to, but he will restrain himself. Your family will stand behind you. I know that. What are you going to do now? Have you told Chad yet?"

"I don't know. I just don't know what to do. I don't want an abortion, but I don't want my baby to grow up without a father either. I don't want Chad in my life any longer. There's nobody I know who might marry me—nobody except you, that is. I know you loved me, Bart, and I am sorry if I broke your heart, but we could still make it work."

"I'm not the man you're looking for, Judith. It's true that I fancied myself in love with you, but now I realize it wasn't really love. It was infatuation. You can't build a relationship on that. Besides, there's someone else I'm interested in now."

She looked a little sadder but managed a half-smile. "Somehow, I knew you might say that, but I had to give it a try. It's that secretary of yours, isn't it?"

"Well, maybe," he admitted.

"I can see she has a thing for you. Women know these things. Have you told her how you feel?"

"Not yet. We haven't really dated. I'm not sure how things will go because there are a lot of problems I can't get into right now."

"Don't wait too long."

"I'm sorry, Judith."

"Don't be. I brought the problems on myself. Now I have to face the consequences, and that will start with telling my family."

"If there's any other way I can help you, just let me know."

"You've already been a big help. Talking to you made me aware of what I have to do. I just had to give it a try, but somehow I think I already knew your answer even before I came here."

"Then why did you come, Judith?"

"I guess I just had to be sure; that's all."

Bart heard the garage door going up and realized the crew was returning from lunch. That meant Regenia wouldn't be far behind. Before he could say anything else, Judith stood up. He followed her lead and walked over to open the door for her.

"Thanks for everything, Bart," she said as she leaned over and kissed him softly on the cheek.

Bart watched as she walked out the front door of the garage. He turned back towards the work area and saw Regenia standing at the back entrance. *How much had she seen?* he wondered. All he needed was for her to see another woman kissing him. That would pretty much kill his chances of winning her heart. Was he ever going to be able to have a normal relationship with women?

— ◦◦◦ —

REGENIA COULD HARDLY BELIEVE HER eyes—Bart being kissed by another woman, and a beautiful, sophisticated one at that. How did a guy who was so down-to-earth manage to attract such a woman? Somehow, they just didn't seem to mesh. And why was she worried about it anyhow? Oh, Bart had been nice to her and had gone out of his way to help her, but that didn't really mean anything. He was just a nice guy. That's what he did. He helped people; it was just his nature. It hadn't taken her very long to figure that out. Besides, why should she care if he was involved with another woman? It wasn't like she should be having any romantic notions about her boss. No, not at all. She had too many other problems to worry about. There was Timmy and Marlene and their lack of money, although that situation had improved tremendously since she had gotten this job. But most of all, there was still Ross. They had managed to evade him so far, but she had a feeling he was on their trail. Eventually, there would be a big showdown, and she wasn't looking forward to it.

She walked back to the office slowly, lost in thought. Suddenly she heard someone yell, "Watch out!" Before she knew it, she found herself in Bart's arms as he pulled her out of the way of a tire that had just come loose from one of the vehicles that was suspended on a lift.

"Are you okay?" he asked.

She drew a shaky breath before responding. "Yes, I'm all right. What happened?" She noticed that she was still in his arms, and he didn't seem to be in any hurry to let her go.

"Looks like Justin let a tire get away from him. That's why we don't allow customers in the shop area. Accidents happen."

"Sorry, boss," Justin apologized.

"I'll be fine. Let me get back to the office and back to work."

"Sure thing but watch where you're walking next time." He released her as he spoke.

She wouldn't have minded if he had kept on holding her, but her pulse was racing at twice its normal rate, partly from the near-accident and partly from being so close to him. It was the first time they had ever gotten so close. She usually made it a point to stay a safe distance away. She wondered what it would be like to have him kiss her. She tried to put that picture out of her mind as she went back to work.

Bart took a deep breath just to calm his nerves as she went into the office and closed the door. Evidently, he was over Judith, as her visit had no effect on him, and his heart was still intact. But now he had another problem—Regenia Whitworth.

"So, are you going to let her get away?"

He turned to face Jim, who had walked up behind him. "You think I should just kiss her in front of God and everybody here?"

Jim grinned. "Well, if that's what the situation calls for, go for it, brother."

"I prefer to do my courting in private. Besides, if you knew anything about Regenia you would know that she can't be rushed. She has a lot of problems right now, and I think she'll have to deal with them before she's ready for any new man in her life."

"I guess you know what's best. But don't wait too long, brother. I don't want you to get your heart broken again."

"I know what I'm doing this time. Trust me. Now get back to work before I have to fire you," Bart teased.

"Okay, okay, I'm going," Jim grumbled. "Slave driver," he muttered as he walked away.

Bart glanced around and saw that everybody appeared to be working hard on their assigned jobs. But he was sure they had viewed the whole scene. In fact, he wouldn't be surprised to learn of a betting pool about when he was going to hook up with Regenia. *Well, they will just have to wait. I'm going to take my time and do things right this time,* he decided.

A sudden noise at the entrance door drew his attention. It was Amy Phillips, the wife of Judge Jeff Philips, along with their two children, Michael and Sophie. She hurried towards him, the children running in front of her.

"Slow down, kids," she called out. "Hello, Bart. I'm having car problems. It seems to be overheating. Can your men take a look at it? I'm afraid it will go out on me in the middle of traffic."

The children screeched to a halt in front of him and looked up expectantly. He grinned down at them. "Hi, kids. How about a lollipop?"

"Thanks, Mr. Bart," they echoed in unison.

He walked over to the office door and opened it. "Regenia, do we have any lollipops for our visitors? And please escort Mrs. Phillips to the lounge while we take a look at her car."

Regenia looked up from her computer. "Of course." She grabbed two lollipops from the jar on her desk. "Here you go, kids." She smiled as she handed over the candy. The children eagerly unwrapped them and stuck the suckers into their mouths.

"Now, kids. Put those wrappers in the trash can. We don't want to see litter," their mom reminded them.

"If you'll follow me, I'll show you our waiting area," Regenia told her. "We have free coffee and also a Coke machine. She switched on the TV set, turning it to a channel that featured cartoons. "Maybe this will keep the children occupied while you wait."

"Thank you so much. I'm just a little overwhelmed right now," Amy commented. "My babysitter just quit on me and I haven't found another one yet."

"Oh, really? I have a younger sister who might be interested in the job. However, she would have to bring my son along, as she's his caretaker while I'm working."

"Both of the kids are in school, so I just need somebody to watch them for about three hours in the afternoon until I get home. I'm an elementary teacher, so my hours are pretty regular. How old is your son?"

"He's two and his name is Timmy. Does she need references?"

"If you're working for Bart, that's reference enough for me. I've known Bart for years. I know he wouldn't hire somebody he didn't trust."

"Let me check with my sister, and if she agrees, I'll give you a call tonight if you give me your number."

"No problem. I'll just write it down for you." Amy pulled a notepad out of her purse and quickly wrote down the information. She handed it to Regenia.

"Okay. Make yourselves as comfortable as possible while you wait. I have to get back to the office," Regenia told her.

Regenia tried to contain her excitement. She didn't want to seem too eager about the job, but this might be exactly what they needed to supplement their income. She just hoped Marlene would agree to it. Her sister was good with kids, but she didn't know if watching two more kids after keeping Timmy all day was going to work or not. She would just have to see when she got home. That sort of thing was best discussed in person.

━❖❖❖❖━

REGENIA COULD HARDLY WAIT TO tell Marlene the news after work. She rushed home and walked in to find Marlene in the kitchen preparing the evening meal. Timmy was in the living room watching cartoons on the old TV set that Bart had scrounged up for them.

She was glad Timmy had something to do besides color and read all day. Plus, it gave Marlene a little free time also.

"I can't believe my eyes. Have you actually taken up cooking?" she exclaimed as she entered the kitchen.

"It's nothing fancy—just some omelets with canned biscuits and bacon," Marlene informed her. "I decided to give you a break from cooking. Besides, I got bored just sitting around all day."

"Anything will be good as long as I don't have to cook it! I've had quite a day today, and I'm completely exhausted," Regenia told her. "But I might have some good news for you—something that would make your days a little more exciting. And, should I say, a little more profitable?"

"What? What kind of scheme have you cooked up for me now?" Marlene asked.

"I think I found a job for you if you want it. A lady came into the shop today and she's looking for a part-time babysitter for her two kids after school. What do you think? Are you interested?"

"Interested? You mean I could get out of this place for a few hours every day? You bet I'm interested. So, how old are the kids?"

"I don't know exactly, but early elementary age. One looks to be in kindergarten, and the other one maybe first or second grade. Still pretty young and full of energy."

"That's the way I like them. Young ones are easier to manage. They don't talk back so much, and I can make up some games to play with them."

"I told the lady we would call her tonight if you want the job. She gave me her number."

"Let's do that right after supper. The omelets are ready and I'm about to take the biscuits out of the oven. We should eat before everything gets cold."

By seven o'clock they had finished the meal and cleaned up the kitchen. Regenia felt that the Phillips family should also be through with their evening meal by that time, so it seemed like a good time to call. She placed the call and got all of the information about the time and location. Amy was going to meet Marlene on the first day and give her a key. Then Marlene would be able to let herself and Timmy in to wait for the children to ride home on the bus.

"How am I going to get there?" Marlene asked.

"You'll take the car, of course. But please be extra careful. I just got through working off the payment for repairs, and I don't want another repair bill. I won't need it while I'm at work, and you should be home shortly after I get off."

"I'll be careful. I promise. I can't wait to get started. Then I might have a little extra spending money of my own. But don't worry, sis. I'll chip in with my fair share of the expenses," Marlene exclaimed.

"I know you will. Maybe now you could actually go out on a date with somebody like...hmm...Jim, for instance."

"Jim! Like I would be interested in a mechanic."

"I've seen the way he looks at you when you and Timmy come down to the office. He can't keep his eyes off you. I think he might have dropped a wrench or two when you walked by."

"Well, he is kind of cute," Marlene admitted. "But a mechanic? Get real!"

"Okay...I'm just saying," Regenia teased.

DURING THE NEXT FEW WEEKS they settled into their new routine, with Marlene leaving in the afternoon for her babysitting job. Regenia had to assume all the cooking duties, but she didn't mind because of the extra income. Besides, Marlene did the dishes every night while she got Timmy ready for bed and read him his bedtime story.

BEFORE LONG, BART FINALLY WORKED up the nerve to ask Regenia out on a date. They went to a movie, a comedy that had them both in stitches. He thought she could use a laugh, and by the end of the night he could see that he had made the right choice. She was more relaxed than she had ever been since coming to work for him. They shared a bag of popcorn and drank Cokes as they watched the movie. More than once, their hands touched when they both reached into the bag at the same time. He felt his pulse beat a little faster every time it happened. *My heart must have finally thawed out again*, he decided.

After the movie, he thought it might be a good idea to drive her out to the lake. There was nothing better than moonlight over the water to put a girl into a romantic mood.

"There's something I want to show you," he told her as he headed his truck in that direction.

"What?" she asked.

"I can't tell you. It's a surprise, but I think you're going to like it. Close your eyes and don't open them until I tell you to, okay?"

She laughed. "I'm always holding on tight when I'm with you because I never know what you have planned."

"That's what makes me such a fun guy," he teased.

He pulled up in front of the lake and stopped, overlooking the view. "Well, here we are. You can open your eyes now."

She peeked between her fingers and then removed her hands entirely from her face. "It's beautiful, but why did you bring me here?"

"I just wanted you to see it at night. We are very proud of this lake. People come out on weekends for all kinds of outings. They have cookouts, go water skiing and sailing. I have a friend who has a sailboat, and I thought you might like to go with us sometime."

"Sailing…oh, no! I couldn't! I just couldn't!" she exclaimed, her voice quivering slightly.

"Why not? Regenia, what's wrong? You're trembling." He didn't know why she was so upset, but he felt really bad about bringing her here now.

"It's a long story. I'm not sure if I'm ready to tell you about it."

"I've got all night. There's no better time than the present. Please, Regenia, you can trust me." He reached over and took her hand. It felt so cold. He wanted nothing more than to take her in his arms, but he didn't dare risk it. He didn't want to upset her any more.

She drew a deep breath before speaking. "It's a long story, and not a happy one. If I tell you, everything must be kept in the strictest confidence. If you tell anybody—anybody at all—Marlene, Timmy, and I could be in danger."

"I won't tell anyone. Is it something illegal?" he asked, his heart almost stopping at the thought.

"No, not exactly. Well, not all of it, anyhow." She paused before continuing. "I don't know where to start. You see, we are running away, trying to escape what was a terrible fate for Timmy. His father and I are divorced, and a nasty custody battle ensued. We had joint custody, but his dad comes from a very rich family, and he was suing for full custody. Timmy was going for weekend visits, but I found signs of abuse. Timmy came home with unexplained bruises, and one time I found the remains of duct tape around his mouth, like his mouth had been taped shut."

"Didn't you tell that to the judge?"

"Yes, I did, but the judge didn't believe me. He assigned a psychologist to evaluate Timmy, and the psychologist sided with the judge. They said Timmy was too young to tell them what was going on. Ross, Timmy's dad, managed to explain it all away, like nothing really happened. But something tells me that his family probably bribed the judge."

"Why didn't you take it to an appeals court?"

"I was going to, but then something else happened. My family was also rich, so money was no problem for us. My dad was going to pay for everything. I had no worries about the legal costs. He and my mom loved to sail, and they went out one weekend on their sailboat. It was just before the new trial, and they wanted to relax. We didn't go with them because I wanted some time alone with Timmy. My dad was always so careful about checking on the weather before he went sailing, but an unexpected storm came up. Their boat capsized, and their bodies were never found."

"Oh, I'm so sorry. I had no idea," Bart lamented. *That explains some things*, he thought. He knew Regenia had class from the moment he laid eyes on her. That's why he couldn't understand how she could be so broke and down on her luck. It was all starting to come together now. "But what about their money? Surely you and Marlene inherited it. Couldn't you still fight the case in court?"

"There's more to the story. After my parents went missing, Marlene and I learned that their estate was totally bankrupt. The lawyers had run through their money. There was nothing left for us. We both have trust funds, but we won't get them until we turn thirty. I had to drop the appeal. We had to sell the house and barely had enough left for a car and a little money to live on. I had to drop out of college and look for a job. We were in the process of moving into an apartment when I got a court order to hand over Timmy to his dad. The social worker was coming the next day to pick him up. That's when Marlene and I decided to make a run for it. We wanted to get as far away from our home on the East Coast as possible. So, we finally ended up here in Summerfield, and you offered me the job. My main regret is that we didn't change our names. I'm afraid Ross will still be able to track us down. It's just a matter of time."

"So, Ross's last name is Whitworth? I'm confused."

"No, I went back to my maiden name after the divorce. His name is Ross Cambridge. We were married just a little over a year, and we got married only because I found out I was pregnant. I lost a little time in college due to the pregnancy and after Timmy was born. My parents were very disappointed, but they didn't disown me. I thought I was in love with Ross. I thought we could make it work. But then I discovered I didn't really know him at all. He had been so charming when we were dating, but he was a nasty drunk, and he liked to drink a lot. When I sued him for divorce, it wounded his pride. He never got over it. That's why he was trying to punish me by gaining total custody of Timmy. It wasn't because he loved Timmy. He hardly gave the boy a second glance once I brought him home from the hospital."

"That's a real shame. Timmy is a wonderful little boy, and you're a great mom. You deserve better."

"Thank you," she whispered.

"I'm so sorry I brought you here and brought up the topic of sailboats. I had no idea."

"It's not your fault. You had no way of knowing. The lake is lovely, especially in the moonlight. It's just that I can't go sailing again because of what happened to my parents. I don't want to get close to a sailboat."

"I understand. Let's get you home now." He patted her hand as he spoke, suddenly realizing that he had been holding it the whole time she had been talking. She seemed to realize it at the same time because she quickly withdrew it and sat with her hands tightly clasped together, as if to stop them from trembling.

They drove home in silence, both trying to sort out their feelings. He was still trying to digest the information she had shared with him. She, on the other hand, was wondering if she had done the right thing. It was the first time she had opened up her heart to anyone since fleeing her hometown. She just hoped Bart wouldn't get into trouble for hiring her and renting his apartment to them.

He dropped her off at the apartment and left after walking her to the door. He had hoped for a goodnight kiss, but that was out of the question now. There was just too much raw emotion floating in the air, and he didn't want to add any more to the mix. It was going to take some getting used to, but he was seeing Regenia Whitworth in a whole new light. Not only was she beautiful, but beneath that exterior was a backbone of steel. It took guts to do what she had done, and he couldn't help but admire her for it. But sooner or later, her past was going to catch up with her. He just hoped when it did, he would be able to think of some way to help her.

—◆◆◆◆◆—

REGENIA WALKED INTO THE APARTMENT slowly, closing the door softly behind her. She knew Timmy would already be asleep, and she didn't want to wake him. She hoped Marlene was already in bed, but no such luck. Marlene was sitting in front of the TV in her nightgown and bathrobe, like a mother hen waiting on her chick.

"Well, how was the date?" Marlene inquired as she grabbed a handful of popcorn out of a large bowl sitting in her lap.

"The movie was a lot of fun. I haven't laughed so much in a long time. Bart is a really funny guy and fun to be with," Regenia responded.

"Kind of late for just going to a movie. So, was that the only place you went?"

"No, Bart drove me out to the lake. He wanted to show me the view."

"Some view, I'll bet," Marlene joked.

"It was beautiful, but that's not all that happened."

"Oh, did he finally kiss you? Tell the truth!"

"No, that didn't happen."

"Why not? What's wrong with the guy?" Marlene demanded to know.

"I think he probably wanted to, at least at first. But something came up that changed the whole outlook. After that, we weren't in the mood."

"So, don't keep me in suspense. What happened? Did a cop show up and run you off like two teenagers?"

"No, nary a cop in sight. But Bart suggested I might like to go sailing sometime with him and his friend."

"Sailing? Oh, dear God, no!" Marlene exclaimed.

"I know. It totally blew my mind. He couldn't understand why I wouldn't want to go sailing with him, so I had to explain."

"Just how much did you tell him?"

"Everything," Regenia admitted.

"Everything? Every single little detail of our whole sordid affair?" Marlene asked.

"Yes, when I started, it just all came out. I couldn't help myself."

"Oh, no. Do you realize what you have done?" Marlene groaned as she spoke. She set the bowl of popcorn on the lamp table and stood up to face her sister.

"I'm sure Bart won't tell anybody. He promised he wouldn't," Regenia assured her.

"Oh, I trust Bart. But did you think about the fact that before you told him, Bart was just an innocent bystander? He hired you totally unaware of your background. We are being hunted by the law. Now he could be arrested for aiding and abetting a criminal. We're all going to jail, and Timmy's going back to Ross. I just know it!" Marlene began to pace the floor as she spoke.

"Keep your voice down," Regenia warned. "Yes, I know that, and I'm so sorry. But he wouldn't let it go. I felt I owed him an explanation."

"Well, what's done is done. But it's like waiting for the other shoe to drop. Sooner or later, either Ross or the law is going to show up here, and when that happens, it won't be a pretty scene. Maybe we should leave now and get out while we still can."

"I like this town, and I like Bart. We are going to stay here, and that's all there is to it. I'm the oldest, and I will make the decision that's best for the family," Regenia informed her, speaking firmly.

"All right, Miss Hoity Toity. Have it your way. I've gone along with you up to now. No sense in changing anything at this point. Now that you're home safe and sound, I'm going to bed. Help yourself to the rest of the popcorn."

Marlene marched down the hall and into the bedroom, head held high. Regenia had to smile. Her little sister could be a pain, but she was a real trouper when it counted. She had grown up a lot in the past few months. Too bad she had missed out on her senior prom and her chance to go to college, but someday it would all work out. Regenia didn't know how she was going to manage, but if and when the court case ever got straight, Marlene still deserved a chance for a college education. *And I still need to finish my degree. Just one more semester and I'll be through. We're both going to make it somehow. That's a promise I intend to keep. Please, God, watch over and protect our little family and someday let our dreams come true,* she sent up a silent prayer.

She grabbed a handful of popcorn from the bowl and settled down on the couch with the TV control in the other hand. She was too restless to sleep. Maybe there was something on she could watch for a little while, at least until Marlene had fallen asleep, and then she could crawl into the bed beside her without further ado.

⬥ ⬩◆◈◆◈◆◈◆⬩ ⬥

BART WAS AS JUMPY AS a squirrel on the first day of hunting season. On one hand, he almost wished Regenia hadn't told him the whole story, but on the other hand, he was glad she did. It was just unnerving, knowing that somewhere out there was a man who was chasing her and Timmy as if they were some kind of prize. If he ever got his hands on Ross Cambridge, he would give him something else to think about besides Regenia and Timmy. Several weeks had passed without incident, and he almost let his guard down. Almost, but not quite.

REGENIA APPEARED TO BE AS nervous as he was. She had started jumping every time the office phone rang. The sadness was back in her eyes, and she rarely smiled. He wished he could do something about that. Maybe it was time to take her to another one of those comical movies. He didn't know if she would go or not, but he would give it a try after work today, he decided.

The workload at the garage had been extra heavy for the past few weeks. Regenia had been busy answering the phone and keeping up with the orders for parts. She was glad because it took her mind off Ross. But there was always that little niggling in the back of her head, reminding her that she and Timmy and Marlene were still in danger. What she needed was an escape plan if he should happen to appear. They should have their bags packed to leave at a moment's notice, along with a substantial amount of cash to live on until she could get another job. *I'll work on that tonight just as soon as I get home,* she thought.

Bart looked up as a stranger walked through the door. He knew most of his customers, but this guy was entirely new. *Who could it be?* he wondered. Bart walked forward to meet the man before he got into the work area of the garage.

"I've been told that you have my car in storage here at your place," the man told him, drawing a paper out of an envelope as he spoke.

"I don't know. I might have it. A few cars have been here for quite a while without their owners claiming them. What's your name?" Bart asked.

"Ross Cambridge," the man replied.

"Ross Cambridge. Why, you..." Bart dove at him and hit him squarely in the jaw with his fist. The man staggered backwards, landing against one of the cars parked and waiting for service. He recovered enough to lunge back at Bart, but Bart was ready for him and took another swing, hitting him in the chin. The man appeared dazed, and Bart continued to pummel him as he fell back against the car again.

Regenia heard the commotion and looked out the office door to see what was going on. "Ross," she whispered. She slipped out quietly and headed towards the apartment. Marlene hadn't left for her babysitting job yet. Maybe they could get away before anybody noticed. She began to run as soon as she was out of the garage.

She burst through the door of the apartment, yelling as she entered, "Marlene, grab Timmy. We've got to get out of here!"

"What's going on?" Marlene asked.

"It's Ross. He's here. We have to go!"

Marlene ran into the bedroom to awaken Timmy from a nap, while Regenia gathered all the spare cash they had on hand. There was no time to pack. She grabbed their coats out of the closet. They would have to get some more clothes later.

"Where are we going?" Marlene asked after they were all safely buckled in and ready to leave.

"I don't know, but we have to get away," Regenia replied as she backed the car out of the garage. She glanced in the rearview mirror just in time to see flashing lights coming up behind her. It was too late. They were trapped!

"Stop the vehicle and get out of the car," came a warning over the police speaker.

Regenia stopped the car and shut off the engine. She and Marlene looked at each other. "It's over," she said. Timmy began to cry. "It's okay, Timmy. Remember, no matter what happens, Mommy loves you."

She exited the car with her hands up, while Marlene got out on the other side in a similar fashion. The police made short work of frisking them and securing both of them with handcuffs. They soon found themselves sitting in the back of a police car. Timmy was removed from their car and placed in a separate police vehicle.

"Mommy," he cried just before a policeman shut the door.

"Timmy, my poor baby," Regenia called through the glass. "Don't take my son away from me. Please!" Tears streamed down her face as she sobbed uncontrollably.

Marlene sat on her side of the car crying quietly. "It's no use. Give it up, sis. Ross won, and we lost."

"Oh, God! Oh, God! Why?" Regenia asked.

"I don't know. I just don't know," Marlene replied sadly.

⊷⊱◈⊰⊶

BART HADN'T FARED MUCH BETTER than the two sisters. The brawl had spilled outside into the parking lot, and some passersby had phoned the police. His men had managed to pull him off Ross, but not before both of them were sporting black eyes. Bart had scored more punches, but Ross had managed to get in a lick or two. Someone had also called an ambulance. Bart had refused treatment, but Ross had made the most of the scene, agreeing to be taken to the hospital after giving his statement to the police.

Bart had been happy to see that Ross appeared to be missing a tooth or two after the EMTs had gotten the bleeding stopped. He hoped they were lying around somewhere on the parking lot. It would serve the sorry sucker right to lose a little of his slick, handsome profile.

At Ross's insistence, Bart had also been handcuffed and arrested. The officer had been reluctant to do so, but he had to follow through because it was the law. Ross had spotted Regenia as she exited the garage and alerted the police as soon as they arrived. They had responded immediately, giving Regenia and her family little time to escape.

Bart caught a glimpse of Regenia's face through the glass of the police car as the car exited the parking lot. "Don't worry," he shouted. "I'm going to fix this. Everything will be all right."

But can I fix it? he wondered. His mind raced ahead as he was shoved into another police car to be taken downtown for booking.

"Don't worry, Bart. We'll get you out," Jim yelled after him.

"Take care of the shop," he yelled back.

<hr />

REGENIA AND MARLENE SAT DESPONDENTLY in a jail cell with little hope of making bail. They both dabbed at their eyes, trying to hold back the tears. It was a far cry from the life they had been accustomed to when growing up. Regenia glanced at the other prisoners. There was quite a variety from what appeared to be prostitutes to drug dealers and even some hardened criminals. She was surprised to see so much crime in such a small town.

"I thought this was a peaceful place," she commented to Marlene.

"Crime is everywhere now," Marlene replied, glancing around at the dismal setting.

They were astonished several hours later when a policewoman appeared and unlocked their cell door.

"Okay, you two are free to go. Someone has posted your bail," she informed them.

"Looks like somebody's got a Sugar Daddy," one of the apparent prostitutes taunted as Regenia and Marlene stood up and walked to the cell door.

"What? I don't believe it!" Regenia exclaimed, addressing her remark to the policewoman who had let them out of the cell.

"Oh, no mistake. We don't release anybody unless they make bail. I suggest you get out of here as quickly as possible," the policewoman advised. She didn't have to tell them twice. They checked out and got their belongings. The officer who released them gave them instructions not to leave town or they would be arrested again.

Regenia looked around, wondering what to do next. Then she spotted Bart coming through the door.

"Hi, are you about ready to go home?" he asked.

"Yes, I can't wait to get out of this place. But were you the one who posted bail? I don't understand."

"It was Jim. He got the money for my bail, and I asked him to get it for you and Marlene also. I saw you being hauled off in the police car. You looked really scared, and I was so worried about both of you."

"Thank you so much. I'll repay you somehow," she assured him.

"Yes, thank you," Marlene chimed in.

"But what are you doing here?" Regenia asked.

"I'll tell you when we get outside. Don't say another word," Bart instructed.

They walked outside, where Jim sat waiting in Bart's truck. "My brother came to pick us up," Bart explained as he led them towards the truck. He opened the door to let them in the back of the extended cab. "It'll be a tight squeeze, but I think we can all fit."

"I would ride in the bed of this truck just to get away from here and get back home," Regenia declared.

"That would be a sight to behold," Marlene told her as they climbed inside.

Bart closed their door and climbed into the passenger seat. "Let's go, brother," he said, and Jim pulled away from the curb.

"Okay, now we can talk," he told them. "There's no use keeping any more secrets, as it will all be coming out with the arrests. I told Jim about the situation with Timmy, so he's up to speed. We came up with a plan."

"Where is Timmy? I need to see him!" Regenia exclaimed.

"That's not possible right now. He's in protective custody and has been placed in a foster home. We barely got you out of jail. The FBI was on the case because you have been charged with kidnapping," Bart told her.

"Oh, God! What else is going to happen to me? This is just terrible!"

"So, how did you manage to get us out of jail?" Marlene asked.

"You work for a judge's wife, remember?" Jim asked.

185

"I called in a special favor to Judge Phillips. He has no real jurisdiction in the case because it originated in another state, but he called a judge he went to law school with who lives there. You're going to need a lawyer, so I called up one of my old classmates, Luci Clark. She's one of the best, and she agreed to take your case," Bart informed them.

"Oh, thank you so much, but I have no money for a lawyer," Regenia responded.

"No problem. You can just work it off, like you did with the car repair," Bart assured her.

"It'll take a lot longer than a few months to pay off a lawyer's fees," Regenia lamented.

"So, are you planning on going anywhere?" Bart asked.

"Well...no. I guess not. There's not much point in running anymore since Ross knows where we are now."

"Right, plus, you can't leave town right now either. That's one of the stipulations the judge made when he let you out of jail. What we need now is a plan. You need to meet with Luci tomorrow and see what you can come up with. I have her phone number, and I'll be glad to take you to her office."

"I'm sure I can find the office by myself if you just give me the directions. I don't want to put you out anymore," Regenia told him. "But you still haven't told me about being arrested...and just look at your black eye!"

"That's a souvenir from Ross. When the guy walked through the door and told me his name, I just saw red. All I could think about was Timmy, so I let him have it. Turns out he packs a pretty good punch of his own."

"But what was he doing at the shop? Had he tracked us down? I don't understand," Marlene interjected.

"No, he was coming to get his car. It's the one that we've had in storage at the back of the yard for several months. I had no idea it belonged to him," Bart replied.

"How is that possible?" Regenia asked.

"Well, the police confiscated the car registration at the scene of the accident because he was unconscious and was suspected of drunk driving. He was in a coma for several months due to head injuries. They held the papers, and I kind of forgot about it with so many other things going on. When he got out of the hospital, he paid his fine and got his papers back. That's when he came looking for us," Bart explained.

"But I still don't understand how he knew I was there," Regenia commented.

"He didn't, but he was looking for you. Then he saw you leaving the shop. By then we were fighting. Somebody called the police, and when they arrived he told them about you. They figured you had headed for the apartment, so that's when they showed up at your door, just in time to stop you from leaving."

"Yeah, another couple of minutes and we would have been gone," Marlene observed.

"What I wouldn't give for those couple of minutes," Regenia sighed as she spoke.

"The best thing to do is to get you two girls back home right now. You can sort it all out tomorrow," Jim suggested.

"You're right. I'm completely exhausted, and I'm sure Marlene is, too. What we need is a good meal and a shower and some rest," Regenia agreed.

"Amen to that," Marlene added.

"Plus, I'm giving you the next couple of days off, so don't worry about coming in to work," Bart announced.

"Oh, thank you so much. That's very kind of you," Regenia told him.

"Here we are, back at your own front door," Jim commented as he pulled the truck up in front of the apartment.

"I never thought I'd be so glad to see this place again," Marlene exclaimed.

"It's home to us now," Regenia observed as they climbed out of the truck and headed up the stairs. "But it's going to be lonely without Timmy." She turned and waved to Bart and Jim as their truck backed up and turned around.

"Are you thinking what I'm thinking?" Marlene asked as they walked into the apartment.

"I don't know. What are you thinking?"

"That Bart is a pretty good guy and a pretty good catch...if you are in the market for somebody new in your life, that is."

"I suppose you're right. He is a great guy. I've been holding back because of our situation, but now he knows the whole story. If he sticks around after that, it will definitely give me something to think about. But what about you and Jim? Have you given that any thought?"

"I told you, I'm not interested in marrying a mechanic. I still want a college education someday. I don't know what I want to major in yet, but I have to get some kind of job skills, especially now that we don't have any money."

"That's too much to worry about right now. Let's get something to eat and talk to that lawyer in the morning. We still have plenty of time to make up our minds about men," said Regenia.

⸻ ❊ ⸻

REGENIA'S MEETING WITH LUCI THE following morning proved to be fruitful. The first thing they needed to do was to get the kidnapping charges formally dismissed. Then they could proceed with an appeal for her to regain custody of Timmy. Blood tests done on Ross during his hospital stay had shown that he was driving while intoxicated, far above the legal limit. So, that was a point in their favor. Regenia agreed to return to her home state of New York voluntarily rather than being extradited, so that would help her case. Luci had retained her law license to practice in New York, as her husband, Jeremy, still had business there. She agreed to stick with Regenia through the whole process.

Luci worked her magic, and after a short trial, the kidnapping charges against both Regenia and Marlene were formally dismissed. A few weeks later they found themselves in the appeals court for the custody case. It was quite a different setting from the other courtrooms. A panel of several judges was scheduled to hear the case. Both lawyers had sent in all their papers, and the judges had read them in advance. On the first day of the hearing Regenia glanced around and saw Bart walking into the courtroom. He took a seat behind her, and she turned around and smiled slightly at him without speaking, as the court proceedings had already begun.

The judges found fault with almost every point the other judge had made on the previous ruling in awarding sole custody of Timmy to his father. In addition, they were also troubled by Ross's charge of driving while intoxicated and causing a serious accident that endangered other people. Plus, there was the incident of the fight at the garage that further damaged his character. In the end, after several hours of deliberation, they found in Regenia's favor. She was awarded full custody of Timmy, while Ross was granted only supervised visitation once a month with no overnight stays. She was also granted permission to go back to Summerfield with Timmy. Ross would be the one who had to travel to visit his son.

Regenia let out the breath she had been holding as one of the judges began to read the verdict. She couldn't believe what she was hearing. It seemed almost too good to be true. She was escorted to a room where Timmy was being held during the proceedings. She opened the door, and Timmy rushed over to her as soon as he saw her.

"Mommy, Mommy," he cried as he flung his arms around her knees.

She bent down and kissed the top of his head, gently extracting his arms from the strong grip that almost threw her off-balance. "Timmy, it's okay now. We're going home."

Bart appeared in the doorway. "Anybody need a ride?" he asked, sporting a broad grin.

"That would be very nice," she told him. "Come on, Timmy."

They rode back to the hotel in a taxi and made plans to catch a plane back to Summerfield as soon as a flight was available. They had to wait several days, so Regenia and Marlene took Bart on a tour of the area and showed him their former home.

"Wow, that's quite a place," he commented, emitting a low whistle as he took in the view from the back seat of a taxi, eying the Victorian-style house with its circular driveway and meticulously manicured lawn dotted with trees and accented with colorful flowers.

"It's all in the past now," Regenia noted sadly.

"What I wouldn't give to live there again," Marlene sighed wistfully as she spoke. "Tennis, swimming, friends, fun...I even miss school."

"That's saying a lot coming from you," Regenia teased. "Maybe now I can go back and finish my last semester of college as soon as I can save enough money."

"Do you mean to tell me that you didn't get quite a substantial sum of money when that place was sold?" Bard asked incredulously.

"Most of the money went to pay the lawyers' fees. We got very little of it," Regenia told him.

"I guess you'll be looking for another job, one that pays more," said Bart.

"It all depends on the fringe benefits," Regenia told him, batting her eyes as she spoke.

"Fringe benefits, huh? I'll have to see what I can come up with," he teased.

"You two are going to make me crazy one of these days!" Marlene exclaimed. "Why don't you just go ahead and kiss her?"

"Not a bad idea, especially since she's sitting so close to me," Bart admitted.

He pulled her closer and kissed her soundly while she offered little resistance. Timmy, who was sitting beside her, began to wriggle impatiently, breaking up the effect of the moment.

"To be continued," Bart said, laughing as Regenia pulled away.

"Yes, later," Regenia agreed.

—◆◆◇◆◇◆◇◆◆—

SEVERAL MONTHS PASSED WITHOUT ANY major incidents. Ross had shown up for his visits with Timmy, but they were growing less and less frequent. He had been belligerent at first, but his attitude seemed to soften on the last visit, giving Regenia hope that someday Timmy might have a normal relationship with his biological father. She just hoped he wouldn't ever attempt to harm Timmy again.

Regenia and Bart had settled into a comfortable state in their relationship. They had been on a number of dates, both with and without Timmy accompanying them. For the first time since her parents had disappeared at sea, Regenia felt that Timmy had a stable male figure in his life. Bart was evidently fond of the boy and made every effort to include him in their activities whenever possible. For that, she was grateful.

Timmy seemed equally fond of Bart. He was happiest whenever Bart was around. Somehow, Bart always had the ability to make him laugh. Bart was really good with kids, Regenia noted. She wondered what it would be like for him to have a couple of kids of his own. She tried to picture him married and settled down with the woman of his dreams...whoever that might be. Could she possibly be the one to fit the picture? Or was there still some other woman who held his heart? She regretted throwing away her college years on Ross. She should have dated more. Was she ready for a relationship? That was the biggest question she had to face now.

Bart wondered just where his friendship with Regenia was headed. They worked together five days a week, and now he couldn't imagine ever doing without her. Every time he stepped into the office to ask her about an order, his day seemed to get a little brighter somehow. She was a lot happier now. The sadness had gone from her eyes, and she seemed more vibrant and more beautiful than ever. Not that she had ever been anything but beautiful, but now she had a glow about her that wasn't present before. *Could being around me possibly have anything to do with that?* he asked himself. *Could I really be that lucky?*

Regenia was unlike any other girl he had dated. Even though she had come from a rich background, she was completely down-to-earth. When she laughed, which she was doing more often now, it warmed him clear down to his toes. He never had a chance with Luci. They were just friends now, and that was how he liked it. Judith had been a passing fancy, a beautiful woman who had captured his heart for a time but never really held it. How he ever thought he was in love with her was a mystery. Oh, he was sorry that she had gotten herself pregnant, but it wasn't his problem, and she was smart enough to figure out what to do with her life without his help. No, those two women he had spent so much time dreaming about were all in the past. Regenia was his future—Regenia and Timmy. He couldn't forget about her son. Anybody who even hoped for a chance with her had to include Timmy, and he had no problem doing that. No problem at all. He needed some way to show Regenia how he really felt about her. Then she might look at him in a different light.

What I need is a strategy, he decided. He should get Regenia into a romantic setting and then see what transpired. There were very few women he could consult with about making plans. Both of his parents had passed away, and he didn't want to ask Marlene for fear she might slip and reveal his plan to Regenia. *Who can I ask for help?* he wondered. Then it came to him—Luci. Of course, Luci would know what to do. Besides that, her husband owned the most popular restaurant in town. He was sure Luci could help him with some kind of romantic setting in which he could reveal his true feelings to Regenia.

Luci was ecstatic when he called her with his request. "Of course, I'll help you, Bart," she told him. "You're like a brother to me. Regenia is a wonderful person. I found that out when I represented her in court. You just leave everything to me."

He was greatly relieved, knowing that all he needed to do was show up with Regenia and a ring in his pocket. He was going to ask her to marry him. It was just that simple. He loved her, and that was all it was to it.

Regenia wondered why Bart had been acting so strange the past few days. He had settled down after the trials, but now he was jumpy again. He was usually so jovial and easy-going. She couldn't understand the change in his attitude. She was growing fonder of him. She realized that. He had wedged his way into her heart, and Timmy's, too. They continued their Saturday night movie dates, followed by church on Sunday. They had both realized that they needed God in their lives again and had rededicated their lives to Christ. She just wished her parents were still around to see how different her life was now and how happy she was with a decent man in her life. Her mother had been a staunch Christian, and she had been sorely disappointed when Regenia had gotten pregnant in college. Regenia hoped that somehow her parents knew how she had turned her life around. Maybe they were watching from above.

Bart stopped in late one Friday afternoon just as she was getting ready to close the office. He was in his work clothes, as usual, with grease stains on the front of his shirt. He sported a five o'clock shadow that contrasted sharply with his copper-colored hair. He walked in, wiping his hands on a rag that he kept in his back pocket.

"Hi, Bart. I was just getting ready to close. What's up? Got another late order for me to fill?" she asked.

"No, nothing like that. I was just checking to see if we're still on for our Saturday night date," he responded.

"Of course. What movie do you want to see?"

"No movie this time. I thought we could go to Rosalena's restaurant for a change. We haven't eaten out in quite a while except for fast food with Timmy. I thought it would be a nice change."

"Oh, that sounds like fun. I know they have wonderful food."

"The best in town. I'll have to tell you the history of that restaurant sometime. But let's make it a special occasion. Wear one of your fanciest dresses."

"Really? You want me to dress up? You—Mr. Denim Jeans and Tee Shirt Man?" she teased.

"Like I said, it's a special occasion."

"What are we celebrating?"

"Oh, I don't know. Us. Being together. I just feel like celebrating, so be ready and I'll pick you up at seven o'clock."

"Okay, I just hope I can find a dress fancy enough to suit you."

Regenia hurried home to look through her meager wardrobe. She had managed to buy a few more clothes since she had been working, but fancy dresses were mostly a thing of the past. She didn't know exactly what Bart had planned. He had been so mysterious about it. He was up to something, but she had no idea what it might be.

She walked into the bedroom and began to sift through the dresses hanging in the closet. Somehow, none of them seemed right. She didn't know what she could come up with for a special occasion. But she really didn't have time to think about that. She had to get supper ready before Marlene and Timmy got home. Maybe Marlene could help her put an outfit together from the clothes they had between them. They were about the same size and often exchanged clothes when they wanted a new or different look.

Marlene breezed through the door with Timmy in tow at six o'clock, their usual time of arrival. "Hi, sis, what's for supper? I'm starved. Keeping up with three kids works up an appetite."

"Oh, just some salmon croquettes with a salad and baked potatoes," Regenia told her.

"You look a little flushed. You're not getting sick or something are you?" Marlene asked anxiously.

"No, nothing like that." Regenia smiled as she removed the salmon from the pan and placed it on a serving platter.

"What put that smile on your face? Does it have something to do with Bart? 'Fess up now!"

"Let's eat first and then I'll tell you all about it. I'm sure Timmy is hungry, too, aren't you?" Regenia asked as she bent down to give her son a kiss.

"Yeah!" Timmy nodded vigorously as he spoke.

"Well, run and wash your hands, and then we will be ready to eat," Regenia instructed.

An hour later with the meal over, the dishes washed, and Timmy in his pajamas, Regenia and Marlene sat back on the couch, while Timmy played with some of his toys.

"He's getting to be a big boy. He's so independent now," Marlene observed.

"Yes, they really do grow up fast. The next thing I know he'll be wanting to go out on dates," Regenia responded. "And speaking of dates, that's what I need to tell you. Bart has asked me to go out on what he calls 'a special date' tomorrow night."

"Really? Where are you going?" Marlene exclaimed.

"Rosalena's restaurant. He said to dress fancy, so there's the dilemma. I've already looked through the closet, and no luck. There's not a single fancy dress between us."

"Well, what do you expect? We haven't had any need for such clothes ever since we left our home," Marlene reminded her.

"Yes, I know. I was just hoping I could put some kind of outfit together. Maybe I can run out tomorrow and find some inexpensive dress on sale or something. What do you think?"

RETURN TO SUMMERFIELD

"That might work. There's no sense in worrying about it tonight, and you can't do anything about the accessories until you have the dress."

"I suppose not. I'll just sleep on it and trust the good Lord to take care of it tomorrow. Well, let me get Timmy to bed," said Regenia.

⸺◆◦❈◦◆⸺

THEY ROSE EARLY THE NEXT morning, forgoing their usual Saturday morning sleep-in. Even Timmy was up early, sensing the excitement that seemed to be building. Regenia decided to make pancakes, one of the family favorites. Timmy smothered his in syrup, while she and Marlene elected to top theirs with strawberries and whipped cream.

"I don't know when I've had such a delicious breakfast," Marlene told her as she rose from her chair and started to clear the table. "I'll get the dishes this morning. You already have enough to do."

"Thanks. I appreciate that. I guess I'll throw on some clothes and head out to shop as soon as the stores open. I have no idea of where to start, though."

Just as she finished speaking the doorbell rang. "Now who could that be at this time of day? So help me, if Bart has come over here now, I'm just going to have a fit," she declared.

She opened the door to find a deliveryman with a package. "I have a package for Regenia Whitworth," he announced.

"I'm Regenia Whitworth," she told him. "Do I need to sign for it?"

"No, it's a private delivery. Have a good day," he said as he handed the package over.

"What's going on?" Marlene asked as she walked in from the kitchen.

"I don't know. Somebody just sent me a package, and there's no return address on it."

"Well, don't just stand there! Open it," Marlene exclaimed.

Regenia fetched a knife from the kitchen and cut the tape on the package. She opened the large white box and found a layer of red tissue paper inside. As she parted the layers of paper she came to a red dress, neatly folded. She lifted it out and held it up for Marlene to see.

"It's beautiful," Marlene told her. "But who sent it? Is there a card or anything else in the box?"

195

"Let me see...yes, here's a card. It was under the dress," Regenia informed her. "It's from Luci. It says, 'I heard you have a big date tonight. A dress like this brought me luck once. I hope it does the same for you. Love, Luci.'"

"I wonder how she heard about the date," Marlene mused.

"I don't know. I guess we'll just have to ask Bart. There's still a lot we don't know about this town. But Luci should be a good judge of sizes, so this dress should fit. Let me see if I have any shoes and earrings to go with it. This will definitely save me some money."

Regenia took the dress and held it up in front of her, waltzing into the bedroom as she hummed softly. Marlene refolded the tissue paper and put the lid back on the box. She looked at Timmy, who was taking in the whole scene instead of watching his Saturday morning cartoons. "Timmy, boy, I think your mom's in love," she told him.

"In love," he repeated, nodding his head as though he understood the situation. He quickly turned back to his cartoons. The box and the dress it had held were soon forgotten.

Marlene sighed and shook her head. If only he knew. If things worked out the way she thought they would, Timmy might just have a new daddy before too long. She hoped so anyhow. She couldn't wait to hear what transpired after the date tonight.

—◆◆◆◆◆—

REGENIA HAD MANAGED TO PUT together what she deemed to be a suitable outfit. She had a pair of long rhinestone earrings that set off the dress perfectly. Along with that, she wore her mother's diamond and ruby heart-shaped necklace, the one heirloom she had managed to hold on to. A pair of red heels, a small evening bag, and a small black lace shawl she had found at the Goodwill store a few months ago completed the outfit. She turned around one last time, surveying herself in the bedroom mirror. It was almost time for Bart to arrive.

The doorbell rang right on time. She drew a deep breath before heading into the living room. Marlene was keeping Timmy occupied in the kitchen as they worked to put together some puzzles on the dining table. Marlene had bribed him with the promise of sugar cookies, one of his favorites. *Thank heavens for sisters,* she thought, as she reached for the doorknob.

"Hello, Bart," she said as she opened the door.

She was surprised to see him dressed in a suit, complete with a vest and tie. The only time she had ever seen him this dressed up was at the Christmas church service. She guessed he wasn't kidding about it being a special occasion. He was holding a florist's box in his hand.

"Hello, Regenia, are you ready to go?" he asked. "I brought you some flowers."

She took the box as he held it out. It contained a white orchid, one of her favorite flowers.

"Bart, it's beautiful. Come in and give me a minute to pin it on."

She walked back into the bedroom and stood in front of the mirror, trying to decide on the best location for the orchid. The little red dress didn't leave a lot of room to work with. She finally managed to position it and then draped her shawl over her arms, being careful not to crush the flower. After all, a girl didn't get too many orchids in her lifetime.

"Thank you so much, Bart," she said as she walked back into the living room, where he stood waiting by the door. "You could have sat down, you know."

"I didn't want to wrinkle the suit," he joked. "Come on. I have a surprise for you."

They walked outside, and Regenia spotted a limousine in the driveway. She couldn't believe her eyes.

"Bart, what were you thinking? A limousine in this neighborhood?"

"Nothing but the best for you tonight. Actually, my favorite taxi service, On Your Way, has started a limo service. It's all part of a package deal I made with Rosalena's restaurant," he explained as the driver opened the door for them and they climbed into the car.

"Oh, my. Now you really have my curiosity up. Next thing I know you'll be telling me we're dining on escargot or pheasant under glass."

"Escargot...no. Pheasant under glass doesn't sound so bad, though."

"Good! I don't think I would care for snails. I have eaten pheasant under glass, but it's not one of my favorites either."

They both laughed as the limousine headed back out to the street.

Soft music drifted through the speakers. She couldn't identify the song, but it sounded a lot like Frank Sinatra, or was it Tony Bennett? Whoever it was, she liked it.

"Next I suppose you're going to tell me that this limousine has a minibar."

"As a matter of fact, it does, but I don't want to spoil your appetite," Bart teased.

They arrived at the restaurant a short time later. The driver pulled up to the front door, exited the car and walked around to open the door for them to get out.

"I'm not used to such service anymore," said Regenia.

"It's all part of tonight's package, so sit back and enjoy," Bart told her as he held the door for her to enter the restaurant.

The hostess approached them. "Hello, Bart. Everything is set up just the way you requested. Please follow me to the patio."

"I've never been on the patio," Regenia commented as they headed towards the back of the restaurant and the doors that opened onto the patio. It was a cool night, but not too chilly. She was glad she had worn the shawl.

They stepped outside to what was a small wonderland. Candles were everywhere—from the private dining table set for them to those lining the ledge around the patio. Flowers were also in abundance in every color imaginable. It was a clear night with twinkling stars and a full moon adding to the effect. The patio was deserted except for them and the waiter, who was ready to bring the first course of the evening. *Could things get any more perfect?* she wondered.

"Wow, I can't believe this. How did you manage it?" Regenia asked.

"Oh, let's just say I had a little help from an old friend," Bart replied. "Do you want to order anything special, or shall it be a surprise?" he asked as he pulled out her chair at their table.

"Everything about tonight has been a surprise so far, so why spoil it?"

"Good choice. Waiter, bring in the salads," he instructed.

The salads were soon sitting in front of them. The waiter opened the wine and poured a glass for each of them. They began to eat, and a violinist appeared. He began to play softly, and Regenia recognized the song as a classic from one of the concerts she used to attend.

"Bart, I can't believe you arranged all of this. It's so...so romantic," she whispered.

"Nothing but the best for you," he responded.

They dined on veal Parmesan with pasta and homemade bread followed by spumoni ice cream for dessert. Regenia laid down her spoon after finishing the last bite of her ice cream.

The violinist faded away discreetly, as if on cue. Soft strains of a familiar love song began to filter through the patio speakers. She recognized the song, "Love Is a Many Splendored Thing."

She sighed. "I don't know when I've had such a scrumptious meal. I couldn't eat another bite. It reminds me of the good old days."

"You're living in the present now."

"I'm sorry. I didn't mean to bring that up. It's just that I can't help but thinking about my past life sometimes and wondering what happened to my parents. The mystery was never really solved. We had no closure."

"Sometimes you just can't do anything about your past. You have to live for the present."

"I know, and I'm so happy now. I think I am actually happier than I was when we had money and a different lifestyle."

"What makes you happy, Regenia?" He reached across the table and took her hands as he spoke.

"I don't know exactly. Maybe not being on the run anymore. Having a job. Just lots of things."

"Could one of them possibly be having me around?" he asked, speaking softly.

She looked down, suddenly shy and unable to look him in the eye. *Was this what she really wanted? Was Bart the man of her dreams?* She had waited so long for another chance at love. "Yes...no...maybe. Oh, I don't know. I just don't know anymore."

"Oh, I think you know, Regenia. I know I do. I love you. I think I loved you from the time you climbed into my truck cab and broke the heel off your shoe."

She laughed. "Oh, you remember that, do you?"

"Like it was yesterday. In fact, you've been on my mind since the first time we met. I have something to ask you. That's why I tried to make this a romantic and special evening."

He pulled the ring box from his pocket and got down on his knee beside her. He opened the box and held out the ring as he began speaking. "Regenia Whitworth, I love you. Will you marry me?"

She hesitated before responding. Her heart was beating so fast she could almost hear it thundering in her chest. She felt a little faint. Then she broke into a smile as she replied, "Yes, Bart. I'll marry you. Yes, yes, yes!"

He slipped the ring onto her finger. Then he rose and pulled her up from the chair, taking her in his arms. They exchanged a long, romantic kiss. They began dancing as the music continued to play from the speakers.

"I don't want this night to end," she whispered.

"Me either, but if it doesn't, we'll never get married," he teased.

She stopped dancing suddenly. "Oh, I almost forgot…Timmy… Marlene. We have to break the news to them."

He laughed. "Somehow, I don't think it's going to be a big surprise, especially to Marlene. I can't wait to be a real dad to Timmy. So, when do you want to get married?"

"As soon as possible. I don't need a fancy wedding. Let's just keep it simple. I just wish my parents were here to see me finally truly happy."

"I wish my parents could be here too, but it's just not possible," he lamented.

"Oh, I'm so sorry. I didn't mean to bring up your parents. I remember you told me they are both gone now."

"Yes, it was a long time ago. I still miss them, though."

"I don't think people ever get over the death of their parents. Somehow, it's like losing a piece of their world," she mused.

"You're right, but let's celebrate the moment and realize that they would have been happy for us. That's the best thing to do," he spoke decisively. "So, let's get out of here and break the news to Marlene and Timmy and Jim."

"Jim—I had forgotten about him," Regenia exclaimed.

"Oh, he knows about tonight. He just didn't know what your answer would be. So, M'lady. Your carriage awaits. Are you ready for another ride in the limousine? And this time maybe we *will* have some of that champagne."

***

THE FOLLOWING MORNING, BART WAS reliving the previous night over and over in his mind. He couldn't believe Regenia had actually accepted his proposal. Regenia, the rich girl, the socialite, was going to marry him, a mere laborer and mechanic. It seemed almost too good to be true. But she loved him. He was sure of that. He just wished there was some way he could make her totally happy. Then he had an idea.

He picked up the phone and dialed a familiar number.

"Luci Clark speaking," was the response when someone picked up on the other end.

"Luci, it's Bart. I just wanted to say thanks for everything you did. Last night was a total success. She said 'yes' and we're now engaged."

"Congratulations! I'm so happy for you," Luci responded.

"But now I have another favor to ask of you. You're the only one I know who might be able to help with this." He went on to explain his idea to her.

"I know just who to call," she told him after he had finished speaking. "Leave everything to me."

She hung up the phone and flipped through the Rolodex on her desk until she came to a familiar name. She tapped her forefinger against the card and nodded slightly. Yes. That was the person she was looking for. If anybody could handle the job, he could. She dialed the number and waited for him to answer. She explained the situation quickly after he picked up on the other end. He assured her that he would get onto the case right away. She smiled, satisfied that she had done her best. Now all they had to do was wait.

***

"An engagement party? You want to throw an engagement party? I thought we were going to keep everything simple," Regenia protested as Bart approached her with the idea of holding an engagement party out by the lake.

"I just thought it would be a good way to celebrate and let off a little steam," he told her. "We've all been working so hard lately, and you never really got much of a break after the court case. So, come on. Let's do it. We can invite some of our friends. I know they all want to wish us well, especially after all we've been through."

"I guess you're right. We're not in hiding anymore, and the weather is so beautiful now. But I still want a simple wedding."

"You plan the wedding, and I'll plan the party. How's that for a trade-off?"

"I guess that's fair. I've actually already gotten quite a few details for the wedding worked out. I want a June wedding. June is the month for brides, you know."

"Fine with me. The sooner, the better. I can't wait for you to be Mrs. Bart Murphy."

"I can't wait either," she told him as he bent to give her a kiss.

"Are you sure you don't want to elope?" he teased, wrapping his arms around her waist.

"Quite sure. I want us to share this special day with our family and friends. I've already had one disastrous marriage. I want this one to get off to the right start."

"Okay, sweetie. The engagement party is set in two weeks, and all you have to do is show up and look beautiful." He tapped her nose and then kissed her again for good measure.

"I'll be there, with Timmy and Marlene, of course."

⊷◈◈◈⊶

Regenia couldn't believe how fast the two weeks flew by. She was busy with her usual job at the shop, taking a couple of days off to shop for a wedding dress and making other plans. She found the perfect dress at a vintage shop in the middle of town. Marlene was to be her only attendant, and they found a dress for her at the same shop. After a few stops to pick up invitations and arrange for the cake and flowers, she felt that everything was set. Although it wasn't usually the case on such short notice, their church just happened to have an open date for the weekend they had selected. The reception would be at Rosalena's, so the restaurant would take care of all the other food. She couldn't believe how much simpler things were than for her first wedding. She also couldn't believe how much happier she was this time.

Bart called on the day of the engagement party. It was Saturday, so she wasn't working. Even though they had seen each other the night before, he liked to keep in touch several times a day.

"So, my beautiful fiancée, how is everything going today? Are you ready for the party?" he asked.

"Yes, I'm just finishing getting myself and Timmy ready. We'll be there shortly," she told him.

"What are you wearing?" he asked. Before she could respond he added, "No, don't tell me. Let it be a surprise."

She laughed. "Don't worry. I'll come up with something, but you said to dress casually. I have to go now."

She wondered why he had told her that. Of course, she wasn't going to wear heels and a sequined dress to the lake. She settled on stonewashed jeans, a white knit top with a denim collar, and denim-colored sneakers, reasoning the outfit would allow her to keep up with Timmy, should he decide to try out the remote-controlled toy boat Bart had given him a few weeks ago.

Besides, the affair was to be informal, with a cookout served buffet style. Bart had taken care of all the details regarding food. All she had to do was show up, he had told her. There would be boating for those who cared to participate. It would be nice to watch the boats on the lake, but she had no desire to get into one ever again.

"Are you about ready to go?" she called out to Marlene as she finished tying Timmy's shoes and grabbed a denim purse that matched her shoes.

"I'm not riding with you," Marlene replied as she came out of the bathroom after putting on her makeup.

"Oh? Why not?"

"Jim is picking me up."

"Jim, huh? I thought you weren't interested in a mechanic," Regenia teased.

"Just because we're going out doesn't mean I have to marry the guy," Marlene retorted.

"No, no, not at all," Regenia agreed, shaking her head and laughing as she spoke.

"Oh, shut up," Marlene protested as she flounced out of the room to answer the doorbell. "See you at the party," she called as she walked out the front door, her voice fading in the distance.

"Well, Timmy, I guess it's just you and me. Are you ready for a day at the lake?" Regenia asked as she turned to face her son. "Do you want to take your boat?"

"Yeah," he responded as he ran to the shelf where the boat was stored.

"Here, let me get it down for you," Regenia told him as he reached for the boat.

They quickly gathered the rest of their belonging, which included shades and hats for both of them, sunscreen, and a couple of towels in case they happened to get wet. She couldn't think of anything else they might need. They walked to the car and were soon on their way to the lake. Regenia remembered the way, as she and Bart had driven out there several times.

Bart was waiting for them as they drove to the designated area. People had already started gathering. She could smell the meat cooking as soon as she stepped out of the car. Timmy wriggled impatiently, waiting to be loosened from his seat belt. He couldn't wait to try out his new boat.

"Hi, glad you finally got here," Bart said as they walked over to where he was standing near the food preparation area. He gave her a kiss on the cheek.

"Looks like a perfect day for the party. The weather is so nice. I can't believe how beautiful the lake is," she observed as she looked around the expanse of woods surrounding the lake area. Concrete picnic tables placed at intervals dotted the green grass that gradually gave way to sand near the water's edge. A few boats were sailing on the lake, which was large enough that some of them had disappeared on the horizon.

"Boat!" Timmy exclaimed, proudly holding up the boat for Bart to see.

"Yes, I see that. Are you ready to try it out?" Bart asked as he bent down to the little boy's level.

"Yeah!" Timmy looked at his mom questioningly as he spoke.

"Okay, as long as a grownup is with you. But don't go near the water by yourself," Regenia cautioned.

"I'll take him down to the lake. Why don't you visit with some of our friends? I've already talked to quite a few of them, all offering congratulations on our engagement," Bart told her.

Their conversation was interrupted as several of their friends walked over. Bart took Timmy's hand and headed towards the lake, waving at her as they left. She smiled at the picture, thinking how different it would have been if Bart were Timmy's real dad. She hoped that someday he might be legally. They would just have to wait and see what transpired along those lines. Those thoughts were soon forgotten as she engaged in chatting with the other party guests.

The smell of the meat cooking soon drew everyone close to the picnic area where the food had been set up. As soon as it was done, everybody was ready to dig in, as it was almost noon, and everybody was hungry. Regenia, Bart, and Timmy were the first in line as the honorees. She couldn't help but compare this occasion to her first engagement party, which had been a formal affair, complete with a five-course meal and all the stiffness that accompanied it. She had been uncomfortable then, wondering just how many people knew or suspected she was pregnant. This time she had no such worry. There was an easy camaraderie among the guests that had been lacking at the other party, which had been mostly for show at the insistence of Ross's mother. How she had ever agreed to marry into such a pretentious family was a mystery to her. She knew now that she had never really loved Ross. It had been infatuation, really, and he had been so charming—at least while they were dating.

She shook the thoughts from her head as the meal ended and rounds of toasts began. Bart began by toasting her and making a sweet speech that brought tears to her eyes. That was followed by a toast from Jim, and then toasts from all the workers from the shop. They provided sparkling cider for those who planned to be on the lake and, of course, soft drinks or juice for the children. However, other beverages would be available for those who planned to stay landlubbers, should they desire something stronger.

Just when she thought she couldn't listen to another toast, Bart made a surprise announcement. "I have a special treat planned for my fiancée. It's something down by the lake, so if you will excuse us, I would like to show it to her now," he said, taking her hand as he spoke. He nodded, and she rose from her chair as he began to guide her gently towards the lake.

"Bart, what is it? You know I don't want to get on a boat," she reminded him.

"Close your eyes and I'll tell you when we get there," he instructed. "Just hold my hand and walk carefully. I won't let you fall. I promise."

"Okay, I'm putting my trust in you again."

"You can always trust me, now and for the rest of your life."

"Timmy—what about Timmy? We forgot about him," she suddenly remembered.

"It's okay. He's with Marlene and Jim. He'll be fine."

They walked for what seemed like forever, even though Regenia knew it wasn't that far. *Everything seems to take longer if you have your eyes closed,* she thought. Finally, Bart let go of her hand and put his arm around her waist, drawing her to a stop.

"Okay, you can open your eyes now," he told her.

She looked over to the pier and saw a sailboat that was tied up there. She looked at the writing on the boat and was surprised to see her own name.

"Bart, what is this? What have you gone and done?" she exclaimed.

"I bought this boat as a surprise to you. I know you said you don't like sailing anymore, but the best way to get over a fear is to face it. So, here she is, ready to go, with a captain and first mate to man it for us."

"Oh, Bart, I don't know. I just don't know if I can," she protested.

"Regenia, you're one of the bravest people I've ever met. You went on the run to protect your son. You managed to live on no income for weeks. You made my apartment into a home for you and Timmy and Marlene. You can do it. I'll be with you all the way. We don't have to go out on the lake if you don't want to. Won't you just step onto the boat and meet the crew? Would you do that for me?"

Regenia looked at the boat longingly. Sailing with her parents had always been fun. She tried to see the faces of the captain and first mate, wondering just how friendly they were. But the captain kept his cap pulled low over his face, and the first mate appeared to be busy with the ropes on the other side of the boat. *Just how competent are they?* she wondered.

Bart continued to plead his case. "I know what you're thinking, but you have nothing to worry about. I know you told me your parents' sailboat capsized during a storm, but this is a lake and the weather is perfect."

"Well…" she began to weaken.

The captain motioned for them to come aboard, but he still hadn't called out a greeting. Regenia found this rather strange. Was he friendly or not?

"Okay, I'll give it a try. Maybe just a short trip," she reluctantly agreed.

"That's my girl. Here, step onto the pier and let me give you a hand onto the boat," Bart instructed.

She stepped onto the boat, taking a deep breath to summon up her courage. She did hope she would be able to sail happily again and share that experience with Timmy. Someday she would tell him stories all about his grandparents and the wonderful times she and Marlene had on their sailboat when they were growing up.

There was something oddly familiar about the captain and the way he moved about the boat. She stared at him, trying to sort it all out. Then he removed his cap and she could see his face clearly. It couldn't be…it just couldn't be who she thought it was. She felt faint as the blood drained from her head. She swayed slightly, only to be caught in Bart's strong arms.

"Regenia, honey, are you all right?" he asked anxiously, wondering if he had made the best decision to spring his surprise on her this way.

"Bart...I...I..." she couldn't speak.

"The captain and first mate rushed to her side, laughing and crying at the same time. She opened her eyes again, and this time she knew for sure who she was seeing.

"Mom...Dad, is it really you?" she whispered as they reached out to hug her.

"Yes, baby, it's us, James and Mary Whitworth, in the flesh," her dad answered.

"We're here," her mom assured her, speaking almost simultaneously.

"I don't understand. I thought you were...I thought you were both gone. I thought I had lost you forever!" Regenia told them.

Marlene, Timmy, and Jim, who had been watching from a distance, raced the rest of the way to the boat. They climbed aboard quickly, with Jim assisting Marlene first and then Timmy.

"Oh, God. I could hardly stand it knowing you were both here so close by," Marlene exclaimed.

"Bart swore us to secrecy," Jim added. "He wanted to make this day special for Regenia."

"And he did...you did," Regenia said, hugging Bart tightly as he grabbed her and kissed her soundly.

"Watch it, young man. You're not married yet," James cautioned playfully as they all laughed and exchanged hugs all around.

"Timmy, my little grandson. You're not so little anymore. Just look at how you've grown," Mary noted, giving him an extra squeeze.

"So, please tell me what happened and how you ended up here today," Regenia said, looking at her parents as they stood holding hands on the deck.

"As you know, there was quite a bit of tomfoolery going on regarding our money and investments," James said. "The lawyers and accountants were in it together. They were siphoning money from our accounts. I started to suspect something was wrong when I looked at the last reports. I had a meeting scheduled with the head of the law firm on a

Monday. Your mom and I decided to go sailing over the weekend to let off some steam."

"But we had no idea our trip was going to turn into a nightmare," Mary interjected.

James continued with his explanation. "It was a plot quickly devised because I had just happened to mention to some of the staff that we were going sailing. They decided to kidnap us and hold us hostage on a remote island where one of them had a cabin. It was just to their advantage that the storm came up unexpectedly. They managed to make it look like the boat had capsized and we were missing."

"I know. We had the Coast Guard looking for you. I don't understand why they didn't find you on that island," Regenia mused.

"Oh, it was pretty far away from the site of the accident, and we were kept locked away until all rescue efforts ceased. Even after that, we were allowed outside only under supervision. There was no chance to slip away, and even if we did, there was no place to go and no way to communicate with the outside world," James explained.

"But I still don't understand. How were you found? Who found you?" Regenia asked.

"I'm happy to say it was all due to our future son-in-law," said Mary.

"I called Luci and she got in touch with a detective who tracked down the lawyers," said Bart. "One of them finally broke under police questioning and spilled the beans on the whole operation. They've all been arrested and will face kidnapping charges, as well as charges for fraud and embezzlement."

"I'm so happy now that I can hardly stand it. I wished more than anything that you could both be here for our wedding, and now here you are! I can't believe you kept it a secret from me, Marlene. How could you?" Regenia chided.

"I've known only since this morning," Marlene admitted. "Jim told me the whole plan. I couldn't believe it either."

"Well, for once you did yourself proud. I didn't know you could keep a secret so well," Regenia teased.

"Are we going to try this boat out or what?" James asked gruffly, clearing his throat as he spoke.

"Yes, Dad, let's sail and show Timmy what it's like. He's too young to remember sailing with us before."

They all donned life jackets, and Jim untied the boat. Her dad started the motor to move the boat out into the lake, where they could hoist the sails and make use of the breeze that was now blowing steadily.

"This time I promise there will be nothing but smooth sailing," Bart assured her.

"I'd like that. I'd like that very much," Regenia told him as she reached up to kiss him. They leaned on the railing as the wind hit the sails. They had eyes for only each other and hardly noticed when the water splashed them as the boat gained speed, moving smoothly as it merged with the horizon.

The End

Springtime in Summerfield

Preview to my next book

Part I

"Catnip"
Cody and Jennifer's Story

A DOOR OPENED SLOWLY, AND a short silver-haired lady's head appeared, barely visible, as she peeked through the space of the small crack she had allowed in the opening, her bright blue eyes scanning the street for any possible sign of people present in the usually quiet neighborhood. Seeing no one, she opened the door wider and picked up a yellow-striped cat, one of her favorite pets. She set the cat down on her front porch and began to shoo him towards a tall oak tree in her front yard.

"Go on now!" she exclaimed. "You know what you have to do."

The cat turned his head and looked back at her as if to say, "Not again."

He turned again and reluctantly began to move towards the tree as she shooed him again. She was satisfied that her plot was, once again, underway.

That's my boy, she thought, as she pulled the door almost to a close. She watched as the cat, Toby, began to climb the tree. *Not too far, now, Toby. Don't go too high,* she silently encouraged him as he moved further up the tree.

Confident that her plan was working, she closed the door and moved towards her home phone, which was located in her living room close to her favorite recliner. She picked up the phone and dialed 9-1-1.

"Hello, this is the 9-1-1 operator. How may I help you?" came the response.

"Hello. This is Miss Betty Applewhite. My cat has climbed a tree and can't get down," she stated.

"Miss Applewhite, not again," came the reply.

"Yes, I'm afraid he has a mind of his own. He likes to go up but doesn't like climbing down," Betty responded.

"Okay, I'll send someone to help you. Give me your address for the record," the operator instructed.

"It's 222 Quail Creek Drive," Betty told her.

"Hold on, and help will be there shortly," the operator promised.

"Thank you so much," Betty said, and she hung up the phone, smiling to herself. She didn't have much excitement in her life, but some was about to begin, once more.

Guess I managed to get the cat up the tree again without anyone seeing me, she thought. *I might be eighty years old, but I've still got what it takes when I want to get something done.*

Unaware that she had been observed, she took a seat in her recliner and waited for the sound of sirens alerting the neighborhood that a firetruck and police car were arriving.

JONAS GREEN STOPPED TRIMMING THE shrubs by the side of Miss Betty's house as he heard the sounds of sirens approaching. He pulled a red-plaid bandana from his back pocket and wiped his forehead, as it was a warm day. Even the large, wide-brimmed straw hat that he wore didn't keep him cool. Trimming shrubs always caused him to work up a sweat. Despite that, he always enjoyed working in the gardens, especially in the springtime when the flowers were blooming, birds singing, and bees buzzing about the brightly colored flowers. He usually kept to himself while he was working, but he had just happened to be trimming the shrubs at the corner of the house when he saw the front door opening and the cat being shooed out by Miss Betty.

Miss Betty, what you done gone and did now? he wondered. *So many matchmakers in this here town, and I have to work for one of them.* It wasn't the first time he had heard sirens approaching, and he knew it probably wouldn't be the last.

He had been working for Miss Betty for the past fifty years, starting when he was just twenty years old. Finding work as a black man with little education hadn't been an easy task, but he was a good worker, and he discovered that he had a talent for gardening and growing plants. He had built up a business for himself, and with the recommendations of Miss Betty, a well-respected member of the community, he soon had more customers than he could handle. Now, at age seventy, he had turned over most of the business to his nephew, Adolphus, who had been working with him for years, but he had kept a few select customers, and Miss Betty was his favorite.

He watched as a fire engine and a police car pulled up beside Miss Betty's front yard, almost in unison. He wondered if it would be the usual people or someone different. Almost instantly, he recognized the driver of the police car. It was Cody Hawthorne, the son of the police chief, Jake Hawthorne. Cody had followed in his dad's footsteps and kept up the family tradition by becoming a policeman as soon as he graduated from high school.

The firetruck began to empty as uniformed fire personnel hopped out and surveyed the situation. They were all gazing up at the tree where the cat was stretched out along a wide limb, totally oblivious to the commotion below.

Miss Betty came hurrying out the front door as fast as an eighty-year-old woman could walk. She was wringing her hands as a sign of distress and muttering, "Oh, my stars! That cat has gotten stuck in the tree again. I just don't know what I'm going to do about him."

What an actress, Jonas thought, as he watched the chain of events unfold. He shook his head and headed back around the corner, chuckling softly as he resumed his job of trimming the shrubbery.

"Okay, Miss Betty, we're going to see if we can get the cat down." The remark came in a distinctly female voice from the only female in the bunch.

"Jennifer Clark, is that you under all of that gear?" Miss Betty inquired.

"Yes, Miss Betty, it's me again. You know, you have to keep that cat inside. We can't keep making trips to get him down from a tree. We might miss an important call for a fire," Jennifer admonished her, speaking kindly.

"I know. I'll try to do better. He just slips out sometimes when I open the door," Miss Betty replied, trying to speak in an innocent voice.

Cody stepped forward. "Okay, guys, I'll keep the traffic away while you get the cat down."

"Sure thing," Jennifer responded. "Good seeing you again, Cody."

"Same here," Cody replied. "Now, let's get to work before a crime or a fire occurs."

"Guys, we're going to need the power ladder to get that high in the tree," Jennifer stated, as she estimated the height of the limb where the cat was located.

"Please be careful. I don't want anything to happen to him," Miss Betty pleaded.

"Don't worry. I'll take care of him for you," Jennifer assured her.

Moments later, Toby was down from the tree and nestled safely in Miss Betty's arms.

"Thank you so much," Miss Betty said, as everyone began to pack up their gear to leave.

"Good job, everybody," Cody added, as he stepped forward to shake hands with all of the fire crew. His handshake with Jennifer seemed to last a little longer than those with the men, an act that was not unnoticed by Miss Betty.

The firetruck and police car were soon gone, and Miss Betty walked back into the house with Toby still in her arms.

"Well, Toby, we did it again," she whispered in his ear, as he flicked it back. "I'm going to get that Cody and Jennifer together if it's the last thing I do, and at eighty years old, I probably don't have that much time left to do it.

Lagniappe

FAVORITE FAMILY RECIPES

Mama Rosa's Drop Dumplings, Revised

- 2 c. plain flour
- 1 heaping T. shortening
- 1 egg
- enough water to make a stiff dough

Mix all ingredients and drop by spoonfuls into simmering chicken broth. Add small amount of onion and celery to chicken while boiling. Season to taste with salt and pepper.

Dianne's Chicken Spaghetti

- 3 boneless, skinless chicken breasts
- ½ c. celery, chopped
- ½ green bell pepper, chopped
- 1 can pimentos, liquid drained from it
- 1 clove garlic, chopped
- 1 c. sharp cheddar cheese, grated
- 1 can sliced mushrooms, liquid drained from it
- 1 pkg. spaghetti or other pasta
- 1 can reduced sodium chicken broth
- Salt and pepper to taste

Boil chicken in salted water. Let chicken cool and cut the meat into small chunks. Let broth cool and remove fat from top. (I cook the chicken the night before and store chicken and broth separately in the refrigerator.) Add 1 can of chicken broth to cooked broth and bring to a boil in a large pot. Add spaghetti and cook for 2 minutes. Add celery, green pepper, and pimentos and cook for 10 more minutes. Remove from heat and combine with chicken and mushrooms. Mixture should be *slightly* juicy. Place in large covered casserole dish and heat thoroughly at 350 degrees. Add cheese and heat another five to seven minutes or until cheese is melted. If desired, top with Parmesan cheese before serving. Serves 6 to 8 people.

Dianne's Chow Mein Tuna Casserole

- 1 can mushroom soup
- ½ c. salted cashew nuts
- 1 3-oz can Chow Mein noodles
- 1 7-oz. can tuna
- ½ c. water
- ¼ c. chopped onion
- 1 c. chopped celery
- 1/8 t. pepper

Combine soup and water. Add 1 c. of noodles, tuna, celery, cashews, onion, and pepper. Toss lightly. Place in ungreased baking dish. Sprinkle remaining noodles on top. Bake at 375 degrees for 15 minutes or until thoroughly heated. Serve while hot.

Sallie Rose's Baked Chicken Thighs

- Chicken Thighs, skinless
- Salt and pepper to taste
- Crushed rosemary
- 2 T. butter, melted
- 3 T. olive oil

Use as many chicken thighs as you need, one to two packages. Pour a thin layer of olive oil and melted butter into a baking dish. Rinse thighs and pat dry with paper towels. Lay thighs in pan; turn over so both sides are coated with oil/butter mixture. Sprinkle with rosemary, salt, and pepper. Cover with foil and bake at 350 degrees for 40 minutes to 1 hour. Uncover and bake another 10 minutes.

Dianne's Tropical Ham and Rice Salad

- 1 and ½ c. instant rice
- 1 and ½ c. boiling water
- 2 T. lemon juice
- 2 t. grated onion
- 2 pkg. cooked, diced ham, drained, rinsed, and patted dry with paper towels.
- 2 c. diced celery
- 1 and ½ t. salt
- 1 and ½ c. mayonnaise
- ¼ t. black pepper
- 2 t. prepared yellow mustard
- 2 c. canned pineapple chunks, drained

Add rice and ½ t. salt to boiling water. Remove from heat and stir to mix. Cover and let stand for 5 minutes. Then uncover and let cool to room temperature. Combine mayonnaise, remaining salt, pepper, lemon juice, onion, and mustard in a small bowl. Mix well, cover, and chill. In a larger bowl combine cooled rice, ham, pineapple, and celery. Chill, preferably overnight. Add mayonnaise mixture just before serving, stirring well to coat all ingredients. Serve with crackers of your choice.

Dianne's Easy Crockpot Ribs

- 1 rack ribs, cut into individual portions
- ½ white onion, chopped
- 1 bottle Sweet Baby Ray's Barbeque Sauce
- Salt and pepper to taste

After cutting ribs between the bones into individual portions; add salt and pepper to taste. Brown ribs in broiler pan under broiler until slightly brown on both sides. Do not cook all the way through. (This step can be omitted if desired.) Place chopped onion into bottom of crockpot that has been lined with a plastic crockpot liner. Add ribs. Pour barbeque sauce over ribs. Cover and cook on high for 3 hours or until done. Remove from crockpot after cooking. Strain sauce with slotted spoon to remove any bone fragments before spooning it over the ribs. Sauce can also be placed in a bowl for people to spoon over the ribs as desired.

Dianne's Old-Fashioned Pot Roast

- 1 boneless beef rump roast
- ½ white onion, sliced
- 3 medium red potatoes, peeled
- ½ t. dried basil
- 3 or 4 T. cooking oil
- Salt and pepper to taste
- 2 cloves garlic, peeled
- 2 large carrots, peeled
- 2 bay leaves
- ½ t. dried oregano
- plain white flour
- cooking spray such as Pam

Prepare roast by rinsing off and patting dry with paper towels. Cut off ends of garlic buds and cut garlic into long slivers. Cut small pockets around roast and put a sliver of garlic into each pocket. Mash holes to close them up. Salt and pepper the outer sides of roast. Coat outer sides of roast with flour. Pour oil into large skillet and heat until small sprinkle of flour bubbles when added to it. Place roast into hot grease and brown on all sides. Then place roast into roasting pan that has been sprayed with cooking spray. Cut ends off carrots and then cut carrots in half. Cut halves of carrots into 4 lengthwise sections. Cut peeled potatoes into round slices. Add potatoes, carrots, and onions to roasting pan. Sprinkle with salt and pepper. Prepare gravy and pour over roast.

Gravy for Roast

Add 2 or 3 T. plain white flour to grease left from browning roast. Stir constantly until mixture is brown, but do not burn. Add salt and pepper as desired. Add enough water to mixture to make gravy. Cook until thick. Pour over roast and vegetables in the roasting pan. Add bay leaves, placing them down into gravy on opposite sides of roast. Sprinkle roast and gravy with basil and oregano. Cover roast with top of pan and bake at 350 degrees for 1 to 1 and ½ hours or until done. Remove roast from gravy and let sit for at least 5 minutes before slicing. Remove and discard bay leaves. Remove vegetables from gravy and place in bowl for serving. Pour gravy into bowl for serving. If gravy is too thin, pour into clean skillet and thicken with Magic Thickening Potion before serving.

Dianne's Magic Thickening Potion

This may be used to thicken sauces and gravies as needed.

- 2 or 3 T. plain white flour
- Equal amounts of cold tap water

Place flour in glass measuring cup. Add equal amounts of cold tap water and mix with fork until smooth. Add small amount of additional cold tap water to make liquid texture, stirring with fork until smooth. Temper mixture by adding several tablespoons of the hot sauce you are trying to thicken. Mix thoroughly with a fork. Add Magic Potion to hot sauce, stirring constantly. Cook for several minutes to cook flour.

Dianne's Turkey Meatloaf

- 2 lb. ground turkey
- ¼ c. wheat germ
- 1 (8 oz.) can tomato sauce
- 2 eggs, slightly beaten
- ¼ t. garlic powder
- 1 t. dried parsley
- ½ white onion, chopped
- 6 saltine crackers, crushed
- ¼ t. Tony Cacherie's no salt seasoning
- ½ bell pepper, chopped
- salt and pepper to taste

Mix all ingredients, reserving ½ can of tomato sauce. Place in greased loaf pan or square casserole dish. Bake for 1 hour or until done. Spread remaining tomato sauce on top and bake an additional 5 to 7 minutes. Remove from oven and let cool enough to set. Slice and serve.

Dianne's Eggnog Cake

Cake:

- 1 box white cake mix
- 1/3 c. light cooking oil
- ½ t. nutmeg
- 4 egg whites
- 2 c. commercial eggnog

Mix above ingredients with electric mixer as directed on cake mix box, substituting eggnog for water. Pour into two greased and floured 9-inch cake pans. Bake at 350 degrees for 28 to 30 minutes. Cool cake in pans for 5 minutes. Remove from cake pans and cool completely on cooling racks before frosting.

Frosting/Filling (make twice in small, high mixing bowl)

- 1 pt. whipping cream, chilled
- 1 t. vanilla flavoring
- ¼ t. almond flavoring (optional)
- ¼ c. confectioner's sugar (add more if desired)
- ½ t. rum flavoring

Whip cream until soft peaks form. Do not overbeat or it will turn into butter. Add ¼ c. confectioner's sugar gradually while beating. Add flavoring while beating. Split layers of cake and spread frosting between the layers, stacking them one at a time. Make the second batch of Frosting/Filling and frost sides and top of cake. Top with toasted sliced almonds, if desired. Keep refrigerated until ready to serve.

NOTE: You may also bake this cake in a rectangular pan and frost with just one recipe of the Frosting/Filling and then top with the toasted sliced almonds. It is easier to store and transport than the layered cake. Keep refrigerated until ready to serve.

Mama Rosa's Favorite Rice Pudding

- 2 c. cooked rice
- ½ to ¾ c. sugar
- 1 t. vanilla
- 3 egg yolks
- 1 c. milk (1/2 c evaporated milk and ½ c. regular milk)
- 1 c. raisins (optional)
- ¼ t. nutmeg

Beat egg yolks with fork until lemon colored. Add other ingredients and mix well. Pour into greased casserole dish and bake at 300 degrees until custard is set. Check with a clean knife for doneness. Serve warm or cold, topped with Cool Whip or whipped cream.

Dianne's Crunchy Green Beans

- 2 cans French cut green beans
- ¼ c. milk
- 1 can onion rings
- 1 can cream of mushroom soup
- 1 can sliced water chestnuts
- ¼ t. black pepper.

Drain liquid from green beans. Place beans in a greased casserole dish. Drain liquid from water chestnuts. Slice water chestnuts into lengthwise slivers. Add soup, milk, water chestnuts, and black pepper to green beans. Mix well. Bake for 20 minutes at 350 degrees until bubbly all the way through. Add onion rings to top of casserole mixture and heat another 5 minutes or until onion rings are thoroughly heated.

Dianne's Baked Beans

- 2 cans pork and beans
- 1 slice white onion, diced
- 3 or 4 slices bacon, cut into pieces
- ½ c. dark ribbon cane syrup such as Steen's
- 1/8 t. dried mustard
- dash of black pepper (optional)

Spray casserole dish with cooking spray. Pour pork and beans into dish. Add syrup, onion, and dried mustard. Stir until mixed. Place bacon pieces on top, spacing evenly. Place in oven that is preheated to 350 degrees and bake uncovered for 45 minutes or until bacon is cooked and brown. (Serve as a side dish for Barbequed Crockpot Ribs.)

Dianne's Potato Salad

- 4 large red potatoes
- 3 T. sweet pickle relish
- 3 hard-boiled eggs, peeled
- ¾ c. mayonnaise
- 1 T. white vinegar
- Paprika as needed
- ½ white onion, diced
- 1 or 2 stalks celery, diced
- 2 t. French's yellow mustard
- ¼ c. Miracle Whip Lite
- 2 green onions, chopped
- salt and pepper to taste

Peel potatoes and cut into cubes 1 to 1 and ½ inches in size. Rinse and place in large pot. Cover with water. Add salt and bring to a boil. (Place a wooden spoon across the pot to prevent boiling over.) Reduce heat and cook for about 15 minutes or until tender when tested with a fork. Do not overcook. Prepare other ingredients while potatoes are cooking. Drain potatoes and return to pot for mixing. Add celery, onion, green onions, and pickle relish. Grate egg over mixture. Add mayonnaise, Miracle Whip Lite, and vinegar. Mix thoroughly, adding more mayonnaise if needed. Spoon into serving bowl and sprinkle paprika on top. Chill thoroughly before serving. Best if made the night before it is needed. (Serve with Crockpot Barbequed Ribs.)

Sallie Rose's Peachy Keen Salad

- 16 oz. to 24 oz. cottage cheese
- 1 small pkg. peach gelatin*
- 1 small pkg. orange gelatin*
- 1 can fruit cocktail, drained
- 8 oz. container whipped topping

Empty cottage cheese into bowl. Sprinkle gelatin over cottage cheese and mix. Mix drained fruit into cheese-gelatin mixture. Fold in whipped topping. Chill, if desired, but we like to eat it right away.

*I use one regular package of gelatin and 1 package of sugar-free gelatin; doesn't matter which flavor is which.

Printed in the USA
CPSIA information can be obtained
at www.ICGtesting.com
LVHW050340041023
759973LV00002B/186